THE [barcode: I0664566]

Star Surgeon Conway was used to aliens—strange and wonderfully non-human beings were his colleagues and patients at Sector General. But this alien was different—it was sharing Conway's brain, it was slowly taking over, and it was driving Conway mad. Unable to eat, haunted by nightmares, wildly in love with a crablike creature, Conway was being reduced to a trembling wreck—and the other doctors, even Nurse Murchison, were forbidden to help him.

Then came a medical emergency, and Conway found himself fighting the battle for his brain, before the alien could ruin Conway's career, disgrace Sector General, and cost a patient its life.

Also by James White
Published by Ballantine Books:

ALL JUDGEMENT FLED

AMBULANCE SHIP

DEADLY LITTER

HOSPITAL STATION

LIFEBOAT

MAJOR OPERATION

STAR SURGEON

THE ALIENS AMONG US

AMONG US

James White

A Del Rey Book

BALLANTINE BOOKS • NEW YORK

A Del Rey Book
Published by Ballantine Books

The Conspirators, Red Alert, To Kill or Cure, Tableau and
Countercharm, copyright © 1954, 1956, 1957, 1958 and 1960
by Nova Publications Ltd. for NEW WORLDS SCIENCE FICTION.
Occupation: Warrior copyright © 1959 by Nova Publications
Ltd., for SCIENCE FICTION ADVENTURES.
The Scavengers copyright © 1953 by Street & Smith Publica-
tions Inc., for ASTOUNDING SCIENCE FICTION (now ANALOG
SCIENCE FICTION-SCIENCE FACT).

Copyright © 1969 by James White

All rights reserved under International and Pan-American
Copyright Conventions. Published in the United States by
Ballantine Books, a division of Random House, Inc., New
York, and simultaneously in Canada by Random House of
Canada, Limited, Toronto, Canada.

ISBN 0-345-29171-9

Manufactured in the United States of America

First Edition: March 1969
Second Printing: April 1981

Cover art by Wayne Barlowe

Contents

Countercharm

❖❖❖❖❖❖❖❖❖❖❖❖

FAR OUT on the galactic Rim, where star-systems were sparse and the darkness almost absolute, the vast, angular structure of Sector Twelve General Hospital hung in space. In its three hundred and eighty-four levels were reproduced the environments of the sixty-nine different forms of intelligent life known to the Galactic Federation, a biological spectrum ranging from the ultra-frigid methane life-forms through the more normal oxygen- chlorine- and water-breathing types up to the beings who existed by the conversion of hard radiation. And in a small ward on the two hundred and third level Senior Physician Conway was lecturing to three visiting specialists of physiological classification ELNT, and feeling confused and miserable because he was suffering from a severe dose of unrequited love.

The object of his affection was one of the three ELNTs—six-legged, exo-skeletal and vaguely crab-like beings from Melf Four—and as the lecture proceeded his gaze was drawn to this entity more and more frequently, and became almost lascivious in its intensity. One half of Conway's mind—the sane, human half—kept insisting that getting all hot and bothered about an outsize crab was ridiculous, while the other half thought lovingly of that

1

gorgeously marked carapace and generally felt like baying at the moon.

He had a problem, Conway thought unhappily; and like so many others in the past, this one had begun with a visit to the office of the Chief Psychologist, O'Mara ...

Major O'Mara had opened the interview with flattery of the type which, if Conway had not known the Chief Psychologist of old, would have been indistinguishable from insults. Hitherto, O'Mara had said, Dr. Conway had been pretty much a free agent in the hospital, and with the happy faculty of picking nice, juicy, dramatic cases to work on—levitating dinosaurs, SRTTs with water on the brain, and the like ...

"... But this dashing, melodramatic stuff is not typical of a doctor's existence," O'Mara had gone on, "and now that they've made you a Senior Physician it is time you realised that.

"Not that you'll stop curing people, far from it," he continued, "but now you will be responsible for upwards of fifty patients at a time instead of devoting all your energies to just one. And if some of those cases are straight-forward you won't even look at them, but will delegate treatment to a subordinate. Eventually you will be expected to join in one of the hospital's long-term research projects, a routine business with no glory attached to it at all, and a greater proportion of your time will be spent in teaching duties.

"This will mean taking one or more Educator tapes," O'Mara had ended grimly, "and retaining them for extended periods. You know what that means?"

Conway had nodded, thinking that he did.

Without the Educator tape system a multi-environment hospital such as Sector General could not have existed. No single brain, human or otherwise, could hold the enormous quantity of physiological knowledge required to successfully treat the variety of patients they received. But complete physiological data on any patient's species was available by means of Educator tapes, which were simply the brain record of some great medical mind belonging to the same or a similar species as the patient to be treated.

A doctor taking such a tape had, literally, to share his mind with a completely alien personality. That was how it felt. Because all the memories and experience of the being who had donated the tape were impressed on the receiving mind, and not just selected pieces of medical data. Educator tapes could not be edited.

". . . Hitherto," O'Mara had gone on seriously, "you've experienced tapes for short periods only, during operations or for purposes of diagnosis, after which they have been erased. Even then the mental confusion can be considerable and I've had to give you hypno treatments at times to remind you which of the two occupants of your mind was boss. From now on, however, you will have no help at all."

"Not at *all*?" Conway had repeated, aghast. He had been expecting to get used to this thing in easy stages.

"Senior Physicians are supposed to be big boys," O'Mara replied, smiling in the lopsided fashion which indicated that his amusement was tinged with sympathy, "and capable of fighting their own mental battles. So there will be no drugs or hypno-conditioning, all I may give you is advice which you probably won't consider helpful. But don't worry, your first assignment is comparatively easy . . ."

A new operative technique had been developed recently for the ELNT life-form, O'Mara had explained, and Conway was to have the job of teaching it to a group of visiting doctors of that species, who would then bring the technique back to their home world. The operation was similar to the work Conway had been doing recently, which was one of the reasons for him being chosen. Models, technical assistance and the finer details of procedure would be furnished by the Director's office. It was also in the nature of a test for Conway.

". . . Some odd things have been known to happen to doctors who are taking a long-term Educator treatment," O'Mara had gone on while Conway arranged himself comfortably on the couch and the psychologist fitted the helmet into position. O'Mara's hands, like the rest of him, were blunt, strong and competent. "Some people, ideal in every other way, are psychologically incapable of keeping a tape for more than a day. Pains, skin conditions, perhaps organic malfunctionings develop. All have a psychosomatic basis, of course, but we both know that to the person concerned they hurt just as much as the real thing. At the same time these disturbances can be controlled, even negated completely, by a strong mind. Yet a mind which has strength only will break under them in time.

"Flexibility allied with strength is required," he had concluded, "and it is my job to see if that irresponsible lump of porridge you use for a brain possesses those qualities."

O'Mara had then instructed him to keep his mind as blank as possible during the transfer, and a few minutes later removed the helmet and nodded dismissal. With the first evidence of double-mindedness already becoming apparent, Conway had left for the Director's office to receive the details of his assignment.

And that had been only six hours ago.

Conway brought his wandering mind back to the present to find that the other half of it had been carrying on without him. He shook his head irritably in an attempt to fuse the two personalities together, and began to wind up the lecture.

He said: ". . . In the initial talk of the series I have dealt with the almost insoluble problem of treating the diabetic condition in the ELNT species. To summarise, this condition, or its near equivalent is known to practically all of the warm-blooded oxygen-breathing life-forms. Ideally it can be cured by the restimulation of the faulty or inactive pancreas. Among certain species, which includes the ELNTs, this treatment is impossible due to its disruption of the endocrine balance generally, which is nearly always fatal and invariably destroys the mental processes.

"Earlier and less efficient methods," Conway went on, "which control rather than cure the condition, are also unsuitable for your race. Administering insulin by subcutaneous injection presupposes a thin, flexible tegument underlaid by muscles, adipose and served by a capillary system which will wash the material slowly and evenly into the bloodstream. The ELNT is exo-skeletal, and it is impossible to inject through five inches of bone. The idea of drilling a fine hole and implanting a needle permanently is unsuccessful for various physiological reasons. And taking insulin orally, which relies on a certain proportion being lost as waste and the rest absorbed through the walls of the stomach, is unsuitable for ELNTs because of your digestive tract, whose efficiency varies markedly with the emotional state.

"All of which means," Conway ended simply, "that you Melfans are the only species remaining in which the diabetic condition is fatal."

The three ELNTs made short, complimentary speeches in turn, thanking him for an extremely useful first lecture. Senreth, the being who Conway wanted to think of as *it* but which one half of his mind demanded that he call *she*, was most flattering. Which did not help Conway's peace of mind one little bit.

Ordinarily he would have dismissed the class at this point and used the next twenty minutes or so in pulling himself together, Conway thought wryly; but not this time. These ELNTs were important people on the home world, so he was expected to act as host as well as instructor.

Sitting cross-legged at the two-foot high table in the Dining Hall involved no great discomfort, but shifting the mass of sea-food—both plant and animal—set before him was a problem. Conway was ravenously hungry, he knew that the Catering Supervisor would not have sent him out anything which was likely to disagree with his Earth-human metabolism, and by ELNT standards the stuff was delicious—the Melfan part of his mind *insisted* that it was. But to the Earth-human eye and nose of Conway it was a disgusting mess which stank like over-ripe fish.

He could always order some decent, Earth-human food, of course. But doing so would have been a breach of good manners, because he knew from the ELNT tape in his mind that the sight of steak and potatoes would have done worse things to his Melfan guests than their miniature fish and seaweed was doing to him. It wasn't until he began to relax and let his human identity slip into the background that he was able to eat at all, and then he found himself snapping at the food on his plate with both hands, using his index finger and thumb in imitation of the pincers of his guests. His nosefilters helped a lot, too.

After lunch he showed them around those sections of the hospital which did not require them to don protective suits. Quite a number of races were warm-blooded oxygen-breathers with one-G gravity and pressure, so that the tour lasted over four hours. They talked shop most of the time and Conway tried to keep at least one of the ELNTs between Senreth and himself. He was getting an overwhelming urge to bang his head against its/her carapace just between the neck and left fore-pincer.

Melfans ate every ten hours and took a four-hour sleep between meals, so on his next visit to the Dining Hall Conway could have ordered what he liked. But now the ELNT tape had gained such a strong hold that both Melfan and Earthly wishes were distasteful to him. Yet he was *hungry*. In desperation he ran his eye down the menu, mentally visualising the items and then hastily putting them out of his mind as the Melfan half registered revulsion or nausea. He had to fall back on sandwiches finally, the standby of all Tape-ridden Diagnosticians and Senior Physicians.

Half his mind insisted that they tasted like cork and the other half thought they were just barely better than nothing. *Fuel*, he thought disgustedly, *just fuel*. For Conway all pleasure in eating had gone.

The following three hours Conway spent in his room working on the lectures he would be delivering during the next week. With the enormous mass of ELNT-oriented data and experience on tap, widening his association centres and doubling his brain power, he simply ran through the theoretical aspect of the work. He felt rather awed by himself, even though he realised that this near-genius quality of thinking was normal to one in these circumstances. This was the Ideal—a working synthesis between the knowledge and experience of an entity long dead and the live, original thinking of a practising physician.

Conway prepared material for the next three days. He could not go much further ahead until he had an idea how fast the visitors would absorb the stuff. He was feeling tired by then and decided to try to sleep as quickly as possible, because the ELNT sharing his mind had begun acting up once Conway had stopped concentrating on purely medical subjects. The sooner he could render himself naturally unconscious the better for both of them.

But with that idea he got nowhere at all.

Tossing and turning in his bed, Conway told himself again and again that the entity sharing his mind was just a recording, the memories of a being long past caring about things physical. He, Conway, was the boss and he must put his mental foot down. This Melfan in his mind had no objective reality and its needs therefore were only the barest shadows of desires.

The trouble was, Conway told himself wretchedly, that they did not feel the slightest bit shadowy. Because the ELNT who had made the tape had done so at the height of his professional career, when he was still a comparatively young member of the species, so that all of Conway's objective knowledge that it was dead and gone to the contrary, the personality sharing his mind was as alive and rarin' to go as the day on which the tape had been made. And the Melfans were warm-blooded with a metabolism not too dissimilar to his own. Perhaps *hot*-blooded would describe them more aptly, because they were an intensely emotional and passionate race. Conway *knew*. And the being who had made the tape, even for one of his hot-blooded species, had been a hellion where the females were concerned.

Conway drifted off to sleep finally, his mind seething with the hot, vivid imagery more normal to an adolescent seriously disturbed for the first time by a member of the opposite sex. Only on this occasion the girl of Conway's dreams was a six-legged, intelligent crab called Senreth . . .

He awoke with a yell of sheer panic. A few minutes

later, when his pulse-rate had dropped back to normal, Conway tried to analyse the nightmare which had awakened him. There had been a great and basic fear, vertigo, and the impression of being utterly defenceless. He lay back, closed his eyes ... and five minutes later sat up, sweating.

Normally Conway did not dream, much less have nightmares. The sense of fear which had awakened him could not, he knew, apply to himself, so there must be something in the room or in the situation as a whole which was affecting the Melfan half of his mind. He lay back for the third time and began searching through the ELNT memories for some reason for his panic. It took a long time, because it was such a simple, basic thing that the ELNTs themselves did not think of it consciously. Conway rolled over on to his stomach, and his last thought before going peacefully to sleep was that *of course* any being with a heavy carapace would feel helpless and afraid if it was forced to sleep on its back.

He awoke with long, rumbling explosions and alarm sirens ringing in his ears. Conway was a very heavy sleeper and had found this to be the combination which wakened him fastest. Some of his colleagues awakened themselves with gentle music, but this Conway considered sissy. The act of groping for the cut-off switch brought him fully awake, and he decided that he would like to crawl around the bottom of his private lake for half an hour before breakfast. If he was feeling particularly devilish he might even dine off a couple of ornamental fish, which were becoming fat and lazy these days. He was on his hands and knees trying to push open the sliding door with his head when the realisation came of what was happening. The ELNT had sneaked up on him while his resistance had been low just after sleep.

He remembered to dress. The Melfans did not use clothing.

Like his last meal, breakfast was a compromise. There was another Earth-human doctor at the same table who was also working on an odd selection of dishes with a similar lack of enthusiasm. They exchanged sickly grins and presently Conway left for the two hundred and third level.

That day was bad, and the one that followed it even worse. The lectures had now progressed to the stage of four-way discussions—which was what Conway had hoped for—and occupied him for three hours each morning and afternoon. Inevitably they overflowed into his lunch period and he had to talk shop while dining with the ELNTs. The food did not bother him so much as the fact that he was having to take Melfan company for nearly eight hours at a stretch every day. It was bothering him, badly. He was being thrown up against Senreth too much.

In one of the busier corridors he had stepped aside to avoid being trampled by an elephantine FGLI. He had stumbled against Senreth and grabbed her mid-left leg to steady himself. The touch thrilled him to the core of his being, even though one half of his mind told him that it felt like a warm, slightly damp log. He drew back hurriedly, his face burning.

"My apologies," said Senreth, in Translated and therefore necessarily emotionless tones. "Ours is an unusually clumsy race."

"My fault entirely," Conway stammered, then added with a rush, "On the contrary, you are both dexterous and physically beautiful ..." He stopped himself in time before the Melfans could realise that he was being personally complimentary to Senreth rather than being polite towards their race as a whole. This had been the first time Conway had engaged in anything other than strictly professional conversation with the Melfan female. His hands were shaking badly.

It was then that Conway decided that he would have to see O'Mara. The ELNTs and himself would start working with models tomorrow, and even for that Conway could not afford to have shaky hands.

But O'Mara wasn't available.

"He's gone sick," said Carrington, the young, round-faced psychologist who was holding down O'Mara's desk. "Apparently his plumbing is clogged up with chloresterol and similar gunk, and Pathology wants to tinker with him for a week or so. Can I do anything for you?"

Conway told him yes and began a somewhat edited account of his mental troubles. He ended by requesting permission to take another Educator tape—one belonging to a completely cold and emotionless life-form which would combat the effect of the female hunter currently inhabiting his mind. By playing the hothead off against the frigid type he could, Conway hoped, keep his own human emotions to the fore and so be able to ignore Senreth.

Carrington looked thoughtful, then said, "Chances are it would make you more confused, but then again it might work. That is if I agreed to help you, which I don't."

"But *why*," said Conway angrily.

"Because O'Mara says so," Carrington replied imperturbably. "He left explicit instructions regarding you. No conditioning, shots or any other form of medication aimed at helping you over the rough spots. Your mental confusion is understandable, and I sympathise, but giving help at this stage would not be a good idea. You must find your own methods of fighting or adapting to the situation. All new Senior Physicians have to do it. A psychological crutch now would mean you always needing one, and you could hope for no further advancement.

"If things get too bad," the psychologist went on, watching him keenly, "serious enough to impair your physical efficiency, I'm thinking of violent digestive upsets, loss of co-ordination and so on, you can ask to be taken off the case."

And that, of course, was unthinkable. It would be a public admission that he had neither professional ability nor moral fibre—in short, that he was unfitted for his job. It was the most humiliating thing which could happen to one in his position. Conway shook his head, growled "Thank you" and left.

Mental confusion and overripe seafood Conway could take, but something would have to be done about Senreth. Maybe his earlier fit of the shakes had been a once-only occurrence, and if so then he had nothing to worry about. But he could not afford to make an assumption like that when there would shortly be a living entity under his knife, and with Senreth and the other two ELNTs assisting in the operation. Something would have to be done about that six-legged *femme fatale*, or about Conway himself.

Fight or adapt, Carrington had said, Conway's trouble seemed to be that he was adapting—giving in—too much. But his original idea for fighting the ELNT influence was still a good one, even though Carrington refused to let him take another tape. He could still fight fire, not with fire, but with extreme cold.

Walking rapidly, Conway went to the nearby inter-level lock and donned a lightweight suit. Ten minutes later he was swimming through the cool green of the water-breathing AUGL section. From there, and using the same suit, he went through a series of chlorine-filled wards belonging to the Illensan PVSJs. There were a lot of people he knew among the PVSJ staff, but by his haste managed to discourage conversation. On the next level the cold struck at him even through the fabric of his suit. Conway negotiated the next lock quickly and climbed shivering into a tank-like vehicle which was parked inside. This vehicle—highly insulated, jammed with heaters inside and hung with refrigeration units out—was the only possible method of entering the Cold Section without both freezing himself to death in seconds and blasting the life out of every patient in the ward with his radiated body heat. For these were the quarters of the methane life-forms, an ultra-frigid, crystaline species which inhabited only the outermost planets of some of the coolest suns.

The blackness outside was absolute and the temperature close to that. In his scanner Conway saw another vehicle like his own come rolling up. It belonged to the nurse on duty and he had to explain that he was conducting some general research which did not require either assistance or the direct examination of the patients.

Alone again, Conway wondered briefly who or what had been in the other tank. The nurse's voice had been Translated so it was certainly not an Earth-human. Then he switched off his Translator, cut out two of the heaters, and increased the gain on his outside sound pick-ups: he wanted to hear the patients conversing without being distracted by what they said. The deliberate chilling of the vehicle's interior was designed simply to put him in a more receptive mood.

With his eyes closed and his unseen breath fogging the cabin, Conway listened to a ward full of intelligent crystals talking. Ineffably sweet, incredibly fragile, they spoke like the chiming of colliding snowflakes. This was a race, Conway thought as an elfin carillon of great purity rang out, whose thinking was cool and fragile and gentle. In all of their history there had been a complete absence of violence, and anything like a sex-motivated thought was something of which they were utterly incapable. They possessed a quality which could only be described as coldly spiritual.

And this, Conway hoped, would be just the medicine to quell the Melfan hothead who was influencing far too much of his mind. And body.

Next day began the practical work, with Conway demonstrating the new procedure on an ELNT model which Anatomy had built for him. It was an extremely life-like piece of work containing a functioning heart and circulatory system. The two male ELNTs expressed pleasure and surprise at its detail, and Senreth reacted in characteristic fashion.

"A handsome brute," she exclaimed, giving the model a series of taps on the carapace which were half-playful, half-affectionate. "We don't hatch them like that anymore."

Conway shut his eyes tightly as the ELNT segment of his mind sat back on its haunches and howled, or whatever it was love-sick crabs did in similar circumstances. Desperately he thought back to the previous night in the methane ward, recapturing the chill, ethereal beauty of that environment. He concentrated hard, and apparently the therapy worked. When he opened his eyes a few seconds later and sneaked a look at his hands, they weren't shaking.

Calling for attention, Conway began listing the instruments to be used, handling each one briefly as he discussed it. Some were standard Melfan equipment, others had been designed at Sector General especially for this operation, and all had their handles terminating in the ELNT-type grip—two narrow, hollow cones set at an angle of thirty degrees to each other. These were designed to fit the Melfan pincers, but Conway found that he could use them. The human hand was about the most adaptable appendage known.

From the instruments he moved to an object enclosed in a transparent case which occupied an adjacent table. It looked a little like a large, three-inch pancake which had been pulled and twisted out of shape. Two lengths of narrow plastic tubing sprouted like limp antennae from its upper surface, and the whole occupied a volume of approximately one cubic foot.

"... This is the artificial pancreas," Conway said with a touch of pride. The first model had taken up a whole room, and refining it down to this size had been no mean achievement. He went on, "Its use is made possible by the fact that in your species the vital organs are practically floating in a shock-absorbent fluid and have considerable free play. The device is convoluted both to accommodate and be held in position by the surrounding organs. The arterial blood supply is diverted into the artificial pancreas at a point close to the heart, which maintains the blood-sugar level at optimum.

"Unfortunately," Conway went on, "neutralisation of the excess sugar causes a certain amount of waste to collect in the device, and this must be removed every three or four years. But this is a much simpler procedure than the initial operation."

Continuing, he stressed the importance of fast, accurate work. When the section of carapace was removed and the fluid drained away, the vital organs together with their attached muscle and blood-supply networks were no longer floating in this frictionless medium. Serious displacement and compression was caused both by their own dead weight and that of surrounding organs, also possible interruptions of the blood-supply to several vital areas. The heart especially was placed under an abnormal strain. If death was not to result within a few minutes these organs had to be supported during insertion of the device, which was the reason why three assistants were necessary. Considering the mass of the Melfan life-form, that was the number calculated to give the maximum help with the minimum of overcrowding.

Conway placed a dummy of the artificial pancreas on the instrument tray and pushed it across to the operating frame where their 'patient' was suspended.

"This is to be a full dress rehearsal, but without the time limit," he said briskly. "So if you will take your positions we will begin . . ."

It began fairly easily with the removal of a section of carapace measuring eighteen inches by six and the uncovering of the underlying membrane, which he pierced with a suction probe. As pumps drew the internal fluid into an aseptic container Conway made a long incision and snapped at his three assistants to go in with support pans. These were specially-shaped pans with long, angled handles which were designed to hold the vital organs in position when the fluid had been drained off.

"One at a time, please!" Conway said sharply as six pincers converged on the operative field as one. "You're making a noise like a machine shop! That's better, but remember that I've to get in there, too . . . Senreth, you're not supporting that lung properly. Let me show you . . ."

Conway grasped one of Senreth's pincers in each hand and gently eased them into the correct position, felt his mouth go dry, and began thinking furiously about the patients in the methane ward. He went on shakily, "To clear a path for the device we must first incise the muscle which anchors—"

There was a sudden spurt of red over his gloves and then a great crimson tide welling into the field, obliterating everything. Conway stared at it foolishly, asking himself how *this* could have happened, and knowing all the time exactly how it had happened.

"A shockingly life-like model," said one of the ELNTs.

"And an object lesson to all of us, sir. We obstructed you, of course."

Conway looked up. The ELNT was giving him an out, and he was tempted to take it. But instead he shook his head angrily and retorted, "If there's a lesson it is that Teacher does not necessarily know everything. And now, Doctors, you may go. I'll have a technician repair the model before the next lecture."

Deliberately he refrained from saying *my* next lecture. He was going to see Carrington. He wanted to quit.

But first he would have to find someone who could take over for him. The Melfans had to be considered, too. Another Senior was needed—one with more experience and stability. Maybe Dr. Mannen would take over for him.

He ran Dr. Mannen to earth as he was emerging from the LSVO theatre. His old friend and one-time teacher specialised in surgery of the low-gravity, winged species of this classification and that of their MSVK cousins, and was in permanent possession of these two tapes. Despite this his manner and conversation was quite rational, if a trifle on the breezy side.

"So you're in trouble and need help," Mannen boomed cheerfully. "What is it? Professional, or some sordid emotional involvement?"

"Both," said Conway bitterly.

Mannen's eye-brows climbed. Grinning, he said, "And I always thought you were too straitlaced for that sort of thing. Well, well. But you can tell me the grisly details over lunch, that is if you don't mind watching me guzzle what looks like a plate of bird-seed?"

"So long as it doesn't smell of fish," said Conway with great feeling, then launched into a somewhat incoherent account of his troubles. Both doctors switched off their Translators so that e-t passersby would not overhear them. This was one piece of scandal which just could not be allowed to get out.

"Basically your trouble is that you want to whistle after crabs," Mannen said as they found a table. Before Conway could reply he added quickly, "Female crabs, of course. I did not mean to imply that there was anything seriously wrong with you."

"This is serious," said Conway quietly.

Mannen nodded. "To you it must be," he said sympathetically. "And I think it was a dirty trick saddling you with an ELNT tape for your first long-termer. A completely alien personality would have made it much easier to keep the two sets of data seperate. The Melfans are very close to us temperamentally, which is one of the reasons for your trouble. And has it occurred to you that your subconscious may be aiding and abetting this six-legged Don Juan, that deep down inside our quiet and ultra-respectable Dr. Conway shares its feelings? After all, this is just a set of memories impressed on your brain, and while a certain amount of confusion is to be expected there should be no great difficulty in establishing which is the original you and which the superimposed entity."

Mannen was silent for a moment. When he went on his tone was almost harsh:

"Maybe I'm beginning to sound like O'Mara, but it seems to me if the proximity of the ELNT female gave you the shakes so badly that you botched the demonstration, this is a clear indication that you *want* the superimposed personality to take over. My advice is to straighten yourself out, fast."

Angrily, Conway denied the charge that he was a mental traitor to himself, and went into details regarding his efforts to combat the ELNT influence. Then he stopped suddenly. There was no need to tell Mannen what his greatest fear was; that of botching, not a demonstration but the operation proper, and killing the patient.

". . . I want to quit, Doctor," Conway ended miserably. "Will you take over for me?"

"No!" Mannen snapped, then more quickly, "Use your head, man! You would have to tell the Melfans why you were ducking out, and you'd be laughed out of the hospital. Dammit, there must be some tricks you haven't thought of yet, you're supposed to be the boy with the unconventional ideas, remember. That melting SRTT and the chrysalis lifeform . . ."

Mannen's voice died away and his eyes took on a far-away look. Suddenly he smiled and said, "There's one approach you haven't tried yet. Trouble is, you're not likely to think of it. I would, and a lot of others I know, but not you. And I'm not allowed to tell you."

Conway breathed heavily through his nose. He said, "Stop hedging. O'Mara said you could advise me. Can't you phrase it so it sounds like advice?"

Mannen shook his head. "I'll have to think about it, pull a few strings, and put it through the proper channels. Pity you aren't the type who shamelessly misuses authority for your own selfish purposes, like me . . ."

"Put *what* through proper channels?" Conway practically shouted.

"Eat up," said Mannen, ignoring the question. "Your sandwich is getting cold."

During the four days which followed Conway did not again make a slip, but there had been several very near things. He continued to get the shakes every time Senreth touched him in the line of duty, but not, he thought, quite so badly. This he attributed to Mannen's earlier conversation, which had left him both angry and half hopeful—though what exactly he was hoping for Conway could not say. *Why* was it a pity that he did not misuse his Senior Physician's authority for selfish ends, and what was it that other people could think of but not him? Was his subconscious acceptance of the ELNT personality part of the answer? Conway did not know, and there were times when he suspected that Mannen did not know either, or that the other was simply trying to make him so worried about the state of his own mind that he would be too engrossed to be bothered by Senreth. Yet Mannen had never struck him as being such a devious person.

On the morning of the fifth day the Melfan patient who had been waiting for the operation went into coma and Conway had to set the time for early that afternoon—three full days sooner than he had planned. There was now no time for him to instruct someone else in the job—he was stuck with it, Senreth, the shakes, and all. Then just as he was leaving for the theatre came another calamity—the news that he was to have an Observer. True it was only someone or other from the AUGL section anxious to brush up on their exo-skeletal procedures, but nothing could have been better planned at that moment to wreck Conway's already weakened self-confidence. He hoped that he, she or it was nobody he knew.

But even that small comfort was denied him. When Conway arrived he found Murchison gowned and waiting. Murchison he knew, both personally and by reputation.

During the preliminaries—while the patient was brought in, transferred to the operating frame and strapped down— Conway spoke very little. And yet he wanted to talk, or do anything at all which would put off the moment of beginning—which would grant the patient a stay of execution. For that was how he had begun to think of it now; his hands were shaking already. Then abruptly he stepped into the recessed section of floor beside the frame— necessary because he was so much taller than the Melfans —and signalled that he was ready to start. Unobtrusively, Murchison drew closer.

While the routine business of opening the carapace was in progress Conway glanced across at Murchison. Since being exposed to the ELNT tape he had been given a completely objective view of his own species, and the opinion had been growing in him that they were, male and female alike, shapeless and unlovely bags of dough when compared with the clean, hard contours of the Melfans. Murchison, he thought, would not be pleased if she knew she was being thought of as a shapeless and unlovely bag. Unless covered by a heavy duty spacesuit fitted with an opaque sun-filter, Nurse Murchison possessed that combination of physiological features which made it impossible for any male Earth-human member of the staff to regard her with anything like Clinical Detachment.

But the regards were one way only—she was supposed to have a shoulder that was strictly from the methane section. At least so it was said. Conway had once worked on a case with her in the Nursery, however, and had found her very easy to get along with. At the moment he thought her gown was belted a little too tightly.

Conway incised the underlying membrane and while the pumps gurgled, drawing off the internal fluid, Senreth and the other two ELNTs were already bringing their support pans into position. They had the drill off perfectly—especially Senreth, who possessed a remarkably sure and delicate touch. If they had only had time to work up their speed Conway could have allowed them to conduct the operation while he merely supervised. He would have had only his mental confusion to worry about then. There was still a distinct tremor in his hands.

"Stop that!" Conway raged silently at them. *"Are you trying to kill somebody!"*

This was a living being they were working on, and the internal organs were subtly different in size and placement to those in the model. There was also a complex of secondary blood-vessels and muscle structure which had only been suggested in the practice sessions. Conway sweated while they gently eased the heart, stomach and a section of lung aside preparatory to inserting the artificial pancreas. Shock had sent the pulse-rate away up and Conway thought wildly that the heart itself might pull free. He didn't know how Senreth managed to hold it—it was like a landed fish flopping about on its support pan. He found his eyes drifting to Senreth's pincers, lingering on the sharp, hard contours and the lovely reddish-grey coloration which was enhanced rather than concealed by the aseptic film. Conway felt his face getting hot and his hands trembled, badly. Helplessly he swore under his breath.

"Can I be of any help, Doctor?" Murchison asked suddenly in her low, pleasant voice. "I'm familiar with your written lectures . . ."

"What? No!" said Conway, startled and irritated. "And don't talk, please."

Murchison must be slipping, he thought. A nurse of her experience should have known better. And her belt was definitely too tight. The effect, in other circumstances, would have been distracting to say the least. Conway made an impatient sound, then turned to lift the artificial pancreas from its saline bath.

A few seconds later it was in position, awaiting only to

be linked into the main artery. This had to be clamped above and below the points of entrance and exit, cut, and the severed ends pressed over the two flexible connections coming from the new pancreas. A tight fit was insured by having the connections taper out to a width greater than that of the artery, and special non-corroding bands would secure the join. It was tricky work, complicated both by the tangle of subsidiary blood-vessels in the area and the obscuring effect of three pairs of ELNT pincers.

On two occasions Murchison apparently got excited and started reporting on the patient's condition—information readily available to Conway from the tell-tales beside him—and he had to shush her. After giving her one particularly angry glare he found himself thinking, *Not just the belt, her whole blasted outfit is too tight . . . !* He returned to his work feeling confused, excited and over-stimulated in some odd fashion. And for the last ten minutes he realised that his hands had been steady as the proverbial rock. Even when he was forced to compliment Senreth for a particularly deft piece of work on her part, or was obliged to move one of her pincers to the side while suturing underneath, they remained steady.

He still regarded Senreth's mandibles as beautiful—hard, steady, wonderfully precise appendages which it was a joy to behold in operation. But when he touched one it felt like a warm, slightly damp log, and his emotional reaction was the same as would have been obtained from any other warm, slightly damp log. None at all.

Almost before he knew it they were finished, the internal fluid returned, the membrane sutured and the carapace being wired in. Anxiously then, they watched the analyser. They watched it until there was no possible doubt that the blood-sugar level was coming down, then:

"We've done it!" Conway yelled, practically falling out of his recess with excitement. He jumped up and did a shambling dance around the frame, slapped Senreth's carapace in a most familiar manner and ended up by hugging Murchison.

"Put me down!" the nurse said severely, when the hug

began stretching past the two-minute mark. "This isn't like you, Doctor Conway ..."

Conway eased the pressure without quite letting go. He said seriously, "You don't know how lucky it was for me that you turned up here. Every time I ... she ... you ... Anyway, I didn't even know you were interested in this sort of work."

"I'm not," said Murchison, still trying to push him away, "but it was suggested that I so interest myself, the suggestion being worded remarkably like an order. This is undignified, Dr. Conway."

Suddenly Conway saw the light. It was Mannen's work, of course! His friend had not been allowed to help him, but through devious channels so that the truth would never be suspected he had arranged to have Murchison planted on him at just the time when he most needed a counterweight—or was counter-attraction the word, considering Murchison's physical endowments—to check his emotional imbalance towards Senreth. It had turned out to be the simple answer to a complex psychological problem. First chance he got he would have to thank Mannen for being a true friend and a lecherous old man. And Murchison, too.

The Melfans were leaving. A little wildly he said, "Murchison, I love you all to pieces. You'll never know why, but I've got to show my appreciation somehow. When do you come off duty?"

"Dr. Conway," said Murchison gently, temporarily ceasing her attempts to pull free, "I may never know but I can guess an awful lot. And I flatly refuse to catch someone on the rebound from a six-legged, female crustacean ..!"

Conway laughed and let her go—temporarily, he hoped. So Murchison knew, then. He was going to have to ask her very nicely not to blab it around.

Solemnly, he said, "Senreth was just a silly infatuation, she isn't really my type. Now, what time do you come off duty?"

To Kill or Cure
>◇◇◇◇◇◇◇◇◇◇◇◇◇◇◇◇◇◇◇◇◇◇◇◇◇◇◇◇◇<

THE LOW pressure system centred off the Hebrides was lashing the coasts of Northwest Ireland and Scotland with rain squalls of nearly gale force when Trans-Ocean Airways Flight 317, while radioing her periodic position check, reported engine trouble. The signal was drowned uncompleted by a resurgence of the interference which had been rendering the ether unworkable for the past three hours—unworkable, that was, but for a few short breaks when that peculiar howling vanished with the suddenness of a light bulb going out. During the next such break Flight 317 could not be contacted at all. She was presumed to have ditched and an air-sea rescue operation was mounted forthwith.

But the search depended to a great extent on ease of communication, and that was not possible with the unearthly din screaming out of head-sets and loudspeakers. When consulted, radio and Met experts spoke learnedly and at great length about sunspot cycles and auroral discharges, but they refused to be pinned down.

On a training flight between North Bay on Barra to Londonderry an Anson aircraft found itself—for reasons best known to its navigator, who was, after all, a trainee—over the Derryveagh Mountains of North Donegal, some forty miles west of its intended destination. But the error was fortunate in that they spotted wreckage.

If this was the missing 317 then a near-miracle had occurred. The pilot of the Anson stated that, although he had merely glimpsed the wreck through scudding rain-clouds and there appeared to be smoke coming from it, it very definitely was not burnt out. But this state of affairs could not last indefinitely. Something in the wreck was burning, probably a puddle of hydraulic fluid, and despite the rain falling in the area, that fire must eventually reach the fuel tanks.

The survivors, if any, had to be reached quickly.

The helicopter skidded and bounced across the sky, tossed and side-swiped by the up-draughts and cross-winds from the mountains one thousand feet below. This was no weather for helicopters, Terrins thought ruefully. He grunted and hugged his waistline in an involuntary attempt to keep his maltreated stomach in place.

"Is there a doctor on the aircraft?" he said.

It was a pretty feeble attempt at humour, Terrins knew as soon as he spoke; like himself at the moment, sickly.

On either side of him Malloy and Thompson smiled with the politeness due a Lieut-Commander (Medical) from those of the lower deck, though their eyes never left the rugged terrain unrolling steadily beneath them. Sub-Lieutenant Price, navigating and in charge of communications when the interference allowed them, had his head-phones on. Lieutenant Stephens in the pilot's position was just far enough away from the Lieut-Commander for him to pretend that he had heard nothing.

Suddenly Price stiffened, an attentive expression on his youthful, rather boney face, then he pulled off the head-phones with an angry motion and spoke.

"The people in that Anson can see about as well as they can navigate," he said in disgusted tones. "That was a signal from *Argus* saying that Flight 317 turned up at Renfrew seven minutes ago on three engines. No flap, no panic—the passengers didn't even know that an engine had seized up. Seems 317's radioman put down the interference which interrupted his signal to self-oscillation or something in his own set, and he didn't receive our later messages or know that there was a search on for them because he was taking his set apart to find out what was wrong with it."

He ended, "*Argus* says to return at once."

Terrin's strongest emotion was one of relief. Though he had been senior medical officer on the aircraft carrier *Argus* for two years now, the times he had been up in the ship's pick-up helicopter could be counted on the thumb of one hand. Compared with the bouncing around he was suffering at the moment, the thought of the large and relatively steady deck of the carrier—at present anchored in Lough Foyle with the rest of the squadron taking part in the forthcoming exercises—was a very pleasant one. With luck he would be back on board in another twenty minutes.

But Price had barely finished talking when Thompson shouted, "Wreckage!" and pointed.

"I see it," Lieutenant Stephens acknowledged, then: "Price. Report this to *Argus*. Tell them that under the circumstances we will investigate this wreck before returning." He looked back, seeking corroboration of this from Terrins, who nodded. "All right. Seat belts! Down we go. . . !"

The wreck had not yet caught fire, Terrins saw, though a haze of white smoke around it was being pulled into tatters by the wind. The long, silvery fuselage seemed virtually intact, and there was very little wreckage in the immediate vicinity. Terrins did a startled double-take at that. Where were the smashed and disembowelled engines, the crumpled remains of wings and tail-planes? There was nothing of that nature in the area at all. Only a peculiar difference in the colour and quality of the ground near the wreck . . .

Terrins brought his attention back to Stephens with a rush as the pilot shouted a warning. Stephens had been trying to land on a reasonably flat-looking ledge of rock about fifty yards to windward of the wreck. But close to the ground the wind was a treacherous, unpredictable thing which had to be out-guessed rather than judged. The helicopter was down to within a few feet of the ledge when a freak gust hurled it crabwise into the hillside. An undercarriage leg struck, and snapped off. They canted forward drunkenly. Two more tremors shook the aircraft as two of the rotor blades ground themselves into ruin against the stony hillside. There was silence then but for the whistling of the wind and the angry muttering of Stephens. Finally he raised his voice.

"Tell *Argus* there are two wrecks now," he said glumly. "I'll give you a list of spares I think we'll need to get this thing airborne again . . ."

He broke off as Price shook his head and held one of his earphones outward so that they could all hear the noise coming from it. The interference was back.

Now that they were down, the drill was to first see that any fires burning in the wreck were either put out or kept under control until the casualties were removed. But Terrins' mind was not on the issuing of fire-extinguishers or any other aspect of the rescue drill, it was focussed solely on the wreck.

"That's not smoke coming from it," he said when the silence had lasted several seconds. "That is *steam*!"

"I don't like this, sir," Stephens said nervously. "That isn't an aeroplane. You can see that."

Terrins could—they all could—and he did not like it either. He said, "I'd say it's a rocket, an unsuccessful try at a manned orbital vehicle. What do you think?"

"There are no venturi openings for the rocket motors," Stephens replied. "And no stabilizing fins."

"Let's have a closer look," Terrins said. He had been talking, he realised now, just to fill time until his seething brain came up with something which would fit the observable and highly disturbing facts before them.

Except for the stoved-in appearance of the nose and the long, yard-wide rent where the shock of collision had caused the hull plating to open, the wreck was a streamlined, featureless torpedo-shape roughly two hundred feet long and twenty in diameter. But more disquieting than the sight of this enigmatic wreck was the appearance of the ground for about twenty yards around it.

It was as though a giant sledge-hammer had struck the

rocky hillside, leaving a regular, saucer-shaped depression where the tangle of heather and scree had been literally driven into the ground. A flattened mass of leaves and splinters showed where one small, lonely tree had stood. And in the centre of this highly unnatural depression rested the wreck.

Terrins felt a chill go through him that had nothing to do with the cold, wind-driven rain that lashed at them suddenly from behind. Sunset was still two hours away, and already he was peopling this bleak hillside with bogey men—or bogey somethings. He made a great effort to get his thinking processes straightened out, then spoke.

"Obviously, this is a spaceship of some kind," he said, and swallowed. He waved his hand at the flattened bushes around them. "And this looks as if ... as if it *pushed in* the ground somehow in trying to cushion its fall—as if the shock of collision was absorbed by a large area of ground surface instead of by the ship alone.

"I'm only guessing," he went on, "but I'd say that this meant that it had some control of gravity or inertia. Certainly it is beyond the crude rocket motor stage ..." He broke off, looked at the three men who had accompanied him to the wreck—Price had been left standing by the helicopter's radio—and ended briskly, "Whatever gadget they used, it wasn't quite good enough. They crashed."

And that was a very reassuring thought, Terrins told himself. He was curious about this wreck, intensely curious. But his curiosity had been more than off-set by anxiety regarding whatever form of life it might contain. His imagination had run riot on that particular track. But the ship was, after all, a wreck, and *dead* bogey men could not hurt anyone.

The gaping tear in the hull was wide enough for a man to crawl through. Terrins flicked a wetted finger against the plating. It was hot, but not excessively so.

"You're not going *in!*"

Terrins had not meant to enter the wreck, but something in the shocked, incredulous tones of Stephens touched the mulelike streak of contrariness in him. Always when someone told him that something could or should not be done in that particular tone of voice, an unreasoning urge overtook him to do it just to prove how wrong they were. Usually they had been proved right and himself wrong, but that had not cured him ...

"Certainly I intend going in," he said, bending to look into the opening. "It's dark inside. We'll need lights."

He stressed the 'we' slightly, and took a perverse delight at the sudden fright in Stephens' face as the pilot began expostulating wildly. This was an event of unparalleled importance which had occurred, he insisted. They should report it and await instructions. This sort of thing was a job for specialists, anyway, and so on. There were a lot more reasons, all good ones, why they should not enter the alien ship just yet.

But there seemed to be a devil driving Terrins, a stubborn, angry devil. Stephens was being eminently sensible, and Terrins himself realised that. But he had, he felt, committed himself to a certain course of action and could not back down now. Thompson and Malloy, the two sick-bay attendants who had recently joined the *Argus*, were standing by with carefully expressionless faces. Were they thinking that the Lieut-Commander was allowing Stephens to talk him out of something he was afraid to do, anyway? Terrins clenched his teeth and gestured for the pilot to be silent. One thing he did know, if they were going inside the wreck, then his reasons for going had to appear as strong to him as Stephens' reasons for wanting to stay out.

"Lieutenant Stephens," he said sternly, "let me remind you that we were sent to the aid of survivors of this wreck, and while the wreck did not turn out to be the one we expected, I am specialist enough in my own field to think that our instructions still stand."

A heroic little speech, Terrins thought in sudden self-disgust, *you big ham, you.*

But it stopped the Lieutenant's arguments cold. Terrins watched the pilot's face as he considered this aspect of the affair, and the changing expression as his imagination began painting lurid pictures of the physical forms which these survivors might take. Terrins had not thought very deeply on that point either, and felt suddenly uneasy. What had he talked himself into this time ... ?

A hail from the helicopter interrupted them, followed by the shouted information that Price was in touch with their ship again. Did they have anything to report?

It was not until a good twenty minutes later that Terrins insinuated himself into the gap in the ship's hull and peered about. *Argus* had been not too politely incredulous about their story of finding a wrecked spaceship, though they had eventually been convinced that the helicopter's crew had encountered a wreck of some description. They had phoned through to Letterkenny, the nearest large town, to send ambulances to the spot. Regarding the investigation of the interior of this alleged spaceship, they didn't care who went in. They had been quite short about it.

It had been Stephens' idea that Terrins run a line from the grounded helicopter to a telephone head-set which he would carry with him into the wreck. In this way Price in the helicopter could relay their findings directly to *Argus* with minimum delay. And, of course, if anything should happen to them ...

Terrins deliberately left that thought unfinished and moved a little further into the ship. The torch showed that he was in a large, rectangular compartment with nothing in it that moved. He called for the others to join him.

The pooled light of four torches showed more detail.

Ceiling, three of the walls and the floor they stood on were painted a drab, reddish-grey colour and were relatively free of attached gadgetry. The remaining wall most decidedly was not. Weird-looking mechanisms grew out all over it to a distance of a foot or eighteen inches, and there were trailing wires and torn metal where others had apparently been ripped from their bases by the crash. A broad, shiny black line began at a semi-circular opening in an adjoining wall and looped around each of the machines in turn, crossing and joining up with itself several times before disappearing through a similar opening in the opposite wall.

Terrins was on the point of describing their surroundings to Price in the helicopter when it suddenly struck him that he was standing on a wall instead of on a floor, and the 'wall' with the machinery, black curving lines and opening several feet above the 'floor' was the true floor. The two-foot high, semi-circular opening was a door!

"I'm taking notes, not relaying," Price said when Terrins made the correction. "The interference is back, sir."

It was a struggle for Terrins to get through the opening and into the compartment beyond—the black stuff was both sticky and oily and it came off on his clothes; it did not smell very nice, either. The others, being slimmer, had less trouble.

This was a long, narrow compartment, and the mechanisms growing out of the floor beside and above them were more numerous and complicated. The broad black lines were everywhere. In the middle of the room a descending ramp, with the ever-present black band along its centre, led into the depths of the ship. Terrins was considering ways of climbing to the ramp using the machinery projecting from the nearly vertical floor when an exclamation from Thompson made him swing round.

He saw his first alien.

Terrins was reminded strongly of a tubby, pink and over-stuffed sausage and, because he had been expecting some larger and more grotesque horror, he felt quite relieved as he moved closer. Why, he told himself, he had seen worse things than this while weeding the garden.

He saw that one end of the pink, slug-like body was pinned down by a heavy piece of equipment which had broken free in the collision, and there was a quantity of reddish-brown goo around which was probably the creature's blood. A knob-like protuberance on its other end—a watery blue colour, this—was probably an eye, and two flaps of skin partially covered it. Immediately behind this was a sort of cock's comb which terminated in three pencil-thin tentacles each about six feet long. Two of these were wrapped tightly around the creature's body and the third extended stiffly into the wreckage strewn against the forward bulkhead. The thing was twisted so that a large, oblong pad on its underbelly showed clearly. This pad was black and had a wet shine: Terrins concluded that its method of locomotion resembled that of a snail, and the broad black lines connecting the various items of equipment they had seen were in the nature of prefabricated snail tracks!

Terrins' skin crawled at the thought of that black stuff smeared all over his clothes, and revulsion fought with his intense curiosity regarding the creature. He drew back slightly; he could just imagine what the thing would feel like to touch—cold and wet, and maybe sticky . . .

"Can you do anything for it, sir?"

It was Lieutenant Stephens who had spoken. His face was pale, on the greenish side rather than white, but there was a vindictive gleam in his eye. Lieut-Commander Terrins had entered this wreck against Stephens' advice not to mention all the dictates of common sense, the pilot's tone implied. He had overridden this good advice, moreover, with the flimsy excuse of being a doctor confronted with a wreck which might contain survivors. Now Stephens was calling on him to do the impossible, and looking forward to seeing his superior officer squirm.

Secretly, Terrins could not blame him.

"It may already be dead," he replied ironically. "In which case I doubt if anything can be done for it . . ." As he spoke he forced himself to touch the thin tentacle which stretched stiffly from the creature to a mechanism which was partly buried in the wreckage heaped against the forward wall.

He was surprised to find that it was warm to the touch, then startled as it slid away from his hand and came whipping back. There was very little force behind it, but the tip of the tentacle was roughened enough to lift a narrow strip of skin off the back of Terrins' hand. The tentacle coiled and uncoiled uncertainly, then fell limp. The creature's body began a slow, quivering motion all over.

"Well, it seems to be alive and, er . . ." he forced a smile, ". . . twitching."

He was saved from having to say or do anything else by Price's voice in the head-phones saying, "The interference has gone again, sir. Have you found . . . I mean, is there anything fresh you want me to report?"

"Yes . . ." Terrins began, and brought Price up to date. He ended, " . . . and tell them I intend going as far as possible into the wreck. But from what we can see the ship's outer shell is extremely strong compared with the interior structure—the inside is a shambles, so we may not get very far."

He turned to the creature quivering like a large pink jelly at his feet, and with the help of the others he tried to lift the girder and twisted plating which pinned it down. But the mass of metal extended deeply into the main wreckage and they had to stop in case the whole unstable mass caved in and buried the creature completely.

Terrins began climbing to the ramp in the centre of the nearly vertical floor which led to the adjoining compartment.

Warm to the touch, he was thinking. A high body temperature usually meant a warm-blooded oxygen breather, and the fact that the creature continued to live when the tear in the outer hull had opened the ship to Earth's atmosphere seemed to prove that ordinary air was not harmful—or immediately harmful, he corrected himself—to it. And the reddish tinge of its dark-brown body fluid also indicated an oxygen exchange system similar to that of a human being.

It was sheer stupidity to suppose that he could aid them in his capacity as a doctor—that type of medical miracle was strictly B-feature stuff. But he should be able to deduce something from visual inspection of the creatures which would at least allow him to proceed without harming them further.

They breathed air and they possessed a normally fast metabolic rate. Terrins blew on his skinned knuckles at the memory of that whiplash tentacle. Muscular action of that nature used up energy, and energy lost had to be replaced
. . .

Terrins stopped in the sudden realisation that there was no way for that energy to be replaced. He had noted a small, porous area on the alien's upper surface through which it breathed, but nowhere on the injured creature had he found anything resembling a mouth! A highly developed organism simply could not function by breathing and nothing else.

But apparently these creatures did not eat.

Stephens, who was following him along the ramp, bumped him from behind. Terrins, in a kneeling position with one hand holding his torch, lost balance. He put the other hand out instinctively to keep from falling onto his face and it landed slap on the oily black line which the snail-like aliens used to get about the ship. It skidded to a sticky halt and the unpleasant odour—slightly fishy, Terrins thought, and a little like the smell of seaweed in the sun—struck at his nostrils. He noticed, too, that his sliding hand had wiped some of the black stuff off the metal underneath. Greenish yellow liquid began to ooze through what had seemed to be solid metal until the cleared patch was filled, then it rapidly turned black.

Terrins had the frustrating feeling that the key to the problem puzzling him was staring him in the face if only he could jog his alleged brain into proper working order. But he was still worrying at the problem a few seconds later when the end of the ramp was reached. He helped the others out, then their torches swept this new compartment.

Thompson was briefly and violently sick.

The true floor of this compartment was only about twenty degrees off the horizontal. Terrins did some quick mental calculations and decided that the cylindrical interior of the alien ship was divided lengthways into three decks at one hundred and twenty degree angles to each other, with whatever machinery was used to furnish the artificial gravity operating from the longitudinal axis of the ship. Had the artificial gravity been working he was sure that all three decks would have been 'down' to those occupying them. But the mechanism and occupants had both suffered in the crash, and by the look of things in here the latter had had the worst of it.

This compartment must have been crowded at the time of the crash. The usual debris lay heaped up against the forward bulkheads with the snail-like aliens lying in, on and under it. Had Terrins been immediately interested in the alien internal structure he would have had no trouble in setting to work, because several of the creatures were in more than one piece. The ones who were not all too obviously dead lay in the tangle of metal and quivered silently.

They've no mouths, Terrins thought suddenly. They can't scream and even their breathing is silent. All they can do is lie and shake in agony. All at once he wished desperately that he could do something for them. But what could he do? He had been unable to even discover if or how the things fed, much less finding out a means of patching them up . . .

An idea he had had a few minutes earlier began to take form in the back of his mind. But it dissolved as the voice of Price came hesitantly from his head-phones.

"Excuse me, sir, I thought . . . I mean, I wondered . . ." The navigator's voice stopped. He cleared his throat—a deafening sound in the head-phones—then got out, "The Derry operator—Derry is listening to us, too, now—and I have been talking. Things have changed there, he says. They don't think you're d——" he broke off in confusion, after very nearly having said too much.

Terrins, said, "Drunk, Mister Price?"

"Yes, sir," Price agreed, his voice gaining confidence now that the Lieut-Commander had taken the word out of his mouth. He went on, "Seems that the general feeling in Derry was that Lieutenant Stephens had piled the aircraft up on a cold mountainside and we were keeping warm with alcohol from the hydraulic system. But they don't think that now," he added hastily.

Terrins' mind had been too busy with the immediate problem to wonder what they had been thinking about him on *Argus* or at Londonderry Base. But Price seemed bursting to tell him something, and the roundabout way he was going about it meant that his news could not be official. Terrins made an interrogatory sound in his throat and waited.

"This is only a rumour, you understand," Price went on. "But the Derry operator says that the American Liaison people are in a tizzy over a message they've just received. Seems there's another spaceship, and this one isn't wrecked—"

"*What!*"

At his exclamation, Stephens a few feet away gave him a startled look. Terrins unclipped one of the ear-phones from his headband and motioned for Stephens to listen in as well.

" . . . Yes. Seems the Americans were tracking a Mouse on radar—er, that means Minimum Orbital Unmanned Sat—"

"I know what a MOUSE is," Terrins said irritably. "Get on with it!"

Apparently the team hunting for a Mouse had caught themselves an elephant. An object which was at least one thousand feet long had appeared suddenly on their radar screens, approaching at a velocity that was starkly incredible and braking that same velocity at a simply impossible rate. It had descended to within four miles above the Florida coast, hung there for perhaps three minutes, then headed inland at a speed which left the fastest pursuit ships standing. All armed forces had been alerted, which included the American Naval units taking part in the forthcoming exercises.

The Derry operator knew all this, Price explained, because the Americans in the radio room were talking about it at the tops of their voices. But it was not yet official, though no doubt it soon would be. Then instructions could be expected from the *Argus* for them . . .

Price broke off at that point to say that another signal was coming through, then he said, "It's from *Argus*, for you, sir. Your orders are to remain there and not to damage or disturb any devices or machinery inside the spaceship. They are hoping to learn something from them which might help against the other ship. The latest information on it is that it has reached the west coast of the United States and has turned back the way it had come and is on a track parallel and approximately twenty miles north of the original one, so that they think it may be mapping the area. Other countries are being warned to watch for similar ships—"

"Reconnaissance!" Stephens burst out suddenly. "Of course! The first step in any war. But the ship assigned to this area had an accident and crashed . . ."

He left the sentence hanging as his eyes darted about the shambles around him, seeing it suddenly in a new light. Malloy and Thompson, who had not heard the news by virtue of the fact that the head-phones only had two ear-pieces, shuffled restively and made querying noises. Terrins filled them in quickly then turned to Stephens.

Irritably, he said, "This does not necessarily mean we're being invaded. It could be a peaceful survey or exploration mission. Why—we don't know for sure that both ships are part of the same operation. They may be from entirely different localities, and contain different forms of life with different intentions towards us—"

"That's stretching coincidence a bit, sir."

"I agree. But . . ." Terrins began, then broke off. He wanted to tell Stephens that they should be careful, that everybody should be careful—especially that small, widely scattered section of the Human race with the authority to start something which they might not be able to finish. This was a big thing and it had to be handled properly from the start. But talking about it would do no good where Stephens was concerned. Stephens had an idea fixed in his mind that the Earth was about to be invaded, and it was the kind of exciting idea that a young man of Stephens' temperament would not give up easily. The ones to convince were the higher-ups, and they, unfortunately, all too often thought like Stephens.

Terrins remembered suddenly that Price had still to finish whatever he had been saying when the pilot had interrupted them. He said, "Sorry, Price. Is there anything else?"

"No, sir—except that you are to take charge of and be responsible for the investigation until the Eire Government give permission for us to send a team of experts to relieve you. Meanwhile you are to find out all you can."

"The Eire authorities won't mind that? Why don't they send them now and leave the red tape until later . . . ?"

"Well, actually, they're thinking of sending an armoured column, too," Price replied. He added, "And air support."

"But this thing's a *wreck*. . . !" Terrins began, then: "Oh, never mind."

Stephens had been listening on the other ear-piece. Eyes gleaming in the uncertain light of their four flash-lamps, he rapidly brought Thompson and Malloy up to date on the latest developments. Thompson seemed gradually to become infected with the pilot's excitement—he broke in once to ask if he should search the wreck for gun turrets—but Malloy's expression remained the same as it had been, a sort of resigned, what-will-the-Navy-throw-at-me-next look. He seemed a lot more interested in the aliens themselves than in their wrecked ship, Terrins had noticed, and at the moment he was gazing intently at one particularly battered specimen.

Terrins said, "Well Malloy, what do you think of them?"

"I think we should kill them, sir," Malloy replied after a short pause. Some strong emotion pulled at his facial muscles briefly, then subsided. He added, "That's if we can't do anything for them. They're in pain."

Terrins had not expected a reply like that, and in some subtle fashion he felt ashamed of himself. Malloy, he thought, had probably been the type who brought stray dogs and starving cats home as a boy—or even as a man. Now there were some aliens—some tentacled, slug-like creatures from God alone knew where—who were hurt. To Malloy it was as simple as that.

"Sir," Stephens broke in, "can I take Thompson and look around this thing? If we got an idea of the layout it would save time when the experts arrive, and we might discover something important."

Absently, Terrins nodded assent. His mind was still busy with what Malloy had said. Kill them or cure them, that was the idea. Yet mercy killing was forbidden where humans were concerned, would it not also be wrong in relation to beings who were at least the intellectual equals of mankind? Terrins thought that it would. But neither could he just let them lie there without trying to do something.

Stephens and Thompson moved astern, their torches throwing weird, surrealistic shadows of the wreckage ahead of them.

Terrins said, "Suppose we try to find one of these creatures who is not too badly injured. Maybe we could help a case like that."

Malloy said, "Perhaps so, sir."

And maybe we couldn't, Terrins thought. But they could try anyway. Aloud he said, "That one over there in the corner doesn't look too bad, we'll try him."

This particular alien was battered but apparently still in one piece, and the constant shuddering of its body proved that it was still alive. Its hide was a mass of shallow incised wounds—suffered, no doubt, by its being flung against the forward bulkhead—and its three tentacles lay limp. A human in the same condition would have been a quite horrible sight, but the gore of the aliens was not the primary red of human blood, and it was a little difficult to feel deeply for a shapeless, pink sack which leaked something that had all the appearance of thick drinking chocolate.

He said, "Lend a hand. We'll lift it onto that clear section of deck, then we'll see if we can do something . . ."

Certain types of treatment were indicated, he was thinking as they linked hands under the warm, quivering mass and drew it free, when an organism displayed symptoms of a certain nature, no matter what its size, shape or origin might be. And if these symptoms included bleeding—or, in this case, the loss of a fluid equivalent to human blood—then the idea was to stop it. That course of action could do no harm, Terrins was sure, and it might even do good providing the creature had not also sustained internal injuries which would ultimately prove fatal. At least it was something to do.

He said to Malloy, "Right, we'll clean the brown goo from the wounds, then you push the edges together with your fingers while I cover them with a sterile pad. Better that, I think, than using sulfa or penicillin dressings—they might be poison to its system. A few strips of tape will hold the pad in place and keep the wound closed . . ."

Once Price's voice interrupted the work to report that

no other countries knew of spaceships violating their terri-
tories so far, and that the one over the United States was
now on its second east to west leg. It was making no effort
either to approach or to avoid large cities adjacent to its
course, which made the observers pretty certain that it
was on a mapping expedition. Price added that question-
ing of the radar men who had first noted the arrival of the
spaceship had elicited the fact that the craft had just
popped into view on their screens and had not been
coming from anywhere. This they swore to. Mathematical
experts and science-fiction readers among the high brass
were now throwing words like 'space-warp' and 'hyperdrive' about ...

Shortly afterwards Stephens and Thompson returned.
The pilot reported that the after half of the ship's interior
was impenetrable, due to what seemed to be a large
number of semi-permanent fittings—metal partitions, sections of plumbing which leaked the black stuff, and so
on—being torn free in the crash. The number of creatures
mixed up in the wreckage led Stephens to suspect that the
ship was either a passenger vessel or a military transport.
Whoever had to cut a way through it later was in for a
very nauseating time, he added.

Terrins grunted acknowledgement, passed across his
mike so that Stephens could repeat his report to Price in
the helicopter, then returned his attention to the work in
hand. Thompson bent to do his share, moving the creature
slightly so that the black pad on its underside was partly
exposed. Terrins found his mind going back to the para-
dox of this animal which possessed the powers of respiration and mobility and yet did not eat. Even if they moved
like snails they could not live solely on air.

The pad on which the alien travelled resembled an
oblong of black astrakhan fur, and the pile of the fur was
in constant, waving motion. Suddenly, Terrins thought he
saw light.

The patching-up job, as he had mentally referred to it,
was finished. The alien lay quivering on the metal deck,
an incongruous, strangely pathetic object. Terrins thought
of a Humpty-Dumpty who had been put together again

with sticking plaster. The patient, however, showed no other signs of life.

Malloy and Thompson were bent over it, staring intently as if willing it to do something, anything, besides shudder. After a few minutes silence, Stephens spoke.

"I think it's dying," he said. The remark was somewhat lacking in tact considering the work Terrins and the two sick-bay ratings had put in with it. Positively, the pilot added, "I think they're all dying. It's only a question of time."

Terrins felt his face and neck getting hot, and kept silent with an effort. If his idea about these creatures was correct he would quickly wipe that smug, know-it-all look from Stephens' face. He nodded for Malloy to help him, then together they lifted and moved the alien until it was over one of the broad, black lines which curved and crossed all over the deck. Terrins said, "Gently now, put it down."

Three seconds later he said, "Lieutenant Stephens, your mouth is open. Were you going to say something?"

Slowly, but with an air of great determination, the alien was moving along the black line on which they had placed it. The two flaps of skin covering its eye drew back and it seemed to stare at them, and the three limp tentacles twitched, curled, then rose slowly upwards. The men stepped back hastily, but the creature merely continued slowly along the shiny black line on the deck, erasing it as it went.

Stephens made stabbing motions at the creature with his index finger. His mouth was now opening and closing, but he still had not found his voice.

"Pick out another likely specimen," Terrins said to Malloy and Thompson. "We may be lucky again."

While they worked over another alien who appeared to have only superficial injuries, Terrins explained the seemingly miraculous 'cure' of alien Number One.

"As I see it," he said, "their race must have developed first on the banks of a tidal river—or perhaps a shallow beach—the surface of which was carpeted with tiny forms of edible plant or animal life, animal in this instance also referring to the sea life left high and dry by receding tides. The creatures ingested through the black pads on their undersides, which were also used to move themselves forward when the supply of food immediately below them was exhausted."

Terrins continued by saying that his guess was that the tentacles and eye had originally been a defence against natural enemies, probably of a winged nature. It was also his opinion that the creature's inefficient methods of food intake forced it to eat constantly in order to remain active— he likened it to a man being forced to exist on soup soaking through blotting paper. When they had evolved to their present high level of technology, a constantly renewing food-source and method of getting about was provided by the broad black lines which curved and circled all over the ship. The men could see for themselves how the creature apparently erased, soaked up, the line as it moved along it, and how a greenish fluid which rapidly turned black oozed out to replace the fluid absorbed.

". . . They're an awkward, slow-moving species," Terrins concluded. "When the crash piled them against the forward sections of the ship, even the least seriously injured could not extricate themselves to return to their . . . er, food tracks."

Stephens, looking impressed, turned to regard the alien they had 'cured' again. He pointed suddenly and said, "Look! What's it doing . . . ?"

The alien was moving slowly along the food track which circled one of the few undamaged control panels in the compartment, its tentacles doing business-like things with the grooved, roughened handles which covered its sides.

Stephens said anxiously, "We should be careful about putting too many of these things back on their . . . their feet. There's no telling what they might do—"

Suddenly the lights came on. It was a harsh, greenish light which robbed the men's faces of all colour, given off from what had been a continuous tubular strip just above floor level, though now there were several breaks in it. The alien withdrew from the control panel and approached them again. Thompson jumped suddenly to his feet. The alien, only a few yards away by this time, halted and seemed to shrink backwards.

"Thompson, you horrible two-eyed monster, you," said Malloy derisively. "Stay still, you're scaring the poor thing to death."

Terrins giggled in spite of himself. He said, "That's true, you know. To it we must look pretty fearsome specimens, and big, too." He made his tone more business-like and went on, "Anyhow, this lighting is a lot better than flashlamps, so let's see how fast we can fix up his pal here."

But apparently the alien had other ideas.

Stephens hissed a warning as the creature came suddenly closer and sent a hesitant tentacle towards the three men bent over its companion. Malloy, busy taping up a four-inch gash near the second alien's eye, gave a yelp of surprise as the tentacle wrapped itself gently around his wrists and gave a slight tug before letting them go. This was repeated on the hands or wrists of Thompson and Terrins, then the peculiar process was begun again with Malloy.

After a few minutes of it, Malloy said, "You know, sir, I think it doesn't want us to work on its pal here. It keeps trying to pull our hands away."

He sat back on his haunches.

That was probably it, Terrins thought. One alien would know better than they whether they were wasting time trying to help its injured companion or not. If the case they were working on was hopeless, and the other alien knew it, then the creature's next step would be—*must* be—to indicate to them which of its companions they *could* help . . .

Sure enough, all three tentacles curled around Malloy's arm, and this time they did not let go. Tugging and straining, the alien tried to make Malloy follow it. The rating's face was a study. His mouth was open and one eye-brow had practically disappeared into his hairline. Terrins said quickly, "Better follow it."

During the few minutes the creature was pulling Malloy towards the pile of wreckage forward, Thompson got in a couple of nasty cracks, *sotto voce*, to his friend about taking dogs for walks. But at the tangle of metal and components it stopped, released him, and pointed with all three tentacles at another alien who was partially buried in the debris. While the others were getting it free, Terrins brought Price in the helicopter up to date.

Before relaying the report to Derry, Price told him that there was no fresh news. The other spaceship was still flying in parallel lines back and forward across the southern United States.

The injured alien was free by this time, but the one they had patched up made motions for it to be placed on a food track and would not allow them to work on it afterwards. Terrins watched it move laboriously along the track. It shuddered continuously, and one tentacle had been torn off and the dark brown blood seeped from lacerations all over its body. Terrins thought that Alien Number One was being a little heartless.

Alien Number One was indicating another casualty to be rescued.

Half an hour later there was a total of five aliens moving about the compartment, and some of them were so badly cut up that Terrins was surprised that they lived at all much less moved. Apparently this was a tough breed. He did, however, feel a little bit miffed at their refusal to let him try working on them, but he supposed they were afraid in case he did something wrong and accidentally killed one.

Stephens had grown progressively more anxious as each new alien became mobile. He wanted to leave the rest of them where they were. You could not trust them, he stated. Given half a chance they would overpower or kill the humans, repair the ship and take off to wreak death and destruction all over the country . . .

Terrins was reaffirming for the fourth time that the physical structure and condition of the aliens made the overpowering of anything larger than a kitten impossible, adding that the pilot had been influenced by too many B-features, when the deck beneath him gave a peculiar lurch sideways. He staggered, and had the sudden feeling that he was going down in a fast lift, then everything returned to normal again.

But not quite; the deck on which they were standing was no longer tilted at an angle of twenty degrees or so, it was now level.

"The ship must have rolled over a bit," Malloy said. It was hard to tell whether he was making a statement or asking a question. He added, "I feel funny."

Terrins felt it, too, a queasy sensation of still going down in an elevator and the light-headed feeling that if he was not careful he would drift ceilingwards. Apparently the aliens were feeling light-headed, too, because he noticed them moving along their food tracks at a surprisingly fast pace—fast for snails, that was. Two of them disappeared into the ramp which the men had used to enter the compartment. The other three, led by the taped-up one, made for the human party.

"I don't trust these things," said Stephens again.

Terrins was beginning to have misgivings himself. As the three aliens wriggled nearer he found himself swallowing with a mouth which was too dry for it to be done comfortably. But when Alien Number One stopped before them and, with unmistakable wavings of its tentacles, merely indicated that it would like its companions' hides taped up the same as its own, Terrins cursed himself silently as a coward for being afraid of them.

"I still don't like it," Stephens said doggedly. "I'm going to see what those other two are up to." He disappeared in the wake of the two aliens. Almost immediately they heard an exclamation of surprise and a yell of "Come here, quick!"

Terrins was first into the descending ramp. He was startled to find that he could walk along it instead of having to crawl down it backwards. And when he arrived at the floor of the adjoining compartment, which had been vertical when they had first entered—he found that he could walk upright on it, too. The gaping rent in the hull through which they had entered was now in the wall facing them, and it was sealed by hard-packed earth and rock. Apparently the ship had rolled over, trapping them for the time being inside.

Something cold and tight seemed to grow in the region of Terrins' diaphragm. A well-defined symptom of fear, he thought sardonically, and tried his best to ignore it. He said:

"Obviously they've put their gravity control system back in working order as well as their lighting. More deck area—and therefore more food tracks—are available to them now. You must admit that they're doing all they possibly can to help themselves, or rather, to help us help them." He forced a smile. "I hope we have tape enough for all the patients."

The truth was that Terrins felt much less confident than he had tried to make out. To his general discomfort was added the uneasy feeling that it was the aliens who were running things now; they were *using* the humans.

"How," said Malloy the Practical, "are we going to get out, sir?"

"Our people will cut a way in," Lieutenant Stephens answered for him. "Or jack up this end of the ship if the other way is too slow." He turned to face Terrins. "But I don't like—"

Price's voice in the head-phones interrupted another of Stephens' dislikes.

"The interference is back, sir, bad as ever." He sounded faintly disgusted, probably because the gossiping Derry operator was no longer available to relieve the boredom of waiting. "It's funny, sir, but it disappeared a few minutes after you entered the wreck. I thought it had gone for good."

Coincidence, of course, Terrins thought; it had to be. But his uneasiness increased nonetheless. He asked, "Did you see the ship roll over?"

"No, sir. It's almost dark out here."

Dark! That meant . . . With an unbelieving look at his watch he saw that they had spent over three hours in the ship. No wonder Price was feeling disgusted. He was telling Price to break into the emergency rations for himself when Stephens interrupted him again.

"What's the attraction in that corner there?" he said, pointing. "What are they doing, anyway?"

A few yards away two aliens were huddled against a tangle of wreckage which was pinning down a third. One of them held a tentacle stiffly as though working at something under the jumbled mass of metal which was just barely within reach. There was a strange familiarity about that position and stance . . .

"Price," Terrins said into his mike, "I'm going to make a test." He gave the navigator brief instruction, detached an earpiece and handed it to Stephens, then advanced on the aliens in the corner.

This time he used a long piece of metal to knock away the tentacle, remembering the skinned knuckle he had suffered the first time. As he had more than half expected, the instant he nudged the stiffened tentacle away from whatever it had been touching, Price reported the interference gone.

"Somebody," Terrins said with forced lightness, "is not using a suppressor."

Whatever repairs the aliens were trying to make in that corner was the cause of the country wide interruption in radio communications.

"We can't have this," Terrins said, wagging an admonishing finger at the aliens. "Shoo 'em away from that thing, Stephens. I've got to finish my report to Derry."

But the aliens did not want to be shooed away, it seemed. As the minutes passed and Terrins asked and answered questions relayed through the helicopter's set from Derry, Stephens' efforts to keep the creatures at a distance became increasingly strenuous. And the aliens, despite their injuries, were becoming downright vicious. Stephens, holding a piece of buckled plating before his face to protect it from their lashing tentacles, was reduced to pushing them away with his feet. He was not being gentle about it, either. Whatever gadget lay underneath that wreckage it was clear that the aliens wanted to get at it badly.

Malloy and Thompson, who had been in the adjoining compartment keeping an eye on the three aliens there, appeared, attracted by the rumpus. Stephens snarled, "Help me. Don't just stand there ..."

While pushing at a quivering alien with his foot, Malloy reported that the creature they had patched up was engaged in cutting its way into the stern section of the ship. It was using a gadget similar to an acetylene torch, he stated, but much smaller—and the alien did not have to stand at all close to the metal it was working on. Malloy was quite enthusiastic about the gadget and was wondering if the alien would mind giving it to him, or one like it, as a souvenir, when Price's voice crackled suddenly from the 'phones. He must have been shouting for it to sound so loud.

"Sir! Derry has just had a signal to say that the ship over the United States has suddenly changed course. They plotted its new heading, it's coming this way!"

Stephens had heard it also, the ear-piece still being clipped to the side of his cap. His face went white.

"It's a radio!" he babbled. "The thing they're trying to get at is a radio. They've been contacting their friends—"

"That's the gadget there," Malloy broke in, as yet blissfully unconscious of this latest development. He pointed.

Alien Number One, looking vaguely piratical in its taping, crouched in the mouth of the entry ramp. The gadget so admired by Malloy which cut through metal walls at a distance was held firmly in one outstretched tentacle.

"Don't move," Stephens whispered urgently. "Listen ..." He quickly told Malloy and Thompson what had happened. While he spoke the two aliens he had been fending off wriggled around him and made as if to resume their interrupted work at the radio. He continued, "... Now that other ship must have taken a fix on their last transmission, that's why it's suddenly heading this way. But I don't think it will be able to find us unless the aliens transmit more or less continuously. One fix at three thousand miles is surely not enough to pinpoint us with the necessary accuracy."

He faced Terrins: "You agree, sir? The only way we can escape is for them not to find us. That other ship will be moving fast, too fast for us to dig our way out of here before it arrives. And you know what will happen to us if we're caught—*we'll* be the specimens . . ."

"Interference is back," said Price.

"Get out of there!" Stephens cried, and swung viciously at the alien who had worked its way behind him, his weapon the section of metal plating which was still in his hands. There was a sound like tearing cloth and a foot long rent appeared on the flank of the already tattered body of the alien. The force of his swing—only partly expended by that glancing blow—sent him stumbling. He tripped and fell, to which accident he owed his life.

The wall where he had been standing showed a bright orange patch at what would have been the level of Stephens' waist. Terrins could feel the heat of it from three yards away.

On the human side most of the action was instinctive after that.

It was several minutes later. Terrins and Lieutenant Stephens were making themselves as small as possible behind the remains of a low control desk. Malloy and Thompson had found similar cover a few yards away. Alien Number One was keeping them pinned down with its long-range cutting torch—even in his mind, Terrins balked at referring to it as a heat ray—and, flanked by its companions from the adjoining compartment, was edging steadily nearer. There were three aliens advancing in front of them and two behind. Of the latter, the one which Stephens had sliced with the metal plate had stopped moving. The other one had taken its place at the transmitter. And in the helicopter outside, Price was reporting interference again.

"We've got to stop it signalling," Stephens said.

Terrins did not answer. He was not feeling particularly afraid, strangely enough, but he felt hurt and very, very angry. When he had treated that first alien successfully, Terrins had felt a great sense of accomplishment, almost a feeling of pride—and he had taken it for granted that the being concerned would show a certain amount of gratitude for said treatment. But instead of gratitude they were trying to roast the humans with some weapon or other . . .

Stephens' voice broke suddenly in on his thoughts. The pilot, seeing that no help was forthcoming from the Lieut-Commander, had assumed command of the situation himself.

". . . Malloy and Thompson. Pick up any loose metal near you suitable for throwing. When I give the word, let fly at the alien with the weapon. You've got to distract it for a few seconds. All right? *Now* . . . !"

An assortment of metal began bouncing off and around Alien Number One. Stephens sprang to his feet, a twisted strip of plating in his hands. He brought it over and down like a broad-sword. Terrins glimpsed the quivering body of the alien at the transmitter, and its three writhing stumps of tentacles, then Stephens gave a gasping cry and dived for cover again. The leg of his uniform trousers was a charred rag and the flesh beneath was a raw, bright red, but his pain-distorted face made a grimace that must have been meant as a smile when Price reported that the interference had gone.

The remaining three aliens advanced slowly.

Relayed from Derry came the report that the second spaceship had been sighted three hundred miles off the Irish coast by a weather ship. Its Captain had stated that it was moving very fast indeed, its nose section glowing white hot. In Lough Foyle *Argus* was readying her De Havilland 110's and Scottish Command were dispatching a squadron of Javelins . . .

"If they get another fix on us, we're sunk," Stephens said through clenched teeth. His face was white and sweating, he was going into shock, and Terrins' kit was in the other compartment.

Silently, Terrins wondered whether another fix was necessary. Alien radio might be that little bit different from the human variety. But if that were so then there was no hope at all for them.

Stephens was hanging on to consciousness with his fingernails. He said, "If that thing comes much closer it could pick us off one at a time with no trouble. We've got to spread ourselves out, and jump it from three directions at once." He tried to get to his hands and knees, groaned

as the partly cooked meat that was his lower leg touched
the deck, and subsided again.

"I think I know what you have in mind," Terrins said
gently. He was feeling very much angrier now, and things
like logic or caution seemed to have been crowded out of
his mind. He took off his head-phones and gave them to
the pilot with instructions to keep in touch with Price,
then he turned to the others.

With Terrins showing himself briefly and hurling odd
pieces of wreckage at Alien Number One to distract its
attention, Malloy and Thompson began their outflanking
manoeuvre—the two unarmed aliens being ignored for the
time being. But fully fifteen minutes passed before they
were in satisfactory positions, and Terrins gave the signal
of attack.

One jump carried him to the top of the control desk
and the second to within five yards of the alien—the
lighter artificial gravity in the ship had its advantages, he
thought. The alien's weapon was swinging round towards
the running figure of Malloy, who had gone into action a
split second too soon. He heard Malloy shriek and saw his
arm from the elbow down smoke, shrivel and fall off, then
the weapon was ranging round on him. He took two
running paces forward—they felt as though he was being
filmed in slow-motion—and dived blindly at the huddled
shape on the deck.

It may have been his imagination, but he thought that
the alien held fire for an instant—surely at this stage it was
not having qualms about killing the doctor who had
patched it up? Terrins struck its soft, resilient body with
both hands outstretched, knocking it off its food track and
onto its back. The weapon made a firey zig-zag on the
ceiling, then he heard it clatter to the deck.

When Terrins picked himself up Thompson was beating
at the alien savagely with a jagged strip of metal. The
taping which Terrins and Malloy had applied so carefully
was stained brown or hanging loosely from reopened
wounds. Suddenly, he felt furiously angry with Thompson;
he put his hand on the other's chest and sent him stagger-
ing backwards.

Stephens' voice came then, weak but all too clear.

"Price says there's a big ship above us. It's dropped flares and is coming down . . ."

Terrins looked at the shambles around him, at the aliens injured in the crash and at the others who had all too clearly suffered at the hands of the humans. *They aren't going to like this,* he thought sickly, *they're not going to like this at all* . . .

They should have allowed the aliens to summon help, Terrins knew now; that last struggle inside the wreck had been the cause of needless suffering to Stephens and Malloy, not to mention the aliens concerned. It was a good thing no permanent damage had been done.

Dawn was silhouetting distant Mount Errigal and, although the rain had blown inland, it was cold inside the grounded helicopter. But its occupants were not really feeling it—the condemned man, Terrins thought drily, does not mind if the signature of his reprieve is a bit smudged.

It was all clear to him now: the accidental crash of the spaceship on Earth, the intermittent interference when one of its crew struggled to send a distress call, and his certainty that it was only the fact of the transmitter being damaged that Earth receivers were affected by the signal at all, because it was obviously propagated at a speed thousands of times faster than light. Unfortunately, Terrins' entry into the ship had caused the signal to be cut off just as a rescue ship had appeared above Earth. The ship had begun a search pattern over the nearest land mass—America—until a brief renewal of the signal by a human-revived alien had given it the wreck's position.

The rescue workers had been different from the injured aliens, bigger and with literally forests of arms and legs, and they had been extremely efficient. Practically every occupant of the wreck was showing signs of life before they left, including the ones which the humans had roughened up. But Terrins had put in one very bad moment when one of them had advanced upon Stephens and Malloy with a purposeful look in its nearest eye and waving the alien equivalent of a scalpel. Stephens and Malloy had been carried into the other alien ship, and

Thompson and himself had been shooed out of the wreck and then ignored.

But he had felt much better a few hours later when the two men came out again, dazed, but walking unaided on their feet.

Lieutenant Stephens had not had much to say, but all through the night he had been touching or pinching the perfectly sound though hairless leg which had been burned so terribly by the alien weapon. He had asked Terrins once whether it was possible to dream that one was pinching oneself. Malloy, on the other hand, had rarely stopped talking. He was talking now.

". . . They must have a Health Service, too," he said, waving his right arm and hand in Thompson's face. Terrins had seen that hand burned off and the forearm reduced to a charred stump, and felt like pinching himself, too. Malloy went on, "But it's like ours. They mean well, of course, but they're rushed sometimes and are inclined to overlook things . . ."

He was mighty proud of that hand, a fact which he tried unsuccessfully to hide by continually griping about it. He held it out again for all to see.

Terrins was thinking of the airliners which sometimes were forced down in the jungle, and of the natives who in their ignorant but well-meaning fashion tried to help the injured. But when proper medical assistance arrived, the doctors treated everyone as a matter of course—including the natives whose ignorant meddling had placed them also on the casualty list.

". . . Even the best dentists pull a wrong tooth sometimes," Malloy was saying in withering tones, "But this . . . Well I ask you, *six fingers* . . . !"

Red Alert
>>>>>>>>>>>>>

FOR SEVERAL minutes after the main fleet emerged into normal spacetime somewhere within the orbit of Pluto, the flagship drove through the grey unreality that was hyperspace. They were four days of first-order flight away from the objective which Everra would reach in seconds, and despite his coldly logical evaluation of the rewards and risks involved, he wished suddenly that he'd held to the old and well-tried tactics usual in operations of this sort. A Commander was not supposed to desert his Grand Fleet like this.

Though technically, thought Everra di Crennorlin-Su, Governor of three inhabited solar systems and temporarily Commander of a task force comprising three thousand one hundred and twenty-seven units, he was simply leading them. If the operation was successful nobody would remember how long that lead had been.

The greyness around his ship dissolved into the blue-green globe of Earth three thousand miles below, and he was committed to a course of action which was unsafe, unprecedented, and most probably unsane. Everra made a small noise of self-disgust to himself as he activated the communicator. His particular form of insanity wasn't rare. It was called ambition.

"Have the advance scouts report, please," he said gently, and waited.

Everra had placed the planet under surveillance from the earliest moment after he had been assigned the Earth operation, and it had been one of the initial observations which had given him the idea of his present strategy. During the organisational nightmare of gathering and fitting-out his mighty fleet for their special mission, those reports had continued to come in, and their significance had not changed. Everra had been given a very dirty job—one where a ninety-five per cent loss would be acclaimed as a tactical triumph. But if he could reduce that percentage, or maybe even reverse it, then Everra would go very far indeed. The reports had shown a way in which this might be done.

Five per cent loss, he gloated.

The view-screen on his control desk lit up, and a scoutship Captain hurriedly went through the rituals of respect due to his high rank. "Our analysis of the planet's war potential is complete," he said. "None of the nations maintain large standing armies, but each physically suitable male undergoes at least two of their 'years' military training, so they can be expected to submit readily to authority. The leading 'nations' have large fleets of surface vessels, which we can forget, and a considerable number of transonic atmosphere craft, which we can't afford to—they're dangerously fast and can carry atomic weapons ..."

Unconsciously, the Commander swayed forward in his couch. This was the important part. If Earth should become prematurely suspicious, and use those weapons on his fleet ... Everra didn't like to think about the probable results.

"... We have detected and marked the sites of all their nuclear armories," the scoutship Captain went on. His voice was very brisk, very clear, and very much aware that it was addressing, personally, a Su Grand Fleet Commander. "But these are no longer kept fully alert; the Earth civilisation is in transition between Stage Six and Seven—nuclear power but as yet no spaceflight—and the war tensions common with early Stage Six are dying out."

We'll soon fix that, the Commander thought grimly.

The officer ended by reporting that a Human high-altitude research group had launched an unmanned rocket into an orbit just beyond their atmosphere, and the Commander's flagship would pass near it in a few seconds time.

Interesting, Everra thought. He liked to see the ludicrous mechanisms that a race first put into space. But his pleasure changed to sudden alarm. That was a research rocket, telemetering all sorts of data to its ground control. Suppose it was able to detect his flagship!

"Armaments!" he said sharply.

"Destroy, or take it aboard?" the Armaments Officer asked quickly. He'd been listening, and was already touching a firing stud.

"Destroy, but quietly," Everra said. "An atomic explosion out here would make them suspicious. Use a chemical warhead ... No, wait!"

Everra's mind flashed over the implications of a nuclear explosion out here to the owners of this research rocket, and he abruptly reversed his previous order. He added, ". . . And put out the refraction screen, we don't want to be caught on their ground radar."

A picture of the Earth rocket flicked onto the Commander's view-screen, sharp, clear and dangerously close. Suppose its instruments had already detected his ship, and relayed the information to the ground? Everra suppressed his growing apprehension: he couldn't know whether he was detected or not, so he must proceed as though he hadn't.

His screen darkened suddenly as a filter snapped into place, then blazed white as the missile found the orbiting rocket. There was a slight tremor as some of the vaporised debris brushed the Flagship's hull.

Everra felt pleased with himself. As he now saw it, the destruction of that orbital rocket could mean just one thing to the nation which had launched it—another nation did not want them to achieve spaceflight. A nation, moreover, with the disquieting ability to send an atomic missile into space to destroy it. Only two other nations had the technology capable of doing that, and one of them had quite recently been this nation's idealogical enemy. Could it be that their peace overtures were just a sham, and they were still secretly arming themselves with long-range nuclear weapons?

And the weaker nations would wonder at that explosion, too, and feel suspicious, and afraid. Encountering that orbital vehicle had been a stroke of luck, Everra realised. The seeds of dissension were already well planted before he had even landed on the planet.

The natives had a saying down there: Divide and Conquer. Ever since that accursed trading ship had run through Sol, then returned to investigate and report the Earth civilisation which it had found, The Commander had thought what a brilliant concept that was. It was going to save an awful lot of lives.

Curtly, he gestured to his Communications Officer that he was ready for the next scout's report.

The second Captain was an Elissnian, who required an interpreter, so the Commander's screen remained blank. He didn't mind that at all, because the sight of the Elissnian body, with its multiplicity of legs, arms and appendages, sometimes upset his digestive tract. What bothered him was the unavoidable slowness of communications made necessary by the sign-language they had to use when speaking with non-telepaths. But the Elissni were sensitive to trends and motivations in large and small population groups, an ability which made them the most efficient social technicians and mass psychology experts in the Galaxy. Everra had been lucky to get so many of them at such short notice.

The Elissnian reported that his analysis of the economic and cultural stresses present on the planet—both current and those likely to develop through the Commander's intervention—was almost complete; also, all scoutships and smaller craft now carried at least one Elissnian telepath, so that the Commander could receive detailed on-the-spot reports from any sector.

The reports came in quickly after that. He learned the names of oceans, continents, countries and most of the chief cities, together with their locations. He already had data on their systems of time and distance measurement, and had been forcing himself to think in those divisions for the past two days. It avoided the confusion of constant mental translation when overhearing data in an Earth language. Everra had to know this planet, its strengths and its failings, like a native. His success depended on it.

As his mighty Flagship slid into Earth's atmosphere and dropped towards the North Polar icecap, Everra thought of the tremendous fleet converging on this third and inhabited planet of Sol, and wondered wryly if it would have a Commander when it arrived.

Three miles above the grey, storm-tossed Atlantic, an aircraft droned steadily across a white monotony of cloud. The whine of its four turbo-jets gave an angry, impatient note to the thunder of its passage, though only a whisper penetrated to the sound-proofed passenger compartment. Neither were its passengers aware of the life-ship from Everra's Arctic base which, rendered invisible by its refraction screen, paced it a few hundred yards away, and they were happily ignorant of the instruments focussed on them which made every thought, word and action plain to the alien observers.

Especially those of a uniformed Human with a diplomatic dispatch case chained to his wrist.

Suddenly the aircraft seemed to stagger in mid-air. The engines died abruptly and it skidded into a spinning, fluttering dive. Control surfaces flapped spasmodically, in a desperate attempt to halt the crazy plunge towards destruction. The effort was wasted.

Trailing the helpless aircraft like a giant kite at the end of its tractor beam, the life-ship continued its dive seawards. It wasn't until angry grey mountains of water, with spray blowing off their peaks, were rolling past a scant thousand feet below that the invisible life-ship released its tractor beam.

Engines roared back to life then, and the aircraft levelled out and slowly climbed towards the cloud base and sunshine again. A female Human began moving along the plane with a cheerful but altogether untrue account of the mishap, adding that the machine was returning to Gander for a check-up.

"Nice work, Captain," said Everra. The whole incident had been relayed to his master screen. The Flagship was now buried in Arctic ice, and while the low temperature suited him, he had no intention of going out to personally supervise operations in the poisonous mixture of oxygen and nitrogen which the Humans called an atmosphere.

"As you know," the Commander went on, "that courier is carrying messages which, if delivered to his chiefs, would greatly ease the tension now developing between those two nations since the destruction of that orbital rocket. Doubtless the courier will try to reach home on another aircraft. You will temporarily disable that plane also, stopping its power plant, then using your tractor beam to make it lose height rapidly.

"This repetition of procedure is deliberate," the Commander explained. "The courier is bound to suspect an attempt on his life, and will communicate these suspicions home. Obviously, his government will conclude, if another nation is trying to kill one of their subjects—and one bearing diplomatic immunity at that—then that nation is not far from declaring war."

As he cut communication with the life-ship Everra thought of the fleet which was now only fifty hours away. Small incidents like this could precipitate a global war, he knew, but could they do it fast enough? There would have to be more such incidents. Some more prodding was indicated.

An attention signal blinked suddenly on his panel just as he was bringing extra levels of his mind to bear on the problem. It was the Ecology Section.

"We have determined the balance between edible flora and fauna necessary to keep the Humans nourished," the Chief Ecologist reported, "particularly such food sources as 'Cattle,' 'Grain' and 'Potatoes,' whose absence or curtailment would lethally affect this balance, and this data has been distributed to the Fleet." He ended, "Atmospheric analysis and tests on specimens we've picked up have shown us the most effective gases to use on these Humans."

Imperceptibly, Everra's mind drifted into a highly plea-surable contemplation of what a successful end to this operation could mean. He checked it roughly, grimly re-minding himself that success depended, firstly, on his bringing the leading nations of the planet to the verge of war—or at least to a state of full mobilisation for it. Secondly, and more important, it required the detonation of a number of politically well-placed Human 'fuses,' hyp-notically primed to function instantaneously all over the planet. These 'fuses' had already been picked out, and needed only the proper conditioning. It was time, he thought as he called up the Elissnian Chief Psychologist, he saw to that.

"We are ready to begin treatment of the first Human ruler," the Elissnian announced, forestalling him. "Do you wish to observe?"

"I do," the Commander said.

It was night. The low, rambling villa was lit only by the reflected sky glow from nearby Peking, and an occasional guard's spotlight playing over the grounds surrounding it. The wall enclosing the summer residence of Mao Hsein-Yan, overlord of all the teeming millions of China and its satellite states, was guarded like a fortress. But this august personage was a mild, studious man who objected to having too many of his drab-uniformed soldiers infesting the place, so the villa itself was relatively empty.

In some ways that made the Elissnian psychologist's job easier. But not much.

The Elissnian dropped like a stone from the hovering scoutship, until its tractor beam abruptly checked his fall and set him gently onto the villa's roof. Carefully, so as not to rattle the instruments hung about his horny body, he scuttled across to the open skylight. Using two gripping arms, he anchored himself to the edge until his four sucker-equipped tentacles were properly attached to the room's ceiling, then he crawled quickly across it and down the wall to the floor.

Fortunately his race was a warm-blooded, oxygen-breathing type, though physically very dissimilar to the Humans, so that a face mask was all the protection he required. He could never have managed such gymnastics in a spacesuit.

Not everyone in the villa was asleep, the Elissnian discovered; he could sense a few clerks working in their rooms, and at each end of the corridor which contained Mao's sleeping chamber stood two guards. They differed from those outside only in that they wore soft felt slippers instead of heavy boots. He began pulling himself in until he somewhat resembled a football with bunches of spaghetti growing from it, and using only his suckers, climbed to where the corridor wall joined its ceiling. It was dark up there. In a few seconds he was at the ventilator above Mao's door, and easing himself through it.

Mao Hsein-Yan lay on a wide divan, and the coat of arms embellishing the silken cushions heaped on it made identification doubly sure. Beside the divan was a low table containing a lamp, and an open book with a set of wire-connected lenses lying on it. The psychologist moved the book and spectacles onto the floor in case of accidents, climbed to the table top, and went quickly to work.

First a needle injected the drug which would place the sleeper in the proper state of trance. While that was working its way through his system, two light, paper-thin metal plates were attached to his temples, and connected to the mental amplifier worn by the psychologist. In a few minutes he would implant the required hypnotic commands. The Elissnian hunched closer.

There was a sharp click and a sudden blaze of light. The Elissnian's movement had knocked on the switch of the table lamp. The sleeper woke. He saw the alien horror poised a few inches from his face, and his mouth opened.

Fortunately, the Human had just exhaled, so his cry of terror was little more than a harsh indrawing of breath. The Elissnian shot up the power of his mental amplifier and viciously held the Human's mind so that a repetition of that or any other noise was impossible. Gradually as the drug took hold, the horror faded from the being's face. The Elissnian switched off the table lamp; his eyes did not require it.

Just below the level of the Human's conscious mind, and with a power and urgency which made them impossible to disobey, the Elissnian psychologist planted his commands. *When you awaken,* he stated with awful certainty, *you will announce that you will speak to your people over the radio networks, at a time exactly fifty-one hours and seven minutes from now. You will order that those without receiving sets will get to one. At precisely fifty-one hours seven minutes from now, you will tell them that they are threatened by . . .*

There was a knock at the door.

In some corner of his mind the Elissnian must have realised that the noise which the Human had made on awakening must have been noticed, and that his stupid switching on and then off of the light had further aroused suspicions. But if he left now he could never finish—Mao Hsein-Yan would be too closely guarded. Grimly he continued ramming data and instructions into that now-defenceless mind. *You will tell them they must not leave the towns and cities, or disperse themselves in any way. After the first wave has hit, you will . . .*

The knock was louder, accompanying an anxiously spoken query.

The psychologist worked on. A whistle shrilled loudly, and he flinched as the door shook to the impact of a heavy shoulder. Whistles were blowing all over the place, and sounds of running feet were approaching the villa when he gathered up his instruments and dropped to the floor. The job was finished.

When the door crashed open he was waiting beside it. Darting through, and between the legs of the still off-balance guards, he made for the room with the skylight, desperately flashing a 'Stand By' call to the hovering scoutship. He was small and fast enough to be mistaken for one of the villa's pets, especially in bad light. But by this time the guards were ready to shoot anything that moved, up to and including their own shadows.

The first bullet tore plaster from the wall beside him. The second smashed through two of his sucker tentacles at the point where they joined the rib cage. Slowly, the Elissnian continued across the ceiling using his remaining suckers, and the adhesiveness of his two feeding orifices to hold him up. It must, the watching Everra thought, have been very, very painful.

Just as the Elissnian was pulling himself over the edge of the skylight, a guard opened up with his machine-gun.

Everra's screen went blank and silent; a bullet had smashed the sound and vision pick-up which the Elissnian had been wearing to relay back his movements.

"Pull him up!" the Commander called urgently. But a new picture flashed onto the screen even as he spoke, the villa roof as seen from the rapidly descending scoutship. The skylight enlarged, as did the tattered, almost shredded, bundle beside it. The bundle was motionless until a tractor beam caught it, whipping it up out of sight. A large, wetly shining stain marked the place where it had been.

"We have lost one of ourselves," the scoutship Captain said. The interpreter could not give Everra the emotional content of the words, but he could understand how a telepathic race must feel about death or injury to one of themselves. The officer ended shortly, "Otherwise we are ready."

"Good. Washington, United States sector, next."

The Commander wanted to say more, but there was no time for sentiment. One thing he did know, the sight of an Elissnian would never disgust him again.

Washington, Paris, Moscow, London—all the capitals would be visited by Elissnian telepaths. And the heads of the smallest countries would also have that mental time-fuse planted in their brains. Not only rulers, but the great statesmen, philosophers and lawgivers would receive the same treatment. In short, every person the people of the world looked up to and trusted would, at a certain instant two days from now, find themselves addressing their largest possible audience, and telling them . . .

The Commander made a small, self-congratulatory noise to himself. That part of his plan should work perfectly. But it would be wasted if he couldn't intensify the present war scare sufficiently for his 'fuses' to have the best results. For the hundredth time he went over in his mind the strategy—that sleight-of-hand on a planetary scale which would, until the right moment arrived, keep the population of a world ignorant of the catastrophe about to overwhelm them, and which should enable Everra to clear the planet of all intelligent life in a matter of hours.

The Humans had to be driven to desperation, to such a state of fear and hysteria that they would accept anything, and do anything, which promised the slightest hope of deliverance. Only one thing could force their minds into that condition of malleability; War. He had to drive them to the point of global war, where civilians and armed forces were both tightly organised and mobilised for defence—and incidently, their considerable array of weapons trained on each other instead of on his Grand Fleet. Then, when they had approached the proper degree of frenzy, despair and sheer nervous tension, only one tiny push in the right direction would be needed for Everra's purpose to be accomplished.

Suddenly the Commander hated the whole business. He felt sickened at the things he would be forced to do to this race. The Su were a highly-intelligent, civilised and sensitive species, and the knowledge that the evil he must do was necessary for the attainment of a much greater good did little to minimise his feelings of self-disgust and guilt.

The Earth operation was not the type of job normally given to a member of the Su race. Occupying all the highest positions in the Galactic Union, they were the ruling class of a civilisation covering several hundred inhabited solar systems, and they were extremely long lived. Physically they were cold blooded and vaguely starfish-shaped entities who had evolved on an ammoniamethane type planet, and they slept only for a few hours each year, and then only when an accident made it necessary to re-grow some part of their body. Mentally they had yet to find an equal anywhere in the galaxy.

Though they ruled, it wasn't altogether the hunger for power that drove them. Rather they felt a pressing need to make everything orderly and predictable instead of chaotic and variable, which seemed to be the natural order of things. And though galactic civilisation was at present about the most disorderly thing imaginable, Everra thought that they were succeeding.

But even among the all-powerful Su there were different levels of intelligence and ability. The Crennorlin-Su—to which class Everra belonged—were a group who traditionally got the dirty work, work more suited to the servants than the masters.

On the Commander's control desk lights winked, but they were not of sufficient urgency for his personal attention. He was thinking of the briefing given him by his superior for the Earth mission, and wondering if he would receive an insult or a compliment.

"For the first time a Su is being given this job," his Sector Co-ordinator had told him, "because you have many times shown a remarkable understanding of individual and group problems facing the lower orders. An operation of this nature calls for this ability in addition to the organisational and logistic proficiency required."

Unceasingly, Everra had striven to attain his present position of Governor of the three solar systems which he ruled—and sickly, uncultured and scientifically-backward systems they were, too, though he was bringing them along nicely. Certainly he understood individual problems. But the function of a member of his race was, or should be, greater than that. Everra wanted to be up where the problems dealt with applied to whole civilisations, where Government was a bright, clean adventure in the exciting realms of probability mathematics, not the dirty, sordid and monotonous solving of the same little dilemmas—with microscopic variations—over and over and over again.

Everra wanted the chance to make policy instead of continually carrying it out.

But if he was to have that chance, Everra thought as the number of attention lights on his panel increased sharply, he had better not forget this particular problem.

An observer from the West Europe sector was waiting to report.

"Due to the severing of diplomatic relations, full mobilisation has been ordered here," the officer stated curtly. "Missile launching stations have been manned and alerted. The civilian defence measures which you predicted are in operation, including preparation of Bomb-shelters built during an older war scare, and tunnels, suitable for conversion to such shelters . . ."

Good! the Commander thought, relieved. If one sector began such preparations, then the others must follow suit out of sheer self-protection. It was only necessary to make sure they did it quickly.

". . . But," the officer continued, "there are certain individuals—their following, though diminishing, is still large—who are preaching ideas such as the 'Unity of Man,' the utter stupidity of War, and stressing the fact that small differences in skin colouration and idealogy are poor reasons for committing racial suicide. There are Humans like this in every sector, and in most places air their opinions unhindered. These persons are definitely retarding the progress of the operation."

Everra seethed quietly. 'The Unity of Man' indeed! He used words picked up from several Human languages, but gained little relief as they referred to body processes and concepts completely alien to him. Difference in colouration and idealogy . . .

Suddenly the Human histories he had been so hurriedly absorbing came back to him. Those two differences had caused high feeling, and even physical violence, many times in the past. He spoke quickly:

"You have an Elissnian on your ship. Connect him to my interpreter at once."

The Elissni were incapable of full telepathic contact with the Humans—only among themselves was perfect communication possible. But they could receive—and more important, transmit—strong, non-verbal feelings and emotions to any warm-blooded oxygen-breathing race. And a member of such a race who was not himself telepathic would, of course, treat those transmitted feelings as his own, and act on them.

Everra knew that among the associates of these sane and peace-loving people whose activities were threatening his master plan must be some who were capable of silencing them. A subtle undermining of moral integrity could do it, but brute force would do it much faster. Briefly he sympathised with these lone crusaders, but there was too much at stake and too little time to do more than that.

As the Commander relayed these instructions to the Elissnian, the general emotional lethargy displayed by the Humans even in the face of approaching war recurred to him. Surely this type of psychological prodding, used in the proper places, could solve that problem, too. Fighting down his sudden self-loathing at this latest tactic, he enlarged on his instructions.

"You will find," he concluded, "that the emotional potential behind such words as 'Nigger,' 'Dirty Red,' and 'Jew-boy' is sufficient, if stimulated correctly, to start a wave of civil intolerance which might accelerate the approaching international breakdown. These feelings of intolerance have been buried for a long time, but——"

"Pardon, sir," the interpreter cut in, "but the Elissnian says 'No'!"

For a few seconds the Commander couldn't say anything. He wasn't used to that word being addressed to him.

"I will not," the Elissnian said—the interpreter having gone back to straight relaying—"attack or undermine the religious or political idealogy of any intelligent being. This is dirty and shameful work . . ."

He continued in the same vein until the Commander called, "Silence!"

The Elissnian stopped. Everra let the silence drag out for precisely the length of time necessary to allow the other to realise the enormity of what he had done, and was doing. Insubordination. Disobedience to superiors while on operational duty—the fact that it occurred at a critical stage of that operation made the crime even more heinous.

Quietly, the Commander said, "This is a combined operation in the widest possible sense of the word. My plan for conducting it has been outlined to every unit in the Fleet, and has been generally approved."

A chaotic picture of the many and variegated life-forms which made up his command swept into his mind, and the incredible amount of organisational detail necessary to make them a single functioning unit, a team.

"However," Everra continued, "there has been no time to allocate the unpleasant jobs to beings who might suffer least in doing them. They have, instead, been given to those I know can perform them most efficiently.

"I do not think that any Elissnian would risk the success of this operation, or have the lives of millions of entities on his conscience should the success be only partial, merely because of ethical hypersensitivity towards a few individuals."

"My apologies, Sir," the Elissnian relayed a few minutes later. "I will begin at once."

"Do so," the Commander said, and settled back. Had he possessed the facial equipment for it he would have sighed with relief.

The Elissni were a peculiar race in some respects. Their telepathy was a curse as well as a blessing; suffering in others affected them almost as strongly as if it had occurred to one of themselves. They were, Everra knew, the Galaxy's most sensitive, moral and sympathetic life-forms, and because of that sensitivity, they were also its greatest crowds. But occasionally, when the incentive was great enough, they could forget what cowards they were.

Again he saw the riddled body of the Elissnian psychologist lying on the roof of that villa near Peking. No matter how this turned out, there would be no disciplinary action against any of them.

But that resolution did nothing to ease his own conscience. He felt anything but proud of some of the things he was doing on this unfortunate planet.

The progress reports were still satisfactory.

An Elissnian-manned scoutship, and life-ships from his own vessel containing Elissnian psychologists, were rapidly processing his Human time-fuses. All national leaders had been treated and they were now working on the relatively less important types—persons who, while not rulers, still commanded a large following for various reasons. The Elissnian lists were long, but the less important—and well-guarded—a person was, the more easily were the hypnotic commands planted in their minds. It was estimated that ninety-one percent of the planet's civilised population—people in backward areas such as Greenland, central

America, and Africa were excluded, of course—would hear the message to be broadcast simultaneously, everywhere, thirty-nine hours from now.

Thirty-nine hours, Everra thought. Progress was more than satisfactory. But that report had posed another problem: the unorganised and decentralised near-savages of Africa, parts of America and the Pacific islands. He wanted to make a clean sweep of the planet, if possible.

The Commander let the problem sink to a lower, almost subconscious level of his mind—where the unique, multi-layer brain possessed by the Su race began breaking it down into large numbers of smaller, and solvable, problems—and considered the other reports coming in.

There were anti-Semitic riots in Paris and Berlin; stonings of several embassy buildings; violence against persons whose skin pigmentation or religious ideals disagreed with the geographical norm. There were increasingly frequent accusations of intolerance and violations against Human Rights being hurled at each other by the leading nations of the planet. Another more than satisfactory report, the Commander thought. He wondered if the situation he wanted wasn't developing too fast.

Before signing off the scoutship officer added that the noted Human broadcaster and critic at large, Hammond R. Bradley, had been found guilty of treasonable activities against his country, and incarcerated. The Human's last broadcast had contained words to the effect that some crazy agency wanted to destroy the Earth, and he refused to believe his fellow men responsible for this madness ...

Everra's limbs curled tightly inwards. His couch creaked with the sudden increase of pressure, but he didn't hear it. *How many people had heard those words?*

... But the Elissnian in charge of Bradley at the time had quickly impressed on the minds of the Humans around him—and which later resulted in its wide-spread publication—the idea that the commentator was not sane.

Everra relaxed again, but not completely. Someone might not believe in Bradley's insanity.

There were more uncertainties in this operation than he had planned for; many more. Everra could feel his limbs and body tightening up—his anxiety had become so in-

tense it was manifesting itself even on the physical level—
and back in the dark and silent corners of his mind there
was growing a nightmare. It was the ghastly picture of
the carnage that would all too certainly occur if those
certainties favoured the Humans, and he was unknowingly
leading his fleet into an ambush.

There was, he reminded himself, the matter of the
orbiting rocket. It *could* have relayed information of his
presence to its ground control, and possibly even a picture
of his ship, before he had destroyed it. Or the whole area
might have been under telescopic observation.

And there was the Peking incident. Suppose someone
found and analysed the blood from the Elissnian psychologist's body. A sufficiently imaginative mind could draw
some dangerous conclusions if both incidents were linked
together ...

Everra's screen lit up. An officer said crisply, "West
Europe sector reports intensification of civilian defence
measures, with frequent Bomb-drill compulsory in all large
cities, and estimates their shelter arrangements adequate
for roughly two-thirds of the population." The officer
paused, his expression suggesting that he expected some
show of surprise at this amazingly high percentage. When
it wasn't forthcoming, he went on, "The only new development is that in certain cities—they are very few—the citizens have refused to take part in these protective exercises, apparently on ethical grounds.

"This situation isn't widespread," he ended, "but it may
require some Elissnian mental work to control it."

A new development, Everra thought wearily. Another
demonstration of Human perspicacity. *Or was it?*

Suppose these stubborn and seemingly rebellious citizens really knew more than the others, knew that there
wouldn't be a war of the type expected, and had been
secretly instructed not to use their Bomb-shelter because
counter-measures were being prepared in them against the
true aggressor, an unearthly enemy of unknown power.

The gory spectre of death and destruction hiding in
Everra's mind began to edge out of the shadows.

Why, the Commander realised suddenly, that commentator Bradley could have been imprisoned, not for his pacifist activities, but because he had unthinkingly given away the knowledge which the higher military authorities of Earth were keeping hidden until they could spring their surprise—whatever hellish weapon that might be—on the fleet which they guessed must be coming.

Everra pictured his Grand Fleet ripped apart, by some weapon which in his hurry he had overlooked, with unpowered wrecks falling incandescent through Earth's atmosphere, or snuffing themselves out like moths as they drifted helplessly into the Sun. And the bloody massacre of the Fleet's surviving personnel. Worse than his own death was the shame to the whole Crennorlin group. The spectre of horror rushed from the shadows and stood plainly revealed. The sight sent a slow, writhing movement along Everra's massive body and limbs.

A simple explanation might be that some of the Humans were all-range telepaths. Such mutations had occurred among non-telepathic races before.

EVERRA was falling into a trap!

Desperately, viciously, the Commander fought to regain control of his mind and body. He was being stupid. He was frightening himself for nothing. Those suppositions were impossible. The Elissni were spread thinly over the planet, but surely they would have detected telepathic Humans, or double-thinking on such a large scale.

The slow undulations in his muscle sheath died as his fear subsided. Everra was very glad that he was alone in the control room where there was no one to witness his shame. Soon he was thinking clearly and analytically again. The spectre was gone—into temporary hiding, at least.

During his instructions to the Elissnian Captain he thought fleetingly of how easy it would be to grab up a few low I.Q. natives from some out-of-the-way spot—to prove he had actually been here—and then take the Fleet back with a story that the Humans had a secret weapon which was too much for them. Nobody would challenge the statements and deductions of a Su, especially when there would be no possibility of returning to check up on them.

The thought recurred as he was energising the transmitters which allowed faster-than-light communication with the approaching fleet, but he drove it from his mind. He had a duty to perform on Earth.

At present the Grand Fleet was coming in high above the plane of the ecliptic—so as to avoid the asteroid belt—at a position slightly within the orbit of Jupiter, and decelerating furiously to kill the tremendous velocity it had built up. Scattered over several billion cubic miles of space, it possessed about as much formation as a cloud of gas. But that would be remedied when the Fleet had braked sufficiently. At the speed they were moving it was better to have some elbow room.

Even when making the jump through hyperspace, ships tended to move with respect to each other, which was the reason Everra hadn't been able to simply take his whole fleet close in to Earth before emerging into normal space. Had it occurred, that materialisation of over three thousand ships out of hyperspace—and into each other—would have resulted in an explosion of stellar proportions, and all life on Earth would have perished there and then.

There was no easy way of manoeuvring such a fleet, otherwise a Su would not have had to take the job. Everra settled himself to absorb the reports which were streaming in, giving to each a very small part of his tremendous and complex mind, and building in it a complete and incredibly accurate picture of the movements and potentialities of over three thousand ships.

Admirals, Marshals, Commodores, and hundreds of other ranks peculiar to individual races—some of which could barely grasp the concept of discipline, or action in concert —reported in. Reports on such wildly varied items as Drive efficiency, morale, bedding, food supplies, and other minutiæ important only when considered as a whole. Occasionally Earthside reports interspersed those from the Fleet, telling of satisfactory progress. To Everra the passage of time seemed to speed up as the Grand Fleet—now pulling itself into a semblance of formation—slowed towards its objective.

He was listening to a commissary report from a Rheslian

transport Captain when, without warning, the screen blanked out. It stayed blank until Everra, more puzzled than angry, asked harshly to be connected to the Commodore of the flotilla containing the ship he had been speaking to.

The Commodore of Flotilla 5, Sub-fleet 87, was a Rheslian whose bony exo-skeleton made his emotions unreadable. But he knew what was required without being asked, and had a picture of the disaster relayed onto the Commander's screen even before he began making excuses for it. Everra didn't care much how it had happened, the sight of it was enough.

The supposedly parallel courses of two Rheslian transports—great unwieldy brutes of ships—had gradually intersected, their lack of manoeuvrability and tremendous velocity making it impossible for their crews to act fast enough to avoid collision. When the two ships had met, their inertia—the product of several hundred thousand tons of ship moving at thousands of miles per second—had fused and partially vaporised them. There was now a small Sun rushing ahead of the still-decelerating Fleet.

Rheslia, thought Everra sadly; a small world, poor in metals and sparse in population. Those two transports were a sizeable fraction of their system's naval power, and the personnel loss had been one hundred percent in each. It was at times like this, the Commander thought rebelliously, that he began to doubt the worth of such expeditions as this.

But mostly he thought of that incandescent mass hurtling ahead of his Grand Fleet. With a flare like that lighting their supposedly secret approach, he might just as well start broadcasting his purpose to the Humans of Earth right away, and forget his devious strategy. But he pictured the confusion, panic and bloody chaos that would occur if he was to use the simple, straightforward method of carrying out his mission. Anything would be better than that. Maybe his original plan could be used even yet.

Quickly he asked the Rheslian Commodore for the course and velocity data of the fused wreckage, then dismissed him. Before the glow had died from his view-screen, Everra's mind was approaching a solution to the problem.

The Fleet had crossed the Solar System and was currently passing the Sun within the orbit of Mercury, thus hiding the flare from its Drive units by approaching Earth from out of the sun. Its acceleration—and subsequent deceleration—had been the highest that its overworked gravity compensators would allow. Lacking guidance, the wreckage of the two ships would move away from the all-concealing Solar glare, and arrive in the vicinity of Earth ahead of the Fleet.

The Commander did some mental calculations—which could have been done by the ship's computer, though not nearly as quickly—then pressed a call-stud on his panel. It wasn't nearly as bad as he had at first thought.

When his interpreter, and shortly afterwards an Elissnian, answered, the Commander told him of the disaster and of the problem it had posed. In approximately eleven hours the wreckage—cooler then, and considerably dimmer—would pass near Earth. It would be brightest for a few minutes before sunset in the Western hemisphere, when it would outshine Venus, and then recede quickly beyond naked-eye observation. Most Humans including astronomers, would dismiss it as a wandering comet. But if some observatory with proper equipment made a spectro-analysis of it, the radio-active and organic components of the wreckage would show, giving a strong indication of its true nature. The Elissnian must therefore take steps to see that bad viewing conditions obtained over the larger observatories.

If direct weather control was impracticable for any reason, the Commander added, hypnosis or sabotage must be used towards the same end.

As he pressed the cut-off stud, Everra was wryly thankful that direct communication was impossible with the Elissni. That race was being severely overworked on this operation; even through the interpreter the Elissnian had sounded annoyed.

To the Commander, time passed at a steadily acceler-

ating rate. He marshalled his fleet into what he hoped was
the most effective formations, and reports from Earthside
scoutcraft continued to pour in. The artificial comet, fu-
neral pyre of two full crews of Rheslians, passed. The
Humans who saw it were inclined to regard it as an omen
foretelling the doom to come, rather than bring any degree of detached, scientific curiosity to bear on it—a possibility which the Commander had not foreseen, but which
eased his mind considerably.

But there was always doubt. Right up to the end there
would be doubt. Someone might have seen that wreckage
and analysed its radiations. The spectral lines of elements
not found in ordinary cometary bodies would have shown
up: strange metals, highly-unnatural radio-actives, and
most of all, the tell-tale traces of Carbon which could only
mean the recent presence of organic life.

There was the destruction of the orbital rocket, and the
other unavoidable slips which had been made. It wasn't
probable, Everra knew, but it was *possible* that a secret
power group on Earth knew, or thought it knew, practically everything, and was keeping this knowledge from the
public so as not to arouse his suspicions. They might even
allow their people to believe in the approach of a global
war to further lull those suspicions, only informing them of
the truth at the last moment when it would be too late for
the Commander to alter his strategy.

Such a ruse, though unlikely, was possible. The Commander's present plan depended on a very similar one.

Grimly he fought back a repetition of his earlier fear,
paralysis. It was time that he issued final instructions to
his Fleet. It had now left the orbit of Venus behind and
was thirteen hours and seven minutes from Earth. The
Commander plunged into that ocean of detail, fiercely
trying to convince himself that everything was going as *he*
had planned it.

To the Pacific sector he assigned two whole Sub-fleets—
light, fast ships capable of dealing with the widely-scattered
population of those unarmed islands. To China—despite
his psychological priming of its ruler, Mao Hsein-Yan—he
directed three. Population density was high there, and
many would be unable to act on those broadcast instruc-

tions. Other sectors of Asia required similar action. Everra
ordered the necessary units to see that it was carried out.

During a brief lull his Earthside screen lit up and an
officer made an abbreviated salute. "War tension is increasing as predicted," he said rapidly, "with the smaller
'nations' allying themselves with one or other of the major
powers. Attempts at reconciliation have ceased." The
screen blanked out.

Suddenly and for no apparent reason, that section of
Everra's mind which he had so carefully trained to think
and react as would a Human's of Earth, looked out at the
state of the planet. *What a hell,* it thought sickly, *for a
civilised race to be in.*

Hastily the Commander brought his attention back to
the approaching Fleet. They were now seven hours away.

Africa, South America and areas like Greenland and
Iceland would require special treatment. In under-
developed and sparsely-populated sectors civilian defence
organisations would be nil. Offensive weapons should be
negligible also—which, the Commander thought feelingly,
was a very good thing. Carefully husbanding his resources
—the Fleet, while large, was not unlimited—he continued to assign Sub-fleets, Squadrons, and often single units,
to the sectors which he thought needed them.

Some of the Humans were bound to escape his net,
Everra knew, but he wanted to make the number to do so
as low as possible.

His screen brightened. A voice rattled, "The situation is
deteriorating rapidly. Sealed orders have gone to Humans
in charge of several missile launching stations, alerting
them for instant use, and psychologically, the personnel
manning them have become very unstable. No official
orders have been given to open hostilities anywhere as
yet, but more and more of the Humans are reaching the
point where war, or some other release, will be necessary
purely for the relief of tension."

That's more like it, the Commander thought, his uneasiness fading. That couldn't be pretence out there; one
could almost feel the hate building up. He had merely the
logistics of a planetary seizure to worry him now.

Four hours to go.

Small nations and cities who remained determinedly neutral were another problem, one needing many individual solutions. But there was so little time left.

It would be dangerous, the Commander realised, very dangerous, but the only answer was to bring in a section of the Fleet ahead of time, to deal surreptitiously with areas not closely in touch with the more advanced nations.

Central Africa, for instance.

Quickly choosing crews who could take acceleration pressure far above the norm, he ordered their Captains to cut deceleration so as to arrive an hour before the rest of the Fleet. If he couldn't manage everything at once, then he must risk spreading the time out a little.

He had barely finished that when another report came in. A party of Human scientists investigating cosmic radiation above the North Magnetic Pole had reported fluctuations in the brightness of the Sun, and numerous points of light shining to one side of it. Unknowingly, they had spotted his Grand Fleet. He sent one of his remaining life-ships to deal with them. Nobody, he hoped, would have time to examine their report too closely during the present emergency.

One hour and seventeen minutes. The advance section of the Fleet was less than half an hour away.

Suddenly the whole panel blazed with attention signals, and the picture of a long, silvery torpedo trailing flame and climbing rapidly, flashed onto his screen. A voice recited its point of origin and course, and suggested a method for dealing with it. Everra hurriedly signalled approval, and watched as the missile wobbled off course and dived into the sea without exploding.

No, he chided the unknown Human whose jitters were responsible for launching the first atomic missile, *you mustn't go off half-cocked like that.*

For the best results, the dammed-up tensions of fear and black desperation had to approach bursting point everywhere simultaneously. Only then could Everra channel it into the direction he wished it to go.

Suicides, murders and rioting had increased sharply, his scout reported; and individual and group excesses of a kind which Everra did not care to think about—he was, after all, a highly civilised being. It was the picture of a society on the rack, being stretched to its elastic limit. The Commander thought briefly of the chronometers used in his ship. They could be wound, and the tension on the spring would gradually dissipate itself along the gearing of the mechanism as it did its work. But wind it too tightly and all the stored power was delivered with a single explosive *snap* as the spring broke.

Earth was wound up far beyond the limits of safety for any culture. Everra continued to wind.

Fifty minutes. The advance guard of his Fleet was due.

The village of Kwali Seywa was important to nobody and even the local chieftain rarely visited the place. Only doctors were mad enough to do that. A thin whistling noise made the few villagers in sight look up.

High in the sky a cluster of black dots were increasing rapidly in size. The natives watched them until they couldn't believe they could grow any bigger, then flame and thunder erupted from the undersides and they realised with a shock that the objects were still many miles up. Paralysed with terror, they saw the things grow until they darkened the sky, and saw swarms of smaller objects burst from them and scatter. One of the big ones landed about three miles to the west. It towered like a black metal mountain above the jungle.

Even before one of the alien small ships—with its all too revealing transparent nose section—shot across the village and circled abruptly back, the natives were running for shelter. But their panic was of little avail as the alien ship had begun to spray a heavy yellow fog over an ever-widening area, which quickly engulfed them in its rolling tide.

Armed with detectors from which nothing that lived could hide, and virtually unlimited supplies of the gas, the life-ships from Everra's advance squadron sectioned off the area and cleared it. Everything that moved was touched briefly by the gas, whereupon the living creatures stopped moving. The new metal mountains spewed out streams of land vehicles which spread out in the wake of the far-flying life-ships, quickly and efficiently dealing with the life-forms lying flaccidly about.

Goats, Humans, cows and a few mangy dogs received precisely the same treatment. Time was too short for distinctions.

From the Flagship, Everra signalled approval of the handling of the operation, and broke contact. Similar events, he knew, were taking place in the Amazon Basin, Bataan and other areas where communications were bad and the level of technology low. He also knew that some of the landings had been seen. But there was an epidemic of object-sightings due to the war which was boiling up, and it would take some time to check them all.

The main Fleet would arrive in twenty-six minutes.

From the Urals this time, another atomic missile streaked skywards and made a long curve down—another Human gunner had reached breaking point. The Commander watched without comment as a life-ship shot after it, and the missile, de-activated, crashed to earth.

But generally, the tension building explosively upwards in billions of Human nervous systems had reached a level just below breaking point, and held there. The reason for this was that they were waiting. Black, white, brown, yellow and red, the people were waiting to hear the voices of their rulers and counsellors.

And of them, Everra would have complete mental control.

The Humans were balanced on a knife edge. They were strung up as tight as they could go. Sick with fear for themselves and their loved ones, their critical faculties almost gone, it required just one tiny push in the right direction to make them do what Everra wanted.

In eight minutes, the push would come.

Everra sweated. The temperature of his massive, sprawling body remained at its customary minus 112 degrees Fahrenheit, but similar physical changes due to extreme worry took place; so Everra sweated. The whole operation, his future, everything, depended on this working right. He hoped desperately that the Elissnian hypnotists had done their work well: they, and their unusual mental abilities, were his chief reason for this unprecedented departure from normal strategy. That, and the current state of armed peace on Earth, had given him the original idea.

Five minutes.

In Alaska, a Second Pilot stood by the frost-smeared window of the briefing hut, looking with frightened disbelief at the long blank shadow of his ship, and at the bulge made at its underbelly by the Hell-bomb, waiting and listening. In Afghanistan, a radio set was surrounded by fiercely bearded, gesticulating hill people, most of whom still regarded the device as a work of magic. But the owner of the house was a wise one, and would explain the difficult words which their leader sometimes used. They also waited.

Three minutes.

Under mountains and plains, in Man-made caverns echoing to the metallic sounds of lethal torpedoes being run into position, other men waited. Their eyes were on radar screens, their fingers on firing studs and their ears cocked towards the extension loud-speakers nearby. All over the planet their thoughts were much the same.

Their King—or President, or Dictator as the case might be—would begin by saying that they did not want to fight. That no person in their country from their ruler down to the poorest beggar wanted to fight. But a terrible war was being forced on them by the insane actions of their enemies, and there was no choice but to defend their country. The end result of these words that all their rulers were saying about each other would, the people knew, be planetary destruction.

And neither the Bomb-shelters, the civil defence drills nor anything else would save them.

But why, *why*, they asked themselves helplessly, had everyone gone mad like this? And all within a few days.

Two minutes.

Announcers in radio stations all over the planet cleared their throats, nervously aware of the power and authority of the individuals waiting to speak beside them, then began, simultaneously, their hundreds of introductory announcements.

One minute.

Everra's Flagship burst from its icy covering and shot southwards. His carefully prepared Human time-fuzes, designed to shock the population of a world into simultaneous, concerted action were about to function, and the spearhead of his Fleet was already screaming into Earth's atmosphere.

Now!

A myriad mouths whose lightest word was law opened to address their people. But the messages appealing to loyalty and exhorting them to defend their rights were not delivered. Instead, reflected in strained faces and tormented eyes, a bitter mental struggle raged as hundreds of the world's most powerful men tried to fight back the words which forced themselves from their lips. In his speeding ship Everra listened, already tasting the joy of success.

Suddenly the lines of strain melted from the faces of the mighty. Their eyes still reflected pain, and shock, but now it was from the complete and accurate understanding of what was about to happen to their planet. They continued speaking, with renewed urgency.

The wave of relief that rose from the listening billions of Earth was almost tangible. There would be no war, their leaders assured them. Something inconceivably worse threatened their planet. But there was help coming, in the form of a great Fleet from space ...

The Commander stopped listening. All at once he had thousands of things to do.

Two days had passed, and the number of Humans waiting to be moved from Earth was less than a million, all of them in the city below. Protected by a fifty-mile circle of utter blackness—the maximum area which the Flagship's refraction screen could cope with—they enjoyed the relative coolness of ninety-seven degrees Fahrenheit.

To the limit of visibility around Everra's ship, the land burned. The sky was a white glare of superheated steam, caused by the boiling top-surface of the seas, and though the scalding, all-enveloping fog hid the Sun, he was fearfully aware of its presence—twice as large as life and ten times hotter.

Fortunately, Earth's atmosphere had made a good insulator. Two hours after the first blast of heat from a suddenly unstable Sun had swept the planet, parts of it were still liveable—provided, of course, that one was far enough underground, or had the protection of a refraction screen.

When the leaders of Earth had relayed the information—which had been hypnotically impressed on their minds by the Elissnians—about the imminent instability of their Sun, and the nature of the rescue fleet coming to remove them to another planet, very little resentment had been shown at the rather drastic methods Everra had used to ready the Humans for quick evacuation. Instead, they used the civil defence organisation and training which Everra's war scare had forced into being to save themselves, which was exactly what the Commander had planned and hoped for.

Assisted by light units of the Grand Fleet, which also sought out isolated groups who had no means of knowing the true situation, great masses of people were assembled and taken off the doomed planet by the giant transports which made up the bulk of that same fleet. Meanwhile mines, Bomb-shelters and the great underground arsenals were readied for those who could not be taken away before the Sun rendered the surface of the planet unliveable.

It had been the civil defence measures which had made the operation such a complete success. While the backward races were being dealt with—usually by gassing into unconsciousness and loading aboard the nearest available transport—their more advanced brothers were preparing, with a minimum of panic and confusion, to leave their world forever. And when, forty-six hours after they had been told of it, their Sun blasted out a sphere of radiation that roasted and partly boiled the surface of Earth, eighty percent of the world's population—including most of its food animals—had already gone. The rest waited their turn underground, or beneath the protecting screens of heavy units of the Fleet.

Below his ship, the last great transport, packed tight

with Humanity, lifted through the Flagship's screen and streaked for space. Everra withdrew his refraction screen, seeing the unprotected city explode into a sea of fire, and followed it quickly. It was decidedly unsafe to hang about here. He thought, again, of what normal evacuation procedure would have meant to this planet.

With time short, and the population too big to convince otherwise, the Humans would have fought him to the last in the belief that they were being invaded. They would have fought until their Sun cremated them where they stood. And with luck, Everra might have been able to rescue as many as seven or eight percent.

Instead, three per cent had been *lost*. *Three per cent—* when accepted losses on a Nova-ed world was ninety percent. The honour to the Crennorlin-Su would be great, and his own personal advancement considerable. Yet his joy could not make him entirely forget some of the things he had to do to achieve success. The Su were a sensitive race, especially about causing suffering to their intellectual inferiors.

This situation had occurred before, Everra thought tiredly, and it would happen again. So long as there were warp-driven ships whose path through hyperspace accidently intersected points in the normal continuum occupied by suns, disrupting their energy balance and causing them to Nova shortly afterwards. And should the Sun concerned have inhabited planets, then every system of the Galactic Civilisation which could reach it in time would send ships to evacuate the inhabitants ...

An alarm clattered loudly, startling him. Briefly, through his heavily-filtered viewscreen, he saw the doomed Sun brighten and swell hideously, engulfing the inner planets as he watched. None too soon, the Flagship slid into the safety of hyperspace.

Presently Everra began working on suitable messages for the friends of the Elissni who had died while planting knowledge in the brains of the Earth leaders, and of the crews of those two Rheslian transports.

Tableau

The War Memorial in the planetary capital of Orligia was unique, but it very definitely was not a nice object. A great many people—beings of sensitivity and intelligence—had tried vainly to describe their feelings of shock, horror and anger which the sight of it had caused them. For this was no aesthetic marble poem in which godlike figures gestured defiance, or lay dying nobly with limbs arranged to the best advantage. Instead it consisted of an Orligian and an Earthman surrounded by the shattered remnant of a control room belonging to a type of ship now long obsolete, the whole being encased in a cube of transparent plastic.

The Orligian was standing crouched slightly forward, with blood matting the fur on its chest and face. A few feet away lay the Earthman, very obviously dying. His uniform was in shreds, revealing the ghastly injuries he had sustained—certain organs in the abdominal region normally concealed by layers of skin and muscle being clearly visible. Yet this man, who had no business being alive much less being capable of movement, was struggling forward to reach the Orligian. It was the look on the Earthman's face which was the most distressing thing about the whole, horrible tableau.

82

TABLEAU   83

Night had fallen, but the Memorial was lit erratically by the flashes which repeatedly outlined the buildings at the edges of its surrounding park. From all over the city came the sounds of sharp, thudding explosions, while rockets grew rapidly on slender stems of orange sparks to flower crashingly into clouds of falling stars. The city, indeed the whole planet, was in festive mood. With the Orligian love of doing things properly or not at all, this meant the letting off of a great many fireworks as well as the usual merry-making. Sleep was impossible, the populace was going wild.

It was, after all, a great occasion. Tomorrow the Orligians were getting another war memorial . . .

Like most single ship engagements it had proved to be a long-drawn out affair. Normally such a duel led to the defeat of the Orlig ship within a few hours, MacEwan thought with that small portion of his mind which was not engaged in throwing his ship about in violent evasive action. But there was nothing normal about this fight, he thought bitterly; the enemy had begun to learn things, to adopt Earth armament and tactics. They, too, had regressed to throwing rocks . . . !

"Closer! *Closer!*" Reviora's voice squeaked suddenly through his phones. "We're too far away, dammit! They'll get us in a minute . . ."

MacEwan did not have to be reminded of the necessity for sticking close to the enemy ship, and many another Captain would have told the Ordnance Officer so in no uncertain terms. But he had discovered long ago that young Reviora, whose voice had only recently changed and was prone to change back again at times of emotional stress, could exhibit all the outward signs of panic while continuing to use his weapons with incredible accuracy. MacEwan relegated the Ordnance Officer's jitterings into the realm of general background noise and continued to focus all his attention on the controls.

His idea in taking evasive action at extreme range—extreme for his ship, that was; it was nearly ideal range for the enemy—was to lull the Orlig skipper into thinking that he intended breaking off the action. Such a thing was unheard of, simply because trying to run away from an Orlig ship meant certain destruction from their primary weapon, but there was always a first time. Maybe the enemy officer would think that his ship was crippled, or out of ammunition, or that its Captain lacked sufficient intestinal fortitude to ram. Anyway, he would be puzzled and maybe just a little bit inattentive . . .

MacEwan said quietly, "Reviora, ready?" He pulled the ship round in a tight turn, then with the Orlig ship centring his forward vision screen he pushed the thrust bar through the emergency gate and held it there. The target vessel grew slowly, then expanded so rapidly that the screen was suddenly too small to hold it. A dull, intermittent vibration told of Reviora, with the ship holding a steady course and the enemy dead ahead, using his forward turret to the best advantage. MacEwan thought he saw a spurt of fog from a hole freshly torn in the Orlig ship's hull, then the image flicked out of sight to reappear as a rapidly shrinking picture in the aft view-screen.

His hands were slippery and he had to blink sweat out of his eyes. *Check velocity!* his racing brain yelled at his slow, fumbling fingers. *Move! Jump around! And above all, keep close . . . !*

So as to give Reviora a chance to get in a killing burst, MacEwan had made a fast but unswerving approach. He had held his ship steady for fully five seconds. That had been an insane risk to take, but he had gambled on the Orlig ship not using its primary weapon on him for fear of his hurtling ship smashing into it even after MacEwan's ship and crew were written off. Now however, he was fast receding from the enemy ship and evasive action was again indicated. Still on emergency thrust he began weaving and corkscrewing, at the same time trying desperately to kill the velocity away from the enemy he had built up during the attack.

Evasive action at a distance was much less effective than close up because the Orlig primary weapon had a certain amount of spread. Maximum safety lay in sticking close and moving fast. Or had done until now . . .

It had been estimated that the radiation, or force, or

TABLEAU   85

field of stress which was the Orligian Primary Weapon
took roughly six to seven seconds to build up, but once
caught in that field a ship and its occupants were a total
loss. Yet strangely the ships affected appeared unharmed.
Provided one was extremely careful they could even be
entered. But just scratch the metal of one of those ships,
or stick a needle in one of the crew-men, and the result
resembled a small-scale atomic explosion—but again,
strangely, without any trace of immediate or residual
radio-activity. Such ships were now left severely alone,
their orbits not even being plotted as dangers to naviga-
tion because the first meteorite to puncture their hulls
caused them to destroy themselves.

It was a super-weapon, only one of those which had
forced Earth back, so far as tactics were concerned, to the
bow-and-arrow level.

MacEwan only half noticed the shudderings of his ship
as Reviora, using absurdly adolescent profanity, tried for a
deflection shot with the remote-controlled waist turret,
and the harsher, more erratic vibration of Orlig shots
getting home. At the moment he was wishing desperately
that there was some means by which he could simply cut
and run—not, he hastened to assure himself, because he
was overly interested in his own safety, but because this
new development represented a change in Orlig strategy.
It was a change which would have to be countered, and
MacEwan hoped that the Brass back home would be able
to find the answer—he couldn't see one himself.

If only Nyberg had never been born, MacEwan
thought; or failing that, if only he had not grown up into
a stubborn, courageous and idealistic Swede whose
highmindedness had started an interstellar war. Such
wishing was sheerest futility, he knew, but even in the
middle of the hottest engagement he had yet experienced
there was this weak, traitorous segment of his mind which
tried to escape into the world of what might have
been . . .

Five years ago the U.N. survey ship *Starfinder*—crew
of fifty-eight plus seven civilian specialists, Captain
Sigvard Nyberg in command—had, at very nearly the limit

of its prodigious range, made contact with a ship of an alien culture for the first time. A tape left by the late Captain Nyberg told of the excitement of the occasion, and a day-by-day summary gave some indications of the difficulties experienced in widening that contact.

Strangely, the vessel of what were later to become known as the Orligians did not seem to want to maintain contact at first, though neither did they show signs of hostility. *Starfinder's* psychologist, admittedly working on little or no data, had suggested that such behavior might be due either to a high degree of conservatism in their culture or to a simple case of cold feet. He had added that cowardice was not a strong possibility, however, considering the fact that the alien ship was four times the size of their own. But Captain Nyberg had maintained contact—just how he had done so was not known in detail because he was a man who disliked talking about his own accomplishments—and widened it to the point where simple sequences of radio signals were replaced by exchanges of message capsules containing technical data which enabled the two ships to match communication channels.

It was shortly after sound-with-vision communications had been set up between the ships that something went wrong. The last words on Captain Nyberg's tape were to the effect that, far from being horrible monsters the aliens were nice, cuddly little creatures and that their atmosphere and gravity requirements seemed to be close enough to Earth-normal for the two races to co-exist on either of their home planets without artificial aids. A few words, mostly of self-identification, had already been exchanged. But the Captain intended going across to their ship next day, because he had a hunch that the Orligians were beginning to shy away again.

When the nine men in *Starfinder's* tender, who had been investigating a nearby solar system during these proceedings, returned they found that the mother ship had been the scene of a massacre. Not one of the ship's personnel had escaped, and the condition of the bodies seemed to indicate that they had been battered to death with the nearest available blunt instrument. The slaughter had been merciless, the human being obviously taken by sur-

TABLEAU 87

prise because in only a few places was the deck stained with blood which matched no earthly group, and there were no Orligian dead at all.

The nine-man crew of the tender somehow managed to bring their mother ship home. The situation was, of course, highly charged emotionally—much more so than normal because of the fact that *Starfinder's* crew had been mixed—so that Earth, which had known peace for three centuries, found itself at war with the culture of Orligia.

And the war, MacEwan was thinking as he frantically threw his ship all over the sky half a mile from the Orligian light cruiser, had been going on for far too long. The sense of immediacy, where the people back home were concerned, had been lost—and with it the horror and righteous anger which had started it all. Defence spending was heavy and teddybears were no longer stocked in kiddy's toy stores, but otherwise there was very little to indicate outwardly that a state of war existed at all. But maximum effort was being, and would be, maintained simply through fear. Earth, had she chosen to, could have withdrawn her spacefleet at any time, could simply have left and called the whole thing off. Neither side knew the positions of each other's home planets. But that course would have left the situation unresolved and eventually, whether in fifty years or five hundred, the Orligs were bound to discover Earth. The people of Earth were honest enough not to gain peace by dumping the problem in the laps of their many times great grandchildren.

But it was an untidy and very unsatisfactory sort of war. The 'front line' so to speak was in the general volume of space where the original contact had been made, and bases had been set up by both sides on planetary bodies in the region, and supplied by ships taking very great pains to conceal their point of origin. The distances involved made patrolling a joke and any battle a vast, disorganised series of dogfights. Except when raids were carried out on enemy bases it was nothing unusual for three weeks to go by without a single clash, and this at a time when both sides were prosecuting the war with maximum effort.

Altogether it proved what had been known from the first, that the very idea of interstellar war was impractical and downright silly. But the chief reason for the feeling of dissatisfaction was the fact that, slowly but surely, the Earth was losing.

Superiority in offensive and defensive weapons belonged to the Orligs. They had a screen, probably originally intended for meteor protection, which englobed each of their ships at a radius of two miles and which melted anything approaching at a velocity likely to do harm— meteors, missiles, attacking ships, *anything*. This screen could be penetrated only by guiding the ship through it at what was practically a crawl. Once through, however, the missile's remote-control equipment immediately ceased to function and the missile drifted harmlessly past the target. On the one or two occasions when a nuclear warhead had accidently drifted into an Orlig ship, nothing at all had happened.

Earth science had been able to duplicate this screen, but it was no good to them because the Orligs scorned the use of such crude methods of attack as atomic missiles: they had The Weapon.

This the Earth scientists could not understand, much less duplicate. They only knew that it was some kind of beam or field of force which required several seconds to focus, and that its maximum range was about thirty miles. There was no answer to this weapon. A ship caught by it became a lifeless, undamaged but untouchable hulk which needed only sharp contact with a meteorite or piece of drifting wreckage to blast itself out of existence. The Weapon was also thought to be the reason why atomic warheads refused to function in the vicinity of Orlig ships, but this was just a guess.

There had been panic in high places, MacEwan remembered, when the most advanced offensive weapons of Earth had been proved useless. What was needed was some form of weapon which was too simple and uncomplicated for the Orlig nullification equipment to be effective, and a tactic which would bring such a weapon to bear. An answer of sorts had been found. To find it they had to go back, not quite so far as the bow-and-arrow era, but to

TABLEAU 89

the Final World War period and the armour-piercing cannon, and chemically powered rockets used in the aircraft of that period. The tactics which had been developed were the only ones possible with such weapons, but they tended to be wasteful of men.

"Sir! Sir! Can I have the ship?"

It was Reviora, excited but no longer swearing. The tiny, wandering portion of MacEwan's mind came back to present time with a rush. He said, "Why?"

"Ammunition's running out, but we've three Mark V's in the nose rocket launcher," Reviora babbled. "It's working now—I found the break in the firing circuit. They won't be expecting rockets at this stage. We can use that trick of Hoky's—" He bit the sentence off abruptly, then stammered, "I . . . I'm sorry, I mean Captain Hokasuri—"

"Skip it," said MacEwan. He ran his eye briefly over the control panel, then switched everything to the forward conning position. "Right, you have the ship."

Hoky had had lots of tricks. Hokasuri and MacEwan were the Old Firm, the unbeatable, invincible combination who invariably hunted together. But then every team was invincible until one or the other failed to come back. MacEwan squirmed restively. His mind, temporarily freed of the responsibility for guiding the ship, flicked back over the opening minutes of the engagement. It could only have been through sheer bad luck that his partner had been Stopped, the mild-mannered little Japanese with the apologetic grin and the black button eyes was not the type to make mistakes . . .

Hokasuri and he had been searching the nearby planet for signs of an enemy base when they had surprised an Orligian presumably engaged on the same chore. Distance had been about two hundred miles. They had immediately separated and attacked.

The Orligs used fairly large ships; apparently the generators for The Weapon took up a lot of space. Earth craft were very small and fast, and hunted in pairs. Though not one hundred percent successful, this had proved to be the only effective means of coming to grips with the enemy. The Weapon had a range of thirty miles and took six or seven seconds to focus. Two ships, therefore, approaching from different directions, the while taking violent evasive action, discharging 'window' and performing various other acts designed to confuse enemy aim, could be expected to run the gauntlet of The Weapon until the screen which surrounded enemy ships at a distance of two miles was reached. But to penetrate this the attacking ships had to check velocity, and it was at this point that the two attackers usually became one, the reason being that there was time for The Weapon to be focussed on one of them. The surviving attacker then closed with the enemy—its very nearness and extreme mobility protection against the slow-acting Weapon—and slowly battered the Orlig ship into a wreck with solid, armour-piercing shells and rockets.

Once begun such a battle had to be fought to the death, because the Earth ship would be a sitting target if it attempted to escape through the screen again.

MacEwan had not been worried about Hokasuri getting through the screen, they had done it so often before despite all the laws of probability and statistics. They were the invincible ones, the pilots with that little something extra which had enabled them to return together after eighteen successful kills. But he had seen Hokasuri Stopped, seen his ship diving unwaveringly into the planet below them and watched it explode in the fringes of its atmosphere.

For the first time then MacEwan had experienced a sense of personal anger towards this Orlig ship. Indoctrination to the contrary, previous attacks had always seemed more like a big and very dangerous game to him. But then his anger had been pushed into the background by a sudden upsurge of fear that was close to panic. The Orlig ship, which should have been helpless now that he had closed in, was hitting back. What was worse, it was using the same type of archiac weapon for short-range defence that Earth ships had developed for attack, heavy calibre machine-guns of some sort. His ship was in nearly as bad a state as was that of the enemy . . .

Now he watched the Orlig ship spreading out in his

TABLEAU 91

forward view-screen again. The bow-launchers were fixed mount; to line them up on the target Reviora had to aim with the whole ship, and the Ordnance Officer had to do it because MacEwan's fire control panel was dead.

Hokasuri's trick had been to open up the enemy ship with his guns, saving the rockets until he could place them right inside the target. It was a process which called for accuracy of a high order. Perhaps Reviora could match it.

For an agonising four seconds Reviora held the ship on a collision course with the enemy while the fire of two Orlig blister turrets gouged at its hull. Suddenly the rockets were away, streaking ahead and plunging unerringly into the long, dark rent already torn in the Orlig's hull plating by an earlier attack. Everything happened at once, then. Metal fountained spectacularly outwards and the ragged-edged hole in the Orlig's hull lengthened, widened and gaped horribly. Simultaneously there was a sharp cry from Reviora which faded out in peculiar fashion. MacEwan wondered about it for perhaps a fraction of a second, decided that the peculiar sound was due to the sudden loss of the air which carried Reviora's voice from his mouth to the suit mike, then he was reaching frantically for the control panel again.

Reviora was dead. They were still on a collision course!

Desperately MacEwan stabbed control keys—forward and rear opposed lateral steering jets to swing ship, and full emergency thrust on the main drive to get him out of there fast. The ship began turning, but that was all. Controls to the main power pile were cut, probably by the recent Orlig gunnery, and the hyperdrive telltales were dead, too—the ship was a wreck. Now it was skidding in broadside-on and still closing rapidly with the other ship. MacEwan hit more keys, firing all lateral jets on that side in an attempt to check velocity. Uselessly, it was too little and too late. There was a close-spaced series of shocks as the ship ran through the metallic debris blown from the Orlig ship, climaxed by a tearing, grinding crash as the Earth vessel embedded itself exactly in the hole its rockets had blasted in the enemy hull.

The shock tore MacEwan, straps and all, sideways out

of his chair and threw him onto the deck. His head hit something ...

When he was in a condition to think straight again his first thought was for the spacesuit. Captains did not wear protective suits in action for the same reason that necessitated their safety webbing being thin, flexible and generally not worth a damn—too cumbersome, and besides, the control room was tucked away relatively safe in the centre of the ship. But now there was no longer any need for his hands to be unhampered and his body able to move freely; his control board was dead. Two view-screens were still operating for some peculiar reason but that was all. There were no indications of a drop in air pressure, his ears felt normal and respiration ditto, but it was too much to expect that the crash had not opened seams even here. He was about to open the suit locker when his mind registered what his eyes were seeing in the two view-screens.

One was focussed inwards and showed where the lateral jets had practically fused the two ships together before cutting out; some of the Orlig's bulkheads still glowed red hot. The other screen gave a view outwards and showed the planetary surface only a few hundred miles off. As MacEwan watched his ears detected a whispering, high-pitched rushing sound.

There are no sounds in space. The Orlig ship, crippled, a near wreck and carrying the remains of the small ship responsible for its present condition, was trying for a landing. It was already entering atmosphere. MacEwan abruptly forgot about spacesuits and dived instead for the acceleration chair.

He was still scrambling weightlessly above the chair when the first surge dropped him face downwards into it. He had time to fasten just one safety strap, before suddenly mounting deceleration hammered him flat. Briefly, he thought that the Orlig ship must be in bad trouble to want to land in its present state. With the damage inflicted by the Earth ship the Orligian must be an aerodynamic mess, and that without taking into account the wreckage of the aforesaid ship jammed against it like some spacegoing Siamese twin. Then all thinking stopped as he strained

TABLEAU 93

every nerve and muscle to keep alive, to keep his creaking and popping rib cage from collapsing onto his straining heart and lungs and strangling the life out of him.

After what seemed an impossibly long time the deceleration let up somewhat, becoming steady, measured surges of one or two G's which he could take comfortably. Obviously the Orlig pilot had shed most of his velocity in the thin, upper air to minimise atmospheric heating, then was taking her down slow for the last few miles. Not too slow, though, or stratospheric winds might buffet her off vertical despite everything the gyros could do. This Orlig was *good*, MacEwan thought; he deserved to make it. MacEwan also thought that he would like to buy the Orlig pilot a drink, supposing such a thing was possible and that Orligs drank.

The control room was vibrating and heaving in a manner unnerving both to mind and body, as if jerking and swaying in time to the mad cacophony of shrieking air, bellowing engines and a banging, rattling percussion section as deceleration and air resistance tried to shake both ships to pieces. MacEwan was amazed that the wreckage of his ship had not torn itself free long ago.

Suddenly there was a last, violent surge of deceleration, a smashing, jarring shock, then the grinding scream of tearing metal. They were down—but not still. There was a sickening, outward swaying motion and more harsh crepitation of ruptured metal. MacEwan's eyes flew to the view-screen. It showed a stony, desert-like planetary surface swooping up to meet him. One of the Orlig's landing legs must have buckled, they were toppling . . .

The noise was like a pick driven into his brain, and he saw the ship coming to pieces all around him. Bits of sky showed in surrealistic geometric shapes which changed constantly with the shifting of the wreckage. There was a sudden bright explosion, and MacEwan had time only to remember their damaged midships launcher and the primed rocket still jammed in it, then flying, jagged-edged metal ripped all consciousness from him.

When MacEwan came to again there was surprisingly little pain; his strongest impressions were those of numbness and extreme, clammy cold. This must be shock, he diagnosed briefly. But there was a warm wetness overlying the chill of his body that seemed to be localised in the area where he felt the dull, shock-numbed pains. He looked down at himself then, and realised how very lucky he was to be in a state of shock. He knew at once, of course, that he was dying.

The blast had left only a few shreds of his uniform, there was a great deal of blood, and his injuries . . .

A man should not have to look at himself in a state like this, MacEwan thought dully. If he had met an animal in this condition he would have shot it, and had it been a member of his own species he would have turned away and been violently sick. As it was he gazed at the frightful wounds with a strange objectivity until his brain, not quite as numb as the rest of him, re-opened communications with his one good arm. He fumbled open the emergency medical kit that still hung from his belt and used the coagulant spray freely, ending by swallowing rather more than the prescribed dose of antipain against the time when the shock would wear off. With most of the external bleeding checked. MacEwan tried to lie as motionless as possible. If he moved at all he felt that he would burst open along the seams like some great big football filled with red molasses.

It was while he was trying to look around him—and endeavouring to decide *why* he had given himself this inadequate first aid—that MacEwan saw the Orligian.

By what freak of circumstances it came to be there it was impossible to say, but not three yards from MacEwan lay one of the Enemy. It was not a very impressive object, he thought, this small being which resembled nothing so much as a teddybear that had been left out in the rain. But it was not rain which matted the fur on the creature's chest and head, nor was it water oozing from the raw ruin of its face. It was in much better shape than MacEwan, however, it was breathing steadily and making odd twitching movements which suggested returning consciousness. The broad belt to which was attached MacEwan's holster and the pouch containing the medical kit was the only part of his uniform left intact. He carefully

TABLEAU   95

drew the little gun with its clip of thirty explosive bullets
and waited for the Orlig to wake up.

While waiting he tried hating it a little.

MacEwan had always been an unemotional man—
perhaps that was the secret of his success as a Captain,
and the reason for his unusually long period of active
duty. In his particular job MacEwan was convinced that
emotion simply killed you off in jig time. A man making an
attack approach with hate or any other emotion—whether
directed towards the enemy, or something or somebody
else—clogging his mind was leaving that much less of it for
the vital business of evading The Weapon. In battle Mac-
Ewan felt no hatred for the enemy, no anger that his
Ordnance Officer cursed and swore in a highly insubordi-
nate fashion at him—Reviora was invariably full of apologies on their return to base—and none of the softer emotions that could leak over from the times when he was not
in battle.

There had been a girl once, a tall, dark-eyed girl who
had been attached to the base Plot Room. MacEwan had
eaten with her a few times, seen how things were going,
then avoided her. That had been the smart thing to do;
good survival. Now he was realising what an unhappy
man he had been.

Hokasuri had treated the whole thing as a game, too.
MacEwan had had one of his rare moments of anger
when his brother Captain's Stopped ship had exploded in
this planet's atmosphere, and when Reviora had died. But
now he felt only a dull regret. He reminded himself that
the Orlig lying over there was responsible—in part, at
least—for those deaths, but still he could not actively hate
the thing.

It was his duty to kill it, whether he hated the Orlig
personally or not. Why, then, was he being so squeamish
about not wanting to shoot it when it was unconscious,
and trying to work up hatred for it? Was his imminent
demise making him go soft, had Iron Man MacEwan
turned to putty at the end? Phlegmatic, unsmiling and
distant, Captain MacEwan was looked upon back at base
as the embodiment of the soulless, killing machine. Now

he felt as if he was thinking like a woman. Now he was thinking that, just this once, he would like to do something on a basis of emotion rather than for cold, calculating, logical reasons. It would be the last chance he would have, he thought wryly.

But wasn't he fooling himself? Suppose he forgot logic for once, would he use the pistol to blow the Orlig into little pieces out of sheer hate or would he do something stupid? Yellow cowardice was a motivation as well as duty or hate, and MacEwan was coming near his end. He had never been a religious man, but nobody had been able to give him concrete data on what lay on the other side, though a great many believed firmly that they knew. Was he simply scared that doing a bad thing now would have serious consequences later, after he died—even though he did not really believe there was a later? MacEwan swore weakly, the first time he had done such a thing in years.

All right, then! MacEwan told himself savagely. This mind of mine, admittedly dopey from shock and antipain pills not to mention a generous measure of sheer blue funk, will for the first and most decidedly the last time reason on the purely thalamic level. He would not shoot the Orligian. Fear of the Hereafter was only part of the reason, there was the fact that this particular Orlig, or one of his crew-mates, had made a very fine crash landing.

MacEwan said, "Oh, go ahead and live, damn you!" and tossed the gun away from him.

Immediately the Orlig leapt crouching to its feet.

MacEwan only faintly heard the gun sliding down the inclined deck, falling between the ruptured seams of floor plating and clattering down through the wreckage below. He was watching the Orlig and realising that it had been playing possum, pretending unconsciousness and covertly keeping him under observation while he had the gun in his hand. A smart little teddybear, this Orlig, and now that he was unarmed ...

He could not help remembering that the muscles under those soft-looking, furry arms were capable of tearing a man's head off, as the massacre on the *Starfinder* had shown.

TABLEAU 97

"MacEwan," he told himself sickly, "you have done a very stupid thing."

At the sound the Orlig started back, then it began edging nearer again. One of its arms hung limp, MacEwan saw, and very obviously it was having to force itself to approach him. Finally it got to within three feet and stood looking down. It growled and whined in an odd fashion at him and gestured with its good arm; the noises did not sound threatening. Then the arm reached out, hesitated, and a stubby, four-fingered hand touched MacEwan briefly on the head and was withdrawn quickly. The Orlig growled again and retreated. It disappeared behind a nearby tangle of wreckage and he heard it clambering awkwardly through to the remains of its own ship.

MacEwan let his head sink to the deck, no longer willing to exert the tremendous effort needed to hold it upright. The antipain was not working too well and his brain seemed to function in fits and starts, racing one minute and completely blank the next. All at once he was utterly, deathly tired, and it must have been at that point that he blacked out again. When he came to, MacEwan's first impression was of vibration striking up through his jaw from the deck plating. His second was that he had gone mad.

His eyes were closed yet he could see himself—all of himself, including the head lying on the deck with its eyes closed. And there was a constant gabbling in his mind which could only be delirium. MacEwan wanted to black out again but the delirium kept him awake. It was too loud, as if somebody were shouting in his head. But the words, though nonsense, were heard clearly:

. . . *It is wrong to do this. My Family would be ashamed. But my Family is dead, all dead. Killed by the Family of this loathsome thing which is dying. It is wrong, yet here is a chance to obtain valuable data about them, and with my Family dead the displeasure of other Families cannot hurt me. Perhaps my efforts are useless and the creature is already dead, its wounds are frightful* . . .

MacEwan shook his head weakly and opened his eyes. He blinked so as to focus on the odd mechanism which had appeared on the deck about a foot from his head. It was squat, heavy-looking and was dull grey except where clusters of fine, coppery rods stuck out at intervals. A thick power cable sprouted from its base and disappeared somewhere, and just behind the machine the Orlig sat on its haunches. The expression in its eyes, which were the only feature in that ruined face capable of registering any emotion, could only be described as intent.

In his present state it was hard for MacEwan to feel undue excitement or amazement. But he was not so far gone that he could not reason logically, so that he knew quite clearly what it was that he was experiencing.

The Orligs had telepathy.

In the instant of his reaching that conclusion the babble in his head ceased, but there was not silence. Instead there was a bubbling stew of half-thoughts, memory fragments and general confusion, the whole being overlaid by an extreme feeling of antagonism and instinctive loathing which the Orlig was trying unsuccessfully to control. But it *was* trying, MacEwan knew, and that was a good point in its favour. And the main reason for its confusion, he saw, was the fact that having opened communications with a species which was its deadly enemy, the Orlig was at a loss for words.

MacEwan thought that the right thing to do would be to mentally spit in its eye. But he had stopped doing the right things recently—he had gone all emotional. Instead he thought, *That was a very nice landing you pulled off. A very fine landing.*

With the rapport existing between them MacEwan now *knew* that this was the Orlig pilot.

Surprise and increased confusion greeted this, then; *Thank you,* the creature's mind replied. *At the time I did not know I had a passenger to observe it.*

Maybe it was due to an accident of phrasing, but MacEwan thought that there was an undercurrent of surprisingly Human humour in the thought. But it was lost abruptly in an upsurge of the ever-present antagonism and revulsion, and the flood of sight, sound and pain impressions that, although shockingly clear in themselves, were roaring through the Orligian's brain at a speed too fast for words. The screaming hail of metal from the

TABLEAU 99

attacking Earth ship, searching out its Family one by one, ripping them into bloody ruin and continuing to churn horribly at what was left. As the most junior member of the Family with the fastest reflexes it had been in the pilot's position, and relatively safe. But it had felt and seen its brothers being cut to pieces, and when its father had left the control room to take over a firing position, the mentacom had sent him the feelings of its parent gasping frenziedly for air in a compartment which had suddenly been blasted open to space by MacEwan's guns . . .

You started this war, not us! MacEwan broke in, suddenly angry because he shared identical feelings about Reviora and other acquaintances that he had been careful to avoid thinking of as friends. He was remembering the *Starfinder*.

The reply he got staggered him. It was his own race, not the Orligs, who were responsible for the war, and looking at it from the other's point of view he could see that it was so.

What a perfectly ghastly mess! MacEwan thought. And Nyberg, poor, brave, ignorant Captain Nyberg. If only he had realised that a feeling of instinctive friendship towards these newly-discovered aliens—because they were so soft and furry and so reminiscent of a child's first non-adult friend, a teddybear—did not necessarily have to be reciprocated. On the Orlig's home planet there was a species which resembled the Earthmen as closely as Orligs did teddybears. Its habits were dirty, it was vicious, cowardly and possessed just enough intelligence to be depraved. To the Orlig mentality that species was like fat, wet things under rocks, and things that itched and stank. One of their tricks was to play and cavort within sight of groups of Orlig cubs until one or more, intrigued and as yet not intelligent enough to know better, would wander off after them. The species was, of course, carnivorous . . .

And Captain Nyberg, impatient to broaden Earth's mental horizon by contact with an extra-terrestrial civilisation and puzzled by the alien's tendency to shy away, had crossed to the Orlig ship. He had been admitted by beings whose conditioning from earliest childhood towards things like him was diametrically opposed to his feelings for them. But that alone might not have led to war. If only Nyberg had not tried too hard to win friends and influence Orligs by the tactic so beloved of Earth politicians.

If only he had not tried to kiss babies.

The Orligs were a very emotional race and things had happened very quickly after that incident. There were not enough beings on the ship possessing the objectivity to realise that Nyberg's action might only have *appeared* threatening . . .

But why, MacEwan wondered, had not one of the mentacom gadgets been handy. Instead of halting words and actions, both of which were wide open to misunderstanding, there would have been full comprehension of the potentially explosive differences in the backgrounds of both races. The *Starfinder* incident would never have happened, there would not have been a war and he, MacEwan, would not be dying. Even at this late date he wondered what the Earth authorities might do if the true situation was explained to them. They, too, like Captain Nyberg, had been at one time anxious for contact with an intelligent extra-terrestrial species.

But the flood of the Orlig's thinking was pouring over him again. The main torrent roared through his brain, but not so loudly that the small, revealing side streams went unnoticed. Things like the fact that large-scale war had been unknown on Orligia—though small ones, something like feuds, tended to be rugged—because the Family system made them impossible. There were no nations on the planet, just Families, which were small, close-knit groups of up to fifteen who submitted willingly to the near-Godlike authority of the male parent until they showed sufficient aptitude to form a family group of their own.

It was an intensely conservative type of culture with very complicated and inflexible codes of manners, and Nyberg's misadventure proved the severity of punishments for offences against this code. And the mentacom, it seemed, had been recently developed from existing instruments in use by Orligian psychologists. Apparently the noise of a space battle played hob with the delicately

TABLEAU   101

modulated whines and growls which were the Orlig spoken language so that they had been forced to develop a method of mechanical telepathy to solve the communications problem.

Just like that, MacEwan thought dryly, then he concentrated on the main stream of thought being radiated at him. It was so much easier to do that.

He was cold all over now, his mouth and tongue burned with a raging thirst and he could not believe that a human body could feel so utterly and completely weary and still remain awake. Had the conversation been in spoken words MacEwan knew that he could never have carried it on, he was too far gone. His brain felt funny, too, as if a cold, dark something was pushing at it around the edges. Fatigue, loss of blood and oxygen starvation were probably responsible for that effect, he thought, and wondered ironically what particular code he would break if he died on the Orlig in the middle of a conversation.

A sudden new urgency had come into the Orlig's thoughts. They were on the *Starfinder* incident again, and apparently there were those in that Orlig ship's crew who had felt themselves unduly constrained by their home planet's codes of behaviour and of thinking. In their opinion the planet was too hide-bound and conservative and contact with an alien culture was just what it needed if stasis and decadence were to be warded off. The Families in the Earth ship were, it was true, outwardly loathsome to an infinite degree, but perhaps the visual aspect, thought some, was not of primary importance . . .

MacEwan felt a sudden wild hope growing in him as he guessed the trend of the others' thinking. But an equally great despair followed it. What could *he* do, he was as good as dead?

Do I understand, he thought as distinctly as he could, *that you would like peace?*

The Orlig's thoughts fairly boiled out at him. Their centuries-old civilisation was being disrupted. Though warships were generally crewed by one or more complete Families, for technical reasons some Families had to be split up. The pain and tragedy of this process could only be appreciated by an Orligian. And hundreds of other

Families, the very best Families who specialised in the
various technologies, were being lost every year in the
war. Most decidedly the Orlig, and quite a few of his
acquaintances, would like peace!

We, also, thought MacEwan fervently, *would like
peace*. Then suddenly he cursed. A door had been
opened, just the barest crack, and it was heavy with the
inertia of past guilt and blood and misunderstanding. How
could a dying man push it wide and cross the threshold?

MacEwan felt that his mind as well as his body was
packing up on him. It would be so nice and easy just to
let everything stop. But he was Iron Man MacEwan, he
reminded himself goadingly; MacEwan the Indestructible,
the big bodied and even bigger headed Superman, the
perfect killing machine. Now he had something which was
really worthwhile to strive for, and all he wanted to do
was give up because he felt tired. *Think, damn you!* he
raged at himself. *Think, you stinking lousy quitter . . !*

And he did think. Weakly, urgently he pleaded with
the Orlig to relay his suggestions to the other's superiors.
He thought in terms of an Armistice preparatory to peace
talks, and explained how this might be brought about by
using the Earth device of a flag of truce. A raid on an
Earth base in which message containers only were
dropped, followed by a single ship with a white flag
painted prominently on the hull. The Earth forces would
be suspicious, but MacEwan did not think they would
blow the ship out of the sky . . .

At that point MacEwan blanked out. It was as if the
peaks and hollows of his brain waves had suddenly evened
themselves out, leaving him with the knowledge of being
alive but with no other sensations at all. He didn't know
how long it lasted but when he came round again the
Orlig pilot was pleading with him desperately not to die,
that medical help was on the way—together with a flotilla
which was escorting the rescue ship—and that he must live
until the other's superiors talked with him.

MacEwan was icy cold and sick and his thirst was a
dry acid in his throat. The antipain was not working so
well anymore, but he knew that he would never be able to

TABLEAU 103

keep a clear head—or even stay conscious—if he took another dose. He thought longingly of water; he knew the Orligs used it.

But the Orlig sent him a firm, sorrowful negative. He did not know much of Earthmen's physiology, but he was very sure that food or drink would do further harm considering the seriousness and position of MacEwan's injuries. There was a queer, guilty undertone to the thought. MacEwan fastened on it, prised it open, and felt a sensation of hurt which had nothing to do with his wounds. As well as the reasons stated the Orlig had been trying to hide the fact that he did not want to have to touch the Earthman again at any price.

Tell me of yourself, the Orlig went on hastily, *of your world, your background, your friends and Family. I must know as much as possible in case* ... It tried to stop the thought there, but only succeeded in accentuating it: there can be no tact in a meeting of minds ... *In case you die before my superiors arrive.*

MacEwan fought pain and thirst and soft encroaching darkness as he tried to tell the Orlig about Earth, his friends and himself. He was pleading a case, and a successful decision meant the end of the war. But he could not be eloquent, nor could he cover up the unpleasant aspects of certain things, because it was impossible to lie with the mind. Several times he slid into a kind of delirium wherein he fought out the last engagement which had killed Hoky and Reviora, right down to the crash, the explosion and the meeting with the Orlig pilot. He could do nothing to stop it, this recurrent nightmare which just might end on a note of hope.

The Orligian was horrified at MacEwan's personal score of kills, but at the same time he seemed to feel just a little sympathy for the loss of Hokasuri and Reviora. And there was a peculiar thought, which MacEwan did not catch properly because he was slipping into a delirious spell at the time, about the Weapon that was somehow tied in with the strange belief on the Orlig's part that no civilised being could attack knowing he had a fifty-fifty chance of being killed; such bravery was incredible.

But what impressed the other most was the knowledge that the long-dead Captain Nyberg's actions had been motivated by *friendship* towards the Orligians. And that there were creatures on Earth closely resembling the Orligians which the Humans liked and treated as pets, whereas positions were completely reversed on Orligia. It meant that the unfortunate Captain had been slain unjustly, and if it could convince its superiors of that, the groundwork for understanding and eventual peace might be laid.

A severe mental struggle became apparent in the Orlig pilot's mind at that point, so intense that the other seemed deaf to MacEwan's thinking even though he was in one of his rare lucid periods. The being rose to his feet and padded up and down the clear deck area of the wrecked control room. Its mental distress was extreme. Finally it stopped, crouching above MacEwan, and began to bend forward. It was fighting hard, every inch of the way.

A stubby, hairy hand found MacEwan's, held it and actually squeezed it for all of two seconds before being hastily pulled away.

My name is Grulyaw-Ki, it said.

MacEwan could not think of a reply for several seconds because there was a funny tightness in his throat—which when he came to think of it was silly.

MacEwan.

Things were hazy after that. They talked a good deal through the mentacom, mostly about the war and regarding tactics and installations in a way which would have had the security officers of both sides tearing their hair. It came as a shock to see that the control room suddenly contained three more Orligs, who eyed him keenly and touched him in several places without any particularly strong signs of repugnance. Obviously Medics are used to horrible sights since the war. They withdrew and immediately afterwards he noticed a large section of the control room wall being cut away, revealing a blue sky, the slender pillar of the rescue ship and a barren stretch of desert. An intricate piece of electronic gadgetry was being assembled in the gap, with power lines running from it to the wrecked Orlig ship. MacEwan could not ask

TABLEAU   105

about it because the power cable to the mentacom had been taken out and plugged into this new mechanism.

The Orlig medics had cleaned Grulyaw-Ki up but had not been able to do much for his face, and the being had steadfastly refused to leave MacEwan and go to the rescue ship for proper treatment. It seemed that the Orlig felt deeply obligated to MacEwan because of the Captain's earlier decision not to kill it when he had had the gun and the Orlig was lying helpless on the deck. The Orlig had got the memory of that little item from MacEwan when he had been delirius, apparently. He wanted to stay with the Earthman until ...

The mentacom had been disconnected at that point.

Officers of ever increasing seniority arrived and talked with Grulyaw-Ki. Some hurried away again and the others stayed and looked down at MacEwan from positions behind the electronic gadget—still apparently arguing with the Orlig pilot, who seemed to be refusing to move more than a few feet from MacEwan's side.

There was something going on here, MacEwan knew suddenly, something which was not consistent with the things he had expected from reading the Orlig's mind. For instance why, after pleading with him to stay alive until the arrival of Orligian higher-ups had the pilot allowed the mentacom to be disconnected immediately after the arrival of the medical officers? Why weren't they asking him questions over the mentacom instead of whining and growling urgently at the Orlig pilot from behind the now apparently complete mechanism a dozen feet away? What *was* the blasted thing anyway ... ?

Tenuous as mist, with neither strength, directional properties or even clarity, an Orlig thought sequence seeped through his mind. The mentacom beside him was disconnected, but somewhere—at extreme range and probably on the rescue ship—there was another which was operating, and there was an Orligian near it who was thinking about him. There was an undercurrent of excitement in the thought, and hope, and the overall and everpresent problems of strategy and supply—the thought of a very important and responsible Orlig, obviously. MacEwan was a very brave entity, the thought went on, but even so it was

better that the Earth-being should not be told what was
to happen to him ...

Rage exploded so violently in MacEwan that he forgot
his wounds, and his anger was matched only by his utter
self-loathing. He had been a blind, stupid fool! He had
talked too much, betrayed his friends, his race and his
world. He had told *everything* to the Orlig pilot, and with
knowledge of the spatial co-ordinates of Earth a planet-
wrecker or a few bacteriological bombs would soon end
the war. Of course the Orlig had given him equally vital
information, but with the difference that MacEwan was
hardly in a position to pass it on. Now apparently, they
were too impatient even to wait for MacEwan to die,
because the mechanism which had been set up and which
was now focussed on his huddled, near-corpse was nothing less than The Weapon.

The sheer force of his emotions sent him crawling
towards Grulyaw-Ki. Mounting waves of pain pounded
and roared over the small, feeble core of purpose in his
brain, and he dared not look down at his injuries. But the
Orlig pilot was looking, and his companions behind The
Weapon, and a ragged, tortured whine of sympathy and
horror was dragged from their throats at the sight. They
had feelings; he had met one of them mind to mind and
he knew. It didn't fit, what they were going to do to
him—Grulyaw-Ki's mind had not even considered his being
killed out of hand. Maybe that was why the pilot was
electing to go with him, because he disapproved of the
treachery of his brothers.

Out of the corner of his eye he saw certain coils within
the complex mass of The Weapon glow brightly, and he
hunched himself desperately forward. *We're not all bad,*
his mind screamed, in a vain attempt to reach them
without benefit of a mentacom. *Maybe you've tricked me,
but there can be peace ... peace ...* He tried to reach
out and grasp the Orlig pilot's hand, to show them that he
meant what he was thinking, but his stupid, senseless
lump of an arm refused to move any more for him, and off
to one side The Weapon was about ready to project its
radiation, or force pattern, or field of stress ...

... After two hundred and thirty-six years the Orligians

TABLEAU   107

were getting another War Memorial, were being forced to get another War Memorial. And the Orligians were a very emotional race.

It was after dawn when the noisy festivities died down and the crowd—silent now and strangely solemn—began to gather round the protective plastic of the old Memorial, the most gruesomely effective War Memorial ever known. They had remained far away from it during the night's celebrations, it would not have been proper to indulge in merrymaking in this place, but now they were gathering from all over the city. They came and stood silent and grave and still, moving only to let through the ground vehicles of off-planet dignitaries or the numerous other technicians and specialists who had business at the Memorial. Some of them cried a little.

At midday the Elected Father of Orligia rose to address them. He spoke of both the joy and solemnity of this occasion, and pointed with pride at the ages-frozen figure of the mighty Grulyaw-Ki, the Orligian who, despite the urgings of his friends and the orders of his superiors, had determined to discharge his obligation towards this great Earth-being MacEwan.

The time stasis field projector, once an Orligian weapon of war but now in use in hospitals on every planet of the Union, had made this possible. With great difficulty the Stopped bodies of MacEwan and Grulyaw-Ki had been sealed up and moved to Orligia, there to wait while the first shaky peace between Earth and Orligia ripened into friendship and medical science progressed to the point where it was sure of saving the terribly injured Earthman. Grulyaw-Ki had insisted on being Stopped with his friend so that he could see MacEwan cured for himself. And now the two greatest heroes of the war—heroes because they had ended it—were about to be brought out of Stasis. To them no time at all would have passed between that instant more than two hundred years ago and now, and perhaps now for the first time the truly great of history would receive the reward they deserved from posterity. The technicians were ready, the medical men were standing by, the moment was *now* . . . !

The crowd in the immediate vicinity saw the figures come alive again, saw MacEwan twitching feebly and Grulyaw-Ki bending over him, saw the bustle as they were transferred into the waiting ambulance and—temporarily Stopped again until the hospital would be reached by a small and more refined projector—hurried away. The throng went wild then, so that the noise of the previous night would have been restful by comparison. Some of them stayed out of deference to the sculptor for the unveiling of the new memorial, a towering, beautiful thing of white stone that caught at the throat, but only a few thousand. And of these there were quite a few who, when the ceremony was over, went to look through the little peep holes set at intervals around its base.

Through them could be seen a tiny, three-dimensional picture in full detail and colour of the original war memorial, placed there to remind viewers that there was nothing great or noble or beautiful about war.

The Conspirators

SOMETHING HAD gone wrong. It was outside his range, but Felix caught a sharp, incoherent sensation of mingled shock, loss, and panic in the instant that it happened. He floated, outwardly unconcerned, in the middle of the corridor which led to the Biology Section, and waited for the details to come down the line.

A few minutes later the relay who was clinging to the wall-net at the end of the corridor began sending him the facts. The news was very bad.

It seemed that the Small One whose job it was to damage certain tiny but important circuits in the Communications Room for purposes connected with the Escape had had an accident. Singer had seen it happen—Felix had guessed it was Singer. Even on the fourth leg of a relay the thought pattern was unmistakable; all emotion and not enough fact—the Small One had jumped for cover when he heard the crew-man coming, misjudged, and landed on a live section. It was only a couple of hundred volts, but that was an awful lot to a Small One—he was very thoroughly dead. What was left of him was floating in plain sight, and Singer was rapidly killing himself with his frenzied attempts at holding the crew-man's attention, because if the man noticed the body, and the disconnected wiring beside it, he might be suspicious. Singer wanted somebody to do something, *quick*. The message ended with a sense-free garble of fear, urgency, and panic that was almost hysteria.

To another Small One concealed in a ventilator at the other end of the corridor, Felix relayed the message exactly as he'd received it. But he had an addition to make. He sent, "Include this. Felix to Whitey. I think I can handle this. Send someone to replace me—I'm on relay duty half way along corridor Five-C—I'm going to Communications." He wriggled furiously until he made contact with the wall-net, then launched himself down the corridor towards the intersection leading to the scene of the accident.

Usually Felix left important decisions to the Small Ones. They had the brains. He didn't know why he'd taken the initiative this time. Whitey, he thought, might not be pleased.

He was able to enter the Communications Room and get to the Small One's body without the crew-man seeing him. Singer, though impractical in many ways, could create quite a diversion when he wanted to. Singer was fluttering around the man's head in tight circles, and the man was making ineffectual grabs at him and wondering loudly what had got into the blasted thing. He had eyes and thoughts, Felix knew, only for Singer. Good.

The fur on the body was badly scorched, and Felix's nose told him that parts of the underlying flesh were cooked, too. Suddenly a raw, animal hunger stirred inside him and began to grow, but he fought it down. Since the Change had begun, satisfaction of that nature was not for him. Felix batted the tiny corpse towards the opposite corner of the room, well away from those all-important circuits, then launched himself after it.

When he'd retrieved it and had it settled between his paws, he told Singer, "All right, Bird-brain. You can relax. Better leave now—you're supposed to be afraid of me."

A bright yellow streak of motion, Singer flew out the door and down the corridor. Before he was out of range he returned, "I *am* afraid of you . . . You . . . *savage!*"

Seconds later the crew-man caught sight of Felix.

Pleased, he said, "Felix! Where've you been hiding yourself?" He grabbed Felix by the neck with one hand and pulled himself into a seat with the other. Clipping in and settling Felix on his lap, he went on, "So you caught a mouse, eh, Felix? But what have you been doing with it? Having a barbecue or something?" He stopped talking then, but his mind was busy. He began to stroke the back of Felix's neck.

Felix didn't feel at all like purring, but he knew that it was expected of him. After a while he began to enjoy it in spite of himself, but that didn't stop him from reading the crew-man's thoughts.

A sharp, clear thought—characteristic of the Small Ones—brought him abruptly to full attention. Felix couldn't see the other, but he knew that the Small One was within thirty feet of him—that was the maximum effective range of their telepathy—probably in the emergency spacesuit hanging outside the door that Felix had noticed coming in. The thought said, "Felix, your replacement is in position. Whitey wants you to report."

"Right. Relay this. Felix to Whitey . . ."

For a moment Felix felt awed as he thought of Whitey in Bio-Lab Three—more than half the length of the great Ship away—surrounded by Big Ones, and the Small Ones who weren't on relay duties, and all of them working on the Escape. And of the other telepathic relays that linked Lab Three with places like Seed Storage, Central Control, and Engines . . . Catching an impatient thought from the Small One out in the corridor, Felix hastily brought his mind back to the report.

". . . This Human is not suspicious," he sent. "The Small One was so badly scorched that the Lab markings have been obliterated, and he thinks it is a Wild One from Seed Storage section. He thinks that I have knocked it against some live wires while playing with it, and that I'm very lucky I didn't meet the same fate myself—there's that old 'nine lives' concept again—but he is wondering why I didn't eat the thing . . ."

Felix knew that a feeling of shocked revulsion was left in the wake of his message as it went down the line. Felix did not share the deep sorrow that the accident had caused among the more intelligent and highly-sensitive Small Ones. He took a perverse pleasure in shocking them sometimes. Without meaning to they made him feel inferior, envious. Felix wasn't proud of these feelings, but there wasn't much he could do about them. The Change was very slow in him.

". . . He is not interested in checking any of the room's equipment," Felix continued, "but is impatient to rejoin the bulk of the crew who are packed into Astronomy section all trying to get a closer view of the new planet. He is feeling rebellious at having to stand watch here at a time like this, and is wondering sarcastically if the Captain is expecting the natives—if any—of the planet below to just ring him up.

"At the back of his mind he is feeling angry because the scoutship is unable to make a landing. But neither he nor anyone else suspect that we were responsible for damaging its Planetary Drive coils. The fact that the replacements are also missing they blame on a clerical error in storing or checking the equipment back home. They don't know we've hidden them."

The Human stopped his stroking of Felix and pushed him gently off his lap. Felix ended, "He intends trying to sleep now. Nobody will be coming here, he knows, and he's a light sleeper anyway." He waited a little anxiously for Whitey's reply.

"You've done well, Felix."

Even though coloured by the personalities of nearly a score of the relay entities, the thought was still warm, congratulatory. Then it changed subtly. "Come to the Lab at once, Felix. There is a transport problem."

"Right." Felix answered. "But before I go; the Human is asleep now. If you send somebody to arrange those disconnected wires so's they'll pass visual inspection, nothing can go wrong here."

He intercepted the reply when he was already half way to the Lab. He'd been hurrying. It was:

"Thanks, Felix. It is already being done."

When he reached the Lab two of the Big Ones had the

ventilator grill moved aside for him. The door was never used for the reason that the Humans kept it fastened, so that opening it would have aroused their suspicions. Felix wriggled through. As he kicked himself across the small anteroom leading into the lab proper he heard the Big Ones sliding the grill back into position. *Nothing*— especially now that they were so near to success—must be allowed to make the crew-men suspect anything wrong. Even the Big Ones, who weren't too bright, understood that.

Felix hadn't been 'reaching' with his mind—too much telepathy was still inclined to tire him—so he had no warning of what to expect. Weightless, unable to stop himself, he sailed gracefully into the Lab—right smack into the middle of it.

He was hit five times and sent spinning, his nicely timed dive ruined, by flying Big Ones. And he lost track of how often young Small Ones rammed him. Everybody in the place—*and* their young, too, if any—were in rapid motion, sailing from wall to wall, floor to ceiling, and even corner to corner. It looked like a furry snowstorm. When he succeeded at last in reaching a wall-net, he directed a thought at the white mouse clinging to the fur of a Big One on the other side of the room. The thought was wordless, incoherent, an all-embracing question mark.

"They're practising for the evacuation, Felix." Whitey explained. "And that is the problem I mentioned. Some of them—the young, especially—won't be able to make it." Whitey stopped to give instructions to a Big One who was floundering helplessly out in the middle of the lab. He resumed, "Come over here, Felix. We can 'talk' better at short range."

Felix was again hit several times on the way across by flying Big Ones. But being in collision with a guinea-pig wasn't painful, merely disconcerting, and he hadn't enough dignity left for that to be hurt. He had just settled beside the Big One bearing Whitey when Singer flew in and joined them. The canary hung, wings folded and turning slowly in the draft from the air-conditioner, just six inches from Felix's nose. Felix wondered suddenly what it would be like to bite his head off.

Radiating shock and panic, Singer flapped desperately out of range. "Stop that, Felix!"

Whitey was really angry at him, with the helpless, frustrated anger that is inspired by the constant misbehaviour of a backward child. Ashamed, Felix addressed Singer.

"Sorry, I didn't mean that. I wouldn't hurt you for anything. Come on back."

Singer fluttered back nervously, thinking about horrid, insensitive brutes, and great hairy cannibals. He wasn't completely reassured.

Whitey, his anger gone as quickly as it had come, began to state the problem.

"You two know that we intend to evacuate everyone, and you also know how we're going to leave the Ship—in one of the radio-controlled testing rockets. But we've misjudged badly. The distance from the Lab here to the launching slips is a little over five hundred feet, and now we find that there won't be enough time to get everybody to the rocket.

"You see, several trips will have to be made for the young, and the Big Ones are slow and awkward. They've never had the chance to practise long-distance weightless travel like us, and they're very much worse at it than we'd expected. And they're so slow to learn, some of them . . ."

So slow to learn, Felix thought sadly. Just like me. He knew that all three of them were thinking about the Change, and how it had affected them personally, as well as the way it affected their species as a whole.

Not one of them knew for sure just why the Change had come about, but there were theories. The generally accepted one was that the prolonged absence of gravity occasioned by the operation of the Ship's overdrive, or the freedom from their home planet's gravitation, or the removal of some hypothetical radiation given off by the home sun, either singly or taken together had caused a change in the cell structure of the small, relatively simple brains of the animals aboard the Ship. Its result was a steady increase in their I.Q.

The Change, however, did not occur at a uniform rate, but varied with the size of the brain concerned. The small-brained mice were affected first. They developed a high intelligence quickly, and with it the faculty for communicating telepathically. And, as well as reading each other's thoughts, they were able to tap the mind of the crew-man who came to the Lab at weekly intervals to replenish the automatic food dispenser which kept them fed.

They learned a lot from him; his duties, his background, what he thought about the other members of the crew, and, most important, the purpose of the Expedition. Also, because he vocalised his thoughts, they learned the language. This increased their understanding of their environment, but it also caused them to make an important assumption based, though they didn't know it, on too little data.

Because the Ship had only been gone from Earth barely four months, and the awful boredom had not yet set in, this particular Human was full to bursting with the glorious thoughts of this first exploration among the stars, the possible colonisation of newly discovered planets, and a warm, brotherly feeling towards everybody in general. And he was naturally kind to animals. He was also the only Human whose mind was available to the animals for reading—no other crew-man came within the thirty-foot radius of the the Small Ones' telepathy. Their assumption, therefore, was justified.

For six weeks the community of Small Ones existed in the Lab, with servo-mechanisms attending to their every need, happy, contented, and very excited.

They thought they were the Ship's colonists.

Then one day Singer had been put in the Lab. Singer was a completely new species to the Small Ones. He was bright yellow in colour, had 'wings' which made it easy for him to move about in the weightless condition of the Ship, and he produced audible vibrations which were very pleasant to hear. Though he wasn't as bright as the Small Ones, the Change had made him telepathic. He had a lot more information to impart about the Ship and its crew, information that left the Small Ones shocked and horrified. He was able to tell them of their true status aboard the Ship, and of the fate that experimental animals could expect when the time came to test the atmosphere, plant-life, and bacteria of a new planet. Singer also told of a ferocious black monster the Humans called 'Felix' that roamed the Ship, and how the Humans had put him in here to keep the beast from killing him.

Living was suddenly a grim business. They would try to escape, of course, but the Small Ones knew enough about the operation of the ship now to realise how small was the opportunity of doing that. And they couldn't leave the Lab even, because of this thing called Felix. If that had been possible they might have been able to create an opportunity for escape, by sabotage or some other means. But the only thing they could do was wait, and hope that the Big Ones, who also lived in the Lab, would be able to take care of 'Felix' when they became further advanced.

But the Big Ones had been slow, Felix knew, and their bigness was only relative. Luckily they never had to try taking care of him; a scrap between a guinea-pig—or even several guinea-pigs—and a full-grown cat would have been no contest at all.

Felix had been nosing about outside the Lab one day, hoping to catch himself some food 'on the hoof,' when he suddenly realised that the animals inside were 'talking' to him. The reason for the strange ability he'd noticed in himself in being able to understand the Humans—even when they didn't speak aloud—was explained to him, and very soon he had more important things on his mind than a craving to eat Small Ones. All at once he had become an important person, an *invaluable* person. The way the Small Ones explained it, his wider knowledge of the Ship and its crew, together with his aid in guiding them to certain key spots, would make an escape not only possible, but highly probable ...

"Pay attention, Felix!" Whitey radiated sharply. Felix came hastily out of his day-dream, conscious that if he'd been a Human, his face would have been very red.

"I was saying that the Big Ones are slow," Whitey went on, "and awkward. That's partly because we haven't allowed them outside the Lab much; they'd be spotted too easily. But that's the problem now, moving them quickly.

"At the moment I can see no solution. But you two being 'pets,' and having the freedom of the Ship, might be able to suggest something." Whitey paused, and the ghastly wordless images they all knew so well surged up from the back of his mind. Experimentation, vivi-section, *murder*. Grimly, he went on, "I don't want to leave anybody behind, to *that*——"

He broke off as two reports came, almost simultaneously, from opposite ends of the great Ship.

"Relay from Secondary Engines. Quarter G deceleration has been ordered for three minutes."

"Relay from Control-room. Captain has ordered quarter G deceleration . . ." It was practically a duet.

The telepathic link-ups that ran from all the key points on the Ship to the Lab were fast, efficient, and accurate. But they were just a little slower than the Ship's inter-com system. Some of the animals were able to act on the information before the deceleration hit them, and hang on. The rest dropped, an uneven, struggling layer of grey and brown on to the forward wall.

Felix landed the way he always did, crouching, and on his feet. Unfortunately he also landed on a group of eight very young Small Ones. The resultant blast of fear and raw, uninhibited anger from their under-developed minds nearly curdled his brains before he was able to reel off. Then he had to counter the bolts of the outraged parent concerned, even though the adult Small One was intelligent enough to realise that none of it was Felix's fault. There were some things that didn't depend on intelligence, Felix realised, and mother love was one of them.

Abruptly Felix felt awed at himself. He was the muscle man around here—he'd never had thoughts like *that* before. But the feeling left him just as quickly.

While the deceleration lasted Felix listened to the ranting of the Small One, and tried to keep the amusement he felt from showing too much in his mind. He hadn't hurt the youngsters, of course, just frightened them. They were extraordinarily strong for their size, and they were so light that they could take a knocking about that would probably kill Felix. He began to wonder about their toughness, and about the evacuation problem. Suppose ...

The Small One caught his half-formed thought and radiated a horrified negative. Felix tried to reassure her, but just then weightlessness returned and he launched himself towards Whitey again.

While Felix was still airborne Whitey sent, "I heard some of that, too, Felix. Would you expand on that thought about ferrying the young to the rocket?"

Felix took the mental equivalent of a deep breath. He was acutely conscious of the fact that his thinking, when compared with that of the Small Ones, was slow and almost incoherent at times. But he did his best.

"It is this. I suggest we ferry the young to the launching slips *before* the adults go, instead of at the same time. That way the Big Ones would have only one trip to make, and no matter how inexperienced they were, there would be plenty of time for the journey. With Singer here to help me as look-out, I can transfer them six or eight at a time to the test rocket. And even if a crew-man should see me—"

Whitey interrupted: "*How* are you going to move them, Felix?" Every mind in the room was giving him full attention now.

"By pretending to play with them," Felix answered. Hesitantly, he began to explain. "In the old days, before I knew all about the Change, the crew used to give me things to play with. It was great fun ..." He stopped suddenly, feeling ashamed and embarrassed at the confession he'd just made. Hastily, he went on, "That was before I met you, of course.

"But what I want to say is that I know where some of those playthings are. They are soft, spherical, and their fabric is easily opened. The young ones can hide inside them while I push the things along.

"The Humans won't be suspicious of a cat playing with an old rag ball."

Almost before he had completed his thought the objections were coming thick and fast. Felix found it a little frightening; he had never had so many minds thinking at

him all at once before like this. But somehow, after the
first few minutes, it didn't scare him any more. It was a
strange feeling. He still felt awed by their vastly greater
intelligence, but not as much as before. Now he respected
them—and almost *liked* them—as equals. Possibly it was
the nature of the thoughts they were thinking that
brought about the change in him. Felix could understand
their feelings, but those thoughts hurt.

Impatiently, he interrupted the constant stream of protest. They were beginning to repeat themselves.

"Whitey! Tell them I'm not going to *eat* the things . . ."

They didn't believe him.

Oh, the Small Ones knew that he meant what he said,
Felix realised, but they didn't trust his—impulses. The less
intelligent Big Ones still thought of him as a semi-
domesticated carnivore, and wouldn't trust him with their
young farther than they could see him. But, he knew if he
could convince the Small Ones that his plan would work,
they could win over the Big Ones.

Whitey hadn't taken sides in the argument yet, so that
left it up to himself. He signalled sharply for attention and
felt pleasantly surprised when he got it at once. He began
his sales-talk.

"This is the position as I see it at the moment," he sent,
"The Ship is in the process of taking up an eight-hour
orbit around the first apparently habitable planet to be
discovered. The planet, not yet named, is referred to by
the crew as Epsilon Aurigae VII, and they are very
excited about finding it during the first seven months of
their three-year exploratory voyage.

"From our telepathic relay lines to the Ship's control
centres we know that this orbiting manoeuvre will be
complete in just under three hours, after which most of
the crew will be engaged in mapping the planetary surface, studying its weather, or just looking at it through
telescopes. Roughly an hour after the Ship takes up its
orbit, two of the big testing rockets will be sent down
under remote control to the surface, for the purpose of
collecting samples of air, soil and liquid from as many
widely separate points on the planet as possible. These

rockets will be guided automatically, and if everything goes off according to plan, we will be on one of them."

Felix paused. He was thinking about the Small One who had died so recently in the Communications room.

"We have been able," he went on, "to fix the alarm circuits here on the Ship so that the rocket containing us will apparently behave normally, though actually it will be disabled by us at the first suitable landing point so that we can disembark. But we have only an hour—*less* than an hour, to allow for slip-ups—when the crew will be too busy to notice our movements; and during this period all the animals must be got aboard the test rocket. That means that everyone here, all the Small Ones in Seed Storage, and all the relays scattered about the Ship will have to reach the launching slip and find their places aboard in that short time. And most of them will have to make several trips back and forwards for their young, or ..." Felix regarded the untrained and clumsy Big Ones, "... the people who haven't been able to practise weightless travel.

"Whitey says that this is impossible."

The Small Ones knew all this, Felix thought, and the Big Ones should know it, too. But everybody had developed the habit of explaining things several times to the Big Ones—they weren't very bright yet ... Felix got control of himself quickly. That last thought had been tactless. He hoped the Big Ones had been too busy with their own thoughts to notice his slip.

"Now my idea is that we evacuate the young of both species first, and before the orbiting manoeuvre is completed. That way even the clumsiest—" Felix would have liked to use a kinder word, but it was impossible to lie with the mind, "—Big Ones will be able to make their way to the slip in the hour remaining before the test rocket leaves. Also, with everybody making just one trip, the risk of discovery by a crew-man will be practically nil. I think I can handle it, but I'll need a lot of help."

Felix was trying to give them the idea that he'd be under their observation all the time, and that even if he had wanted to, he couldn't pull anything. It was the only way, he knew, to get them to agree to his plan.

"There will have to be Small Ones at both ends of the line to load and unload the young, and I'll need Singer to create a diversion should a crew-man wander by and want to play with me. And I'll need help with other things, too . . ."

Abruptly he wondered why he was taking all this trouble for them. A short time ago he wouldn't have bothered. What was happening to him?

He ended simply, "I don't see any other way of doing it in time."

Later, as he was propelling a lumpy, brightly-coloured ball filled with eight struggling baby guinea-pigs along the corridor towards the rocket, Felix thought how close it had been. When Whitey agreed to his plan Felix had thought everything would be settled—after all, he was their leader. But it hadn't been like that. There had almost been a civil war before they finally agreed to his plan, and they had wasted more than half an hour with their arguing. They just didn't trust Felix, it seemed.

At the intersection leading to the launching slip Felix let his load collide with the wall-net, landing partly on top of it to keep the springy mesh from bouncing it back again. His passengers immediately shrieked that they were being murdered and they wanted their mothers. Luckily, Felix thought, it was on the telepathic frequency; had it been audible, men would have come running from all over the Ship. Hastily he reassured the Small One on relay duty in the corridor who was radiating anxiety like a fluorescent light tube. At the other end of the corridor he saw Singer fluttering around in a slow loop. That was the all-clear signal. Felix settled his burden solidly between his fore-paws and chest and kicked himself off again.

He couldn't really blame them for not trusting him, he thought, as the corridor walls drifted slowly past. There was still quite a lot of the savage in him. Much of it was due to the slowness of his Change, but a lot was due also to the crew-men who had brought him aboard as the Ship's mascot. They were the non-specialists on the Ship. They did most of the donkey work, and they were, to put it mildly, decidedly uncouth. From their minds Felix had learned practically everything he knew until the time of his meeting up with the Small Ones. The result was that he was inclined to think and act like his erstwhile 'masters.' The idiom he used when trying to express his thoughts, and his general air of tough cynicism, made it difficult for the others to trust him completely. It was very hard to convince them that his ideas had changed.

Still, even though he wasn't a nice character, the Small Ones were lucky to have him. They were intelligent, Felix knew; the most intelligent and highly-civilized beings on the Ship—and that included the crew. If they'd only had hands, and a more practical approach to solving their problems, they could have taken over the running of the Ship themselves months ago, and got rid of the Humans. But they weren't tough enough, or practical. When there was any time to spare they used their high intelligence to get into philosophical discussions among themselves, and they were, Felix thought pityingly, terribly unrealistic— soft, even. Like Singer in many ways.

Why, when Whitey had begun planning the Escape he'd told Felix—seriously—that nobody was to be hurt, *not even crew members*.

Felix had thought that very funny.

Just before he made contact with the bulkhead at the end of the corridor a sudden surge of acceleration sent him skidding into the wall. Clinging to a section of wall-net he watched his load roll for several yards, then lodge itself none too gently in a corner. The mental uproar from the passengers nearly drowned out the message from a relay somewhere in the vicinity who reported, "Captain has ordered half G acceleration for three seconds."

Now, Felix thought disgustedly, they tell me.

Singer, who was fluttering his wings slowly to compensate for the half G, hovered a few yards away. Anxiously, he asked, "How many more, Felix? There isn't much time left . . ."

"About a dozen Small Ones, and five of the others." Felix replied as the engines stopped and he began pushing his load through the open air-lock of the Test Rocket blister. "Relax. Two more trips should do it."

But Singer was the worrying type. Supposing Felix was caught at the wrong end of a corridor during a burst of acceleration. A fall of a hundred or more feet, even under quarter weight, would be bad for his passengers ...

And it would be bad for him, too, Felix thought grimly. Possibly it would be fatal. He told Singer rather sharply to be quiet. Felix didn't like being reminded of all the unpleasant things that could happen to him.

Both test rockets lay in their ships. Blunt, grey torpedoes, their access panels lay open, and their stiffly-extended antennae made them resemble twenty foot beetles. Streamlining was unnecessary; the things weren't designed to break speed records, but to cruise about in the atmosphere of the planet being surveyed at a speed that wouldn't damage their sensitive testing gear, and possibly the even more delicate samples they would pick up from time to time. It was this low speed factor that had made the Escape possible. An ordinary missile, or even a message rocket, with an acceleration of fifty or sixty G's would have made a thin stew out of its passengers five seconds after blast-off. He thought the whole thing had depended on luck right from the start. The animals, apart from odd instances like the Communications Room death, seemed to get all the breaks.

Felix didn't like that. He was distrustful of too much good luck.

He gave his load a gentle nudge in the direction of the nearer rocket. It appeared deserted, innocuous, but Felix knew that inside it was a hive of activity. Most of the Small Ones from the nearby Seed Storage section—the 'wild' brethren of the Laboratory mice whose job was the provisioning of the rocket—were already in their positions. The rest were hidden at the open access panels waiting to take care of Felix's passengers.

"Here's another bunch of them," Felix thought at the apparently empty hull. He added lightly, "Fragile. Handle with care."

"Right,"came the curt response. "We see them."

These particular Small Ones had no sense of humour at all where Felix was concerned, and with good reason. Before the Change had made them too smart to be caught, and before that same Change made Felix a reluctant vegetarian where live meat was concerned, he had hunted them a lot. During the early part of the voyage the carnage in Seed Storage had been shocking. They had never forgotten it, or forgiven him. Felix thought sometimes that living on a planet with the Small Ones wouldn't be much fun with a thing like that between them—he was becoming strangely sensitive about his bloody past—but when he thought of what the human minds were like at times . . .

Angry with himself for some reason, Felix kicked off on the first leg of his return journey to the Lab. He kept telling himself that he didn't care what the Small Ones thought of him. He didn't care at all. But he was an awful liar, he knew.

Transferring the remaining young to the test rocket was a simple, if strenuous job. There was only one point on the route that was dangerous—an intersection visible to anyone who might be standing in the entrance to the Control Room. But there had been too much going on in there for anyone to be hanging about the door, so they hadn't been spotted. Luck was still with them.

Felix waited beside Whitey, with an almost imperceptible weight pressing them against the wall. All around, the animals waited, too; not communicating, but thinking their own personal thoughts. He took what he hoped was his last look around the Lab. One of his cloth balls, he saw, had been stuffed with food from the robot dispenser—even though the Seed Storage people were supposed to handle the food supply end. Somebody was taking no chances. All the cages were open, and both of the ventilator grills above the door had been moved aside. As he watched, the door swung suddenly outwards and hung open under its own weight. The Small One who had been working at the latch jumped free and fell slowly across the room. They were almost ready to go.

If a Human should look in here now, Felix thought, it would be just too bad.

Weight disappeared again as the gentle deceleration ceased. Seconds later a Small One in the tensely-waiting crowd announced, "Relay from Control-room. Captain has ordered kill engines. Orbiting manoeuvre completed."

To everyone in the room Whitey sent, "You know the drill. Nothing can go wrong if we're careful, and if we keep our heads. The relays will give warning if a crewman intends coming too close to our escape route, minutes before he arrives." Whitey was obviously thinking at the Big Ones as he went on, "There are lots of places to hide along the route if a Human should come—inside the crew's life-suits, for instance—so there is no real danger if you don't panic. Get to the rocket as quickly as possible. And remember, you're on your own.

"The way is clear now. Move off!"

He added, "You first, Felix."

Felix sprang neatly through the Lab door, caught the corridor wall net, and sprang again. An almost-solid mass of dun-coloured animals erupted behind him and began to pile up against the wall facing the door. He caught the sharp, clear thought of Whitey cutting through the growing confusion, trying to sort the mess out and get it moving again. Felix didn't envy him his job.

Felix took up his assigned position—at the intersection in sight of the Control-room—and waited. There were men in there—he could hear low voices—but the range was too great for him to catch their thoughts. They couldn't have been important anyway, or the relay in there would have passed them on. With a whole new planet to examine, the crew were far too busy to think about the laboratory animals—*yet*.

Eleven Small Ones came sailing along the corridor. They landed against the wall-net almost as one, then launched themselves on the next leg of their journey, still in that tight formation. It was beautiful, Felix thought, but then the Small Ones had had plenty of practice at weightless manoeuvring; besides, one of their greatest sources of pleasure was the execution of the most highly-complicated aerobatics to mind music. They were thinking serious, personal thoughts, but when he asked how the Big Ones were making out, one of them came out of it long enough to send him the mental equivalent of a snort of derision.

When Felix looked back along the corridor he saw what the other had meant.

A kicking, madly-struggling mass of Big Ones had just reached the end of the passage. A few Small Ones were trying to control the resultant pile-up, but without much success. It looked, Felix thought in awe, rather like a cloud of leaves being blown slowly up the corridor by a whirlwind. The Big Ones were moving fast, but they'd no sense of direction at all—they kept bouncing *between* the walls, rapidly, and with a violence that made Felix wince. For every foot they moved forward, they travelled yards sideways, and even at this distance he could hear their panicky squeaking. Some of them definitely weren't keeping their heads. Suddenly worried, Felix sent to the relay near him, "Tell them to stop that noise, or the Humans will *hear* them."

There wasn't much danger of that just yet, of course. His ears were more sensitive than any Human's, but Felix didn't want to take any chances at all.

One of the Big Ones, more by luck than by judgment, came sailing up the middle of the corridor to land on the wall opposite Felix. Pleased, he began to radiate grudging approval, then caught what the other was thinking. "Don't!" he warned desperately. "Not that way——"

But he was too late. The Big One, disoriented and frightened by his trip, had already taken off from the wall, *and he was headed down the corridor leading to the Control-room!* Felix made some hurried calculations of direction and velocity, hoped fervently they were right, and took off after him.

Even with his stronger muscles giving him greater impetus, they were half-way to the Control-room door before Felix caught up with the other—and then he thought he was going to pass him. But with a series of convulsions that nearly broke his back he got close enough to grab a furry leg in his teeth. He hung on desperately as their different masses and velocities sent them spinning rapidly about their common centre of gravity. They smacked hard against the wall, only a few yards from the Control-room. Ignoring the frenzied struggles of the Big One, who was sure his leg was bitten off, Felix transferred his hold to the fur at the back of the other's neck and leapt back the way they'd come. He anchored himself solidly at the intersection.

"*That* way, stupid," he sent angrily, and with a strong jerk of his neck muscles he flung the Big One into the corridor leading to the launching slips.

Abruptly he was sorry. There'd been no time for gentleness, of course, but he'd almost enjoyed mauling the unfortunate Big One back there. The other had been lost, confused, never been outside the Lab before. He shouldn't have ... Felix didn't quite know what he shouldn't have done.

"The thought does you credit, Felix."

Whitey had left the brown maelstrom that was boiling past the intersection, and was clinging to the net beside Felix. He had been in the thick of it, trying to keep the Big Ones moving—in the right direction, if possible—and he looked decidedly ruffled. He had been in collision with inanimate walls and over-animated animals alike more times than he could remember, and his nerves were beginning to suffer, too. Felix got all that from his mind in the brief pause before Whitey continued.

"That was fast, accurate thinking back there, Felix," he complimented. "You did very well—you can be proud of it. And when we reach the planet, you're going to do a lot better ..."

Suddenly uncomfortable and vaguely frightened at some formless meaning that was behind the other's thought, Felix interrupted hastily.

"Is that the lot?" He indicated a few stragglers floundering after the main group along the corridor leading to the rocket blister.

"Yes, that's all of the Big Ones," Whitey replied. "But the others have been told to wait for a bit. There's enough crowding and confusion as it is, and they, being Small Ones, can move quickly and hide more easily if they're spotted. They'll wait in the Lab until the Big Ones are safely aboard."

But Whitey wasn't to be put off by questions. Returning to his praising of Felix, he said, "You don't have to feel uncomfortable, Felix. Or frightened, either ... but tell me, what do you think of the Big Ones? And what, in your opinion, makes them think and behave as they do?"

Felix thought that this was a fine time to start a philosophical discussion, but Whitey tactfully ignored that thought, so he began trying to explain how he felt about the slow, unbelievably impractical, but somehow likeable Big Ones. He didn't take long over it as he'd never really thought about them very much.

"You should have thought about them, Felix. You're wrong, completely wrong, in everything you think about them—" Whitey broke off as a straggler came crashing into the wall beside him. He reassured the frightened Big One, told him to take it easy, and sent him on his way again. Then he returned to Felix.

"They're definitely *not* stupid, Felix. Just slow to develop," he explained. "The Change is very gradual in them. With us Small Ones it was different—we Changed and reached our peak very quickly—in a few months, in fact. But now we've found indications that the Big Ones have a much greater potential I.Q. than we have—they are still changing. In a few months time, Felix, they will be our intellectual equals, *then they will pass us.*" There was no sign of rancour in the thought—Whitey was too highly-intelligent and civilized for that—only a great and burning excitement. "Think what this means, Felix. The size of their brains compared with ours ..."

"*No!*" Felix was frightened, scared. He didn't want to think about it.

"But *yes*, Felix," The other contradicted. He stated solemnly, "You can't avoid the obvious. I am now certain that, barring accidents, you will eventually outstrip all of us. You will be the leader.

"If only," Whitey ended wistfully, "You weren't the only one of you ..."

Felix felt suddenly that his brain had turned into a bubbling porridge and was about to squeeze from his ears. Fear and disbelief gradually gave way to belief, and an even greater fear—the fear of *responsibility*. But before he could form a coherent reply, another interruption drove everything else from his mind.

"Observation Room to Whitey," the relay in the corridor reported. "A Human has just left here. Intends walking in direction of launching slips. No fixed purpose—thinks he's in way of specialist crew members." The Small One stopped, waiting instructions.

Three long, agonising seconds later, he was still waiting.

Felix had never known Whitey to behave like this before. The other's mind was a tight knot of fear and panic. It was an unforeseen and possibly tragic turn of events—just a sheer piece of filthy luck, but, Felix thought with a sudden feeling of pity, Whitey was behaving almost like one of the guinea-pigs.

Suddenly Felix remembered something; he took the initiative.

"Singer! Where's Singer?"

"Here, Felix." Singer was close by, only a few yards around the turn of the corridor.

"You heard that report." It was a statement, not a question. "You've got to intercept that Human, and stop him. Do the same as you did in Communications this morning—but get to him *quickly*. Follow the relay line to Observation, they'll give you his movements.

"And Singer, this is the most important job you ever had. Everything depends on it. You've got to stop that Human from coming here. The Big Ones aren't all aboard the rocket yet, and half the Small Ones are scattered over the Ship on relay duty." He ended grimly, "Stop him, Singer, if you've to peck his eyes out."

"*Felix!*" Singer was shocked again, but he got moving. Felix addressed Whitey:

"Better call in the relays. Singer may not be able to stop that Human, but if he delays him enough to get everyone to the launching compartment . . ."

To the relay beside him Whitey commanded, "Send this. To all Small Ones on relay duty and those waiting in the Lab. Move as quickly as possible to the launching slips—*now*. This supercedes all previous instructions." He paused, then went on to Felix alone, "You really meant that? About blinding the Human?" Horror, and a great sorrow was in the thought. "I cannot allow that, Felix, no matter what happens."

"*You* can't allow it!" Felix was exasperated. Angry yet somehow pitying, he went on, "Listen. You tell me I'm going to be boss eventually. Well, I'm taking over *now*—temporarily. You people aren't equipped to fight your way out of this, or anything else. I don't know how you'll be able to exist on the planet if one of its native life-forms decides to put up an argument—brains aren't everything, you know. You're just too civilised for your own good. You wouldn't hurt a fly, even if not hurting it was to kill you." Felix became more and more heated as he continued, "With me its different. You need someone like me to protect you. Someone who knows Humans well enough to be able to fight them. I ask you, would you let all our friends be caught and killed in lots of unpleasant ways, just to keep a Human from being messed up a little?

"Before *I'd* allow *that* to happen, I would kill that Human." He ended viciously, "There are ways an intelligent, trusted cat could do just that."

"Felix, you wouldn't ... you *can't* take a life—even a Human life—like that." Horror, revulsion, and a terrible shocked urgency were in the other's thought. "Please don't think like that, Felix. Even injuring him ..."

In ones and twos Small Ones were passing them, landing on the wall, and leaping towards the rocket compartment. They were the relays from all over the Ship, making for safety, escape. None of them paid any attention to the argument; they were too busy with their own thoughts.

"... You wouldn't be able to live with a thing like that on your mind," Whitey went on desperately. "You think you could, now. But later, when you've grown more intelligent, more sensitive ... You're still a baby, Felix, a young savage, even if——"

One of the Small Ones passing broke in urgently, "Whitey. Singer's in trouble. Couldn't get details, the relay line is breaking up too fast, but it seems the Human got scared and took a swat at him. Broke his wing. Now the Human is taking him to Sick Bay to patch him up."

The Small One hurried on.

Felix used some thought vocalisations that his old 'masters' would have envied. Then—

"To all Small Ones who can hear me," he sent as strongly as he could. "If you can get to the rocket within one minute, *move!* If you can't *take cover!*"

Sick Bay was next door to the launching slips.

The corridor was suddenly empty as the Small Ones scurried for cover or the launching compartment. Felix knew that less than fifteen minutes remained before the rocket took off. And seconds before that happened, the access panels would close, the inner air-lock would seal itself, and a section of the Ship's hull would swing outwards—all automatically, and pre-timed to a second. If anyone wasn't aboard by that time, it would be just too bad. Felix knew what his own chances of making it were now that this latest crisis had been sprung on them, but he also knew that somebody should take control of the situation at the test rocket. Somebody smart—or in the confusion only a handful would get away . . .

He had no need to finish the thought, Whitey knew what was required.

"I'll go, Felix. But try to make it yourself. We're going to need you." Whitey tried to be commanding, but there was uneasiness in his thought as he reiterated, "And remember, Felix. I won't allow anyone to be hurt."

"I'll try," Felix replied hastily, "And there'll be no rough stuff unless its necessary. Get going, Whitey. Luck."

The soft slap of sandals on the wall at the end of the corridor announced the arrival of the Human. The Man didn't notice the rapidly moving Whitey against the light grey paintwork, he came sailing nearer, still unsuspicious. As the other drew level with him, Felix leapt alongside with just enough power in his spring to keep pace with him. He was getting an idea.

The man reacted as expected.

"Uh-uh, Felix," the Human said harshly, "Don't touch," and hastily he transferred the unconscious Singer from his hand to the safety of the inside of his blouse. He was thinking that if Felix tried any tricks with the injured canary he would kick Felix the length of the Ship. The man didn't like cats.

So the crew-man thought he wanted to get at the bird. Good; that was exactly what Felix wanted him to think.

As they drifted nearer the launching compartment, an urgent thought from Whitey told him that there were still a lot of animals milling about outside the rocket. Felix had expected that. He made contact with the wall-net and, just as the Human was approaching the open lock of the launching compartment, he sprang hard at the Human's chest.

He landed with considerable force beside the bulge that was the unfortunate Singer, sunk his claws into the fabric, and began screeching and spitting for all he was worth. Startled and angry, the Human tried to knock him off, all the time thinking of sneaking, treacherous cats trying to eat poor, defenceless birds. When Felix fastened his teeth into the other's sleeve—and into a piece of his arm, too—the Human began to get rough. It was quite a melee.

It ended when a vicious, open-handed smack sent Felix against the wall with a thump that nearly shook his teeth loose. But it had served its purpose; they'd floated past the open air-lock without the Human seeing what was going on inside.

Feeling more dead than alive, Felix watched the crew-man halt himself neatly at the door of Sick Bay. Once in there, Felix knew, even though the launching slips were only yards away, the animals would be safe, because the Human intended to be busy working over Singer for some time. Maybe Felix would be able to make it to the rocket after all. The thought that Singer and some of the Small Ones still in hiding about the Ship would not make it had a dampening effect on his sudden rise in spirits. But, he told himself, he couldn't do anything about that.

The Human had the door open slightly, and was looking backwards over his shoulder to see that Felix wasn't going to sneak in, too, when he stared suddenly along the corridor. His jaw dropped open.

Felix felt the fur rise along his back. There was no need for him to follow the startled crew-man's gaze—he saw what was happening with shocking vividness in the other's mind.

About twenty Small Ones had landed at the intersection at the other end of the corridor. Felix had forgotten about them; they were the ones Whitey had told to stay in the Lab, and because the relays had been called in, they'd had no knowledge of Singer's failure to stop the Human. Watched by the startled crew-man, they took off again as they'd landed—in a tight, geometrically exact formation—in the direction of the launching room's air-lock. They must have seen the Human half-concealed in the door-way as soon as they jumped, but while rushing along the centre of the corridor in weightless flight there was nothing they could do about it.

Of all the blind, senseless, *lousy* luck. If it had happened just one second later the Human would have been safely in Sick Bay. But no. Bitter rage, born of dispair, flared suddenly in Felix as he thought how near they'd been to escape—the gentle, impractical, too-intelligent Small Ones, and their slow, apparently-stupid, but likeable big brothers. But some of them could be saved yet—the ones already aboard the rocket—if Felix could force himself to act quickly enough.

The initial surprise in the crew-man's mind had given way to an intense curiosity, and there was a slowly gathering suspicion as well. Felix knew he had to act fast. Deliberately he let his rage take root in his mind and grow. He could have controlled it at the start, but instead he fed it with memories, painful and humiliating incidents, anything at all that would fan it to greater heat. For what he knew he had to do Felix would have to be in the proper mood. He no longer trusted himself—or the soft, sentimental way he'd begun to think lately.

From inside the launching compartment Whitey's thought beat at him, desperately urging him to stop, to *think*. But it was like a cup of water on a forest fire. His rage mounted. Hazily he knew that the crowd of Small Ones had landed at the air-lock and that Whitey was giving them orders, but the thoughts didn't register. His rage grew to a blazing, white-hot fury, and his eyes never left the crew-man.

The Human hung about ten yards away, with one hand holding the door and the other inside his blouse, defenceless. Vaguely, Felix knew that all the Small Ones were thinking at him now, but it had no effect at all.

For an instant he tensed for the spring, calculating, watching the Human's face. Then, with black murder in his heart, he leapt at the other's eyes.

He never reached them.

The mass and inertia of a moving Small One is inconsiderable, but twenty of them, leaping together and hitting him as one, was more than enough to deflect his dive towards the Human. Felix crashed into the wall-net amid a cloud of Small Ones, two feet away from the crew-man. He was too shocked by the turn of events to move, but the Human wasn't. Kicking himself free of the doorway he drifted up the corridor, thinking that if he didn't get out of here quick he'd be drowned in living mice; and then thinking that mice shouldn't behave like that, and that Felix shouldn't . . .

Suddenly the Human's thoughts began to jump around. Instances, apparently unrelated, were linking up in his mind. Wires gnawed through, small components missing, tiny but important gadgets sabotaged. Could it be . . . Just then his jump carried him past the open lock of the launching compartment. He saw what was happening inside.

Felix hadn't realised how quiet it had been until the General Alarm siren blared out. Senses dulled with despair he watched the crew-man jabbering into a wall 'phone and holding the Alarm button down with a hard-pressed palm. Voices began approaching from all over the Ship; excited, slightly frightened voices. Thoughts followed them as the crew-man at the intercom broadcast his suspicions—the wary, coldly-implacable thoughts born in the brains of the most ferocious and deadly beast of all, *man*.

But, Felix knew, these beasts were logical. They would realise that they still needed experimental animals for the planets they hoped to find. They would not, he hoped fervently, slaughter all his friends right away.

But if they were too angry, they wouldn't behave logically.

Through the direct observation port Captain Ericsson watched a star that blazed like a gorgeous sapphire against a background of scattered silver dust. Home. He could almost see it coming closer. Smiling, he stroked the cat that sat on his shoulder, serenely following his gaze.

"Good thing your friends didn't make it to that first planet, Felix," he said reminiscently. "That virus . . . They wouldn't have lasted a week. But they should do all right on the world we picked for them. No animal life to speak of, but a semi-intelligent plant-life to keep them from getting too lazy. Unless . . ."

Unless the gravity of their new planet brought about a reversal in the Change that had taken place in space, he was thinking. Even he didn't know for certain whether it was the prolonged absence of weight that caused it, or some enigmatic radiation given off by their home sun, Sol. That was why Felix had elected to remain on the Ship. A cat among a colony of mice and guinea-pigs, and all of them degenerating . . . It wasn't a pretty thought.

As he addressed the others in the room, the tremendous being that Captain Ericsson had become used spoken words. They would be orbiting Earth in three days, and he wanted to become accustomed to communicating non-telepathically again. He said, "We are not going to like the Earth, even though it is our home. We've . . . outgrown it. The Change in we humans, with our larger and more complex brain structure, was very slow indeed—it took almost two years before our maximum development was attained. But even Felix here, who looks on us as near deities, is incapable of realising just how much we have matured." He paused, shaking his head gravely. "No. It is our duty to report the habitable planets we've found, the Change that takes place in space, everything. And they will want some of us for psychological testing. But we will not like Earth. On Earth they fight, and hate, and do violence. They . . . they *kill*.

"I think we will want to leave again as quickly as we can."

The Scavengers
❖❖❖❖❖❖❖❖❖❖❖❖❖❖

THE SHIP was in a hurry. It flashed through the frigid upper reaches of the atmosphere like a great silvery dart. A dart whose needle prow and stabilizers glowed with the furious, angry red of air resistance, and whose flight path was drawn across the dark blueprint of the sky by a thin, perfectly straight white line of vapor condensation. Far below it the planetary surface slid by with deceptive slowness.

In the ship's tiny control room a loud-speaker clicked, hummed, and said, "Flagship to S-Five-Three—" The eyes of the three-man crew flickered briefly towards it, then switched back to their respective instrument panels. A tightness about their mouths and an involuntary jerk of their heads towards the sound betrayed the strain they were under. They relaxed, a little, when it merely stated, "This is the commander. Your ETA over target is nine minutes, fifteen seconds from—now. What have you in mind, captain?"

Spence, the ship's captain, reached out quickly—too quickly—and fumbled the switch to the "Transmit" position. But his voice was quite steady as he replied.

"The usual thing, sir. Direct, high-level approach to within fifty miles, dive, level off at five thousand, spray them, then decelerate and land. Normal procedure from there on in. It should take about two hours."

There was silence for a long moment, broken only by the faint, back-ground hum from the speaker. The miles fled by, a large number of miles. Then the commander spoke again.

"That seems satisfactory, but we are taking too long over this, captain. Hurry it up, please. Have you looked at a clock recently? Off."

Beside the captain, the engineer and servomech officer, Bennett, moved restively. He looked straight at Spence, then at the now quiescent speaker, and inclined his close-cropped, grayish-blond head at two dials on the wide panel before him. The dials showed the hull temperature and the output of the cooling units. They each bore a conspicuous red mark, and their indicator needles seemed to be glued to these marks. Bennett gave a short, interrogatory grunt. It was his way of saying that if they hurried it up any faster they'd probably vaporize themselves, but it was for the captain to decide one way or the other. Bennett was a man of few words.

Spence shook his head curtly. There would be no increase in speed. Then he turned abruptly to the third member of the crew, Harrison, the gunnery officer.

Harrison was muttering angrily, "What did he mean by that last crack? Have we looked at anything else *but* clocks recently? Just who does he think he is—?"

"That's enough," said Spence sharply, as a light flashed urgently on his panel, "I haven't time to listen to you. We dive in three seconds. Brace yourselves." His hands flickered about, checking, then settled on the twin grips of a lever that grew solidly from the floor between his feet. He began to edge it slowly forward.

The great ship curved smoothly downwards into a steep dive. Straining against the straps, the crew hung forward in their seats, their faces pop-eyed, dark red masks of mounting blood pressure. The dive lasted eight seconds, then the pull-out flattened them back into the padding. That was much easier to take, thought Spence. The seats were designed to swing to compensate for any sudden change in direction, but on a planetary operation like this they had, of course, to be in a fixed up-down position.

But it wasn't the ill-treatment his body was being subjected to that was worrying him. No, that was the least of his troubles. It was Harrison.

Harrison was going soft.

Captain Spence couldn't altogether blame him. Harrison had been under a killing pressure, both physical and mental these last few days, but this was certainly not the time to develop a hypersensitive conscience.

Harrison had joined the ship only a week ago, just two days before the current emergency, as a replacement for Walters who was still recuperating with a leg graft after that mess on Torcin Eight. He was a new boy, just out of Basic Training, and like all the freshly-qualified entrants to the Force, he'd worn the dedicated, near-exalted look that sometimes took months to wear off. The great motto of the Force, implying the ultimate in selfless service to humanity, was practically written in letters of light across his forehead as well as being traced in gold thread on cap and shoulder badges. It said, in a language long dead before the motto was even coined, "There is nothing more important than a human life," and Harrison was intensely eager to start saving lives. He was going to save lives if he had to kill himself doing it. Spence had felt the same way at the start, but that idea had been soon knocked out of him. There was no future in it; besides, it was wasteful of highly-trained technicians.

All this did not mean that Harrison had been naïve or unrealistic about things. He'd known that the Force must, by its very nature, be called on to do an occasional little job that was just a shade off-color—for the greatest common good, of course. It was a pity, thought Spence, that his first job had been a five-star alarm, a very big one and the grimmest the captain had ever encountered in his twelve years of service. It was one way of finding out whether a man had what it took, but it was a rather drastic way.

Now Harrison was sitting hunched forward in his seat, staring at the screen which showed the surface ahead and below. From five thousand feet the ground was a dull, reddish-brown carpet unrolling monotonously below the furiously speeding ship. Occasionally there would be a stain on the carpet—an ugly black stain five miles across that had been the site of one of the Crawler cities. The ship had been directly responsible for quite a few of those. There was nothing like a medium-sized H-bomb exploded well underground to really *reduce* a city. The shock-wave left the resultant rubble looking like fine gravel. The placing and detonation of the bombs was the gunnery officer's department, so he was sitting there beginning to hate himself.

Good thing, thought Spence, that the Crawler civilization was concentrated in large, widely-separate cities. It was less wasteful of bombs and made the cleanup job a lot simpler. There were no farms or villages to deal with, but there were groups of survivors, who had somehow managed to evade the first sweep, holing up in various places. It was towards one of these groups, one of the few remaining on the planet, that Spence's ship was splitting the air.

A low range of mountains crept gradually over the horizon. The aliens were behind them. The ship had chosen this course so that the mountains would shield it from radar until the last possible moment, always supposing the Crawlers *had* radar. There was no sense in taking chances. Spence's voice was harsh as he said sharply, "Five seconds to target. Gunnery Officer stand by!"

And, thought the captain, if he flunks it now that he's gone this far, I shall certainly kick him to a bleeding pulp.

The aliens had not got radar, but from bits and pieces of mining machinery they had somehow fashioned a multibarreled antiaircraft weapon. It didn't make the slightest difference, they hadn't a chance. A gray blur streaked across the sky. For a split second they were bathed in a wide cone of invisible radiation. The effect was instantaneous. The group of Crawlers around the gun jerked convulsively as their voluntary muscles reacted to the radiation, then they rolled flabbily to the ground.

And when the lagging thunder of the ship's passage

across the sky beat down on the Crawler mining settlement, the ship itself was a shrinking dot on the horizon, and nothing on the ground was moving. It was as easy as that.

The ship decelerated furiously to subsonic and circled back. It hung motionless over the settlement. From the projector under its nose the radiation again flared out; this time it was maintained for fully two seconds, then the ship settled slowly towards the ground.

That second dose was unnecessary, Spence thought, as the surface expanded below them. It was merely another added precaution. There was not a race known in the galaxy immune to that radiation. It really was the nearest thing to the Perfect Weapon ever discovered; it did not harm the body at all, but struck directly at the brain in such a way that the mind affected was rendered completely unconscious, all the voluntary muscles were paralyzed, and the metabolic rate was slowed to almost nothing. Its beauty lay in the fact that it was reversible. If you potted a friend by mistake, he could be revived. On the other hand, if it was an enemy, you could come back at leisure and burn him, or blow holes in him—he was helpless. The easy way was just to leave him and he'd starve to death.

The trend of the captain's thoughts was becoming too morbid. He pulled himself out of it to find the ship about to touch down. He started doing rapid, complicated things with the controls before him. When he looked up they were down and he hadn't felt it.

"Locks One to Six open. Holds A and B ready for loading," he announced crisply, "Go to it, Mr. Bennett." He sat back tiredly. For the time being he had nothing to do.

Up to this moment the servomech officer had been little more than a passenger, but now he went to work. A stream of robots, functionally specialized, began to walk, roll, or fly out of the opened locks. Some were merely camera pickups, others consisted of a cluster of extensible grabs of various sizes mounted on caterpillar treads, the rest were simply remote-controlled wheelbarrows. The grabs spread out, each trailed by an attentive trio of barrows. When they came to a limp alien, it would be lifted, dumped into a barrow, which would whisk it back to the ship where other types of special machinery would stow it carefully away where it would be sure to keep. Meanwhile, the grab had moved on to the next alien, and the first barrow, now empty, hurried back to wait for a refill.

At various heights above all this activity hovered the camera pickups, constantly sending pictures and pertinent data back to the semicircle of screens around Bennett's control panel. And Bennett, by glancing at a screen and fiddling with a few knobs, would send several tons of highly-complex machinery where it would do the most good. The robots were almost fully automatic, needing only the minimum of guidance, but keeping his eyes on over fifty of the things was a nerve-racking job.

The captain, watching with approval, thought how efficient it was, and how quick. Bennett was good at this. Suddenly he started forward and snapped a reproof.

"Careful there. Take it easy. What do you think you're doing? They're not sacks of flour, you know. Watch it."

One of the grabs in dropping a Crawler into a barrow had misjudged. Its flaccid burden had fouled a sharp-edged projection on its way in. A great, three-foot gash appeared in its side and the treacly goo it used for blood welled out, making a dirty, ever-widening stain on the beautiful, iridescent fur.

"Sorry," Bennett muttered abstractedly, "I was in a hurry." Which was a pretty good excuse, all things considered.

The captain kept quiet. A tricky piece of work had come up and he didn't want to distract the other.

It was one of the Crawler gunners. It had been manning the gun when the projector had caught it, and it was practically tied to its post. The Crawler method of operating their machinery was either to wrap themselves around it or to insinuate themselves right into it, or preferably both, so as to use to the best advantage the five pairs of hands and feet which made them so closely resemble the centipede. This one was so mixed up with the gun that Bennett had brought up another grab to help untangle it. But it wasn't until another specialized servo arrived from the ship and partially dismantled the gun that they were able to draw the alien free. While it was being carted back to the ship the two grabs wheeled about and went hunting again.

But game was becoming scarce. On a large screen in front of the servomech officer a dim gray picture of the mining settlement as seen from the air appeared. Here and there on the picture a hot orange spark burned. Each spark showed the position of one of the Crawlers. It didn't matter if they were out in the open or coiled in some dark corner of their low, dome-shaped shelters. They weren't quite dead, so their brainwaves were detectable and their positions showed plain.

It was another one of the advantages of using the projector—one was able to find the victims without any trouble. When the ship had landed, more than fifty glowing sparks had dotted the screen. Now there were fourteen. Bennett brought thirty of the robots back to the ship, where they automatically sorted and stored themselves away. The job was almost finished and they were only cluttering up the place.

Less than an hour of his estimated two had passed, Spence thought. We've made good time. We should do it comfortably. He began to relax.

Suddenly the wall speaker burst into life again. The harsh voice of the fleet commander pervaded the room.

"Flagship to Scavenger Five-Three. How is it going, captain? Report, please."

Spence took a deep breath, then recited briskly, "Everything going according to plan, sir. We found a sort of mining settlement—the first I've seen here that hadn't a city built over it—with between fifty and sixty Crawler survivors. They had a gun of sorts rigged up but didn't get a chance to use it. We're loading in the last few stiffs now."

He stopped. Bennett was waving at him urgently, trying to attract his attention. Harrison, white-faced, was bending over the other's shoulder and staring at the servo panel as if he didn't believe it. Spence nodded curtly and said into the mike, "Excuse me, sir. Something has come up." He turned impatiently to the others.

"Well?"

Bennett didn't say anything. He didn't need to. His finger indicated five lights burning on the screen before him. A graduated dial showed the depth of the objects which caused the lights to be two hundred feet. Another gave the information that the objects were in fairly rapid motion. He let his hands fall to his lap and looked gloomy.

There were five aliens on the loose.

This was too much to take. Of all the blind, senseless, bad luck. Spence was too angry to be frightened—yet. He'd expected to be clear of this stinking planet in another ten minutes. Now *this*.

The five Crawlers must have been down the mine both times the ship had passed over. The projector lacked the power to penetrate two hundred feet of solid, ore-bearing rock, so the radiation hadn't touched them. They were down there now, five alien snakes with beautiful, shimmering pelts, each of whose bodies measured two feet thick and eight feet wide. Their feelings towards the beings in the ship were probably indescribable, but they were certainly hostile. Spence's voice shook a little as he related this latest development to the waiting fleet commander. When he finished he was sweating.

It was all right while I was busy, he thought, there was no time to be afraid—not really afraid. But this sitting around while the clock ticked off the seconds—He felt almost like asking if the commander had gone to sleep or something, it was taking him so long to answer. He tapped his foot rapidly, nervously against his seat support. When the voice came again he leaned forward anxiously.

"That is bad, captain. Very bad," it said gravely, "but whatever means you use to deal with it, remember that speed must be the first consideration. I will remain in this orbit for exactly fifty-three minutes. You have until then to clear things up." The commander stopped, but he hadn't quite finished. When he went on his tone was just a little warmer and more human.

He said, "I'd better tell you that, if circumstances warrant it, I'll have to leave before the expiration of the time-limit I've just given you. Also, we can't send you any help as you are now the only ship remaining on the planet. When you're through we can all go home. You are last man in, captain. I'll leave you to it. Luck. Off."

Spence had often wondered how it felt to be last man in from one of these clean-up jobs. Now that he knew, he wished that he didn't. But he had only fifty minutes to get something done. He'd have to think, hard.

But he couldn't think of anything but the fact that far below him crawled the last living things native to this planet, and that his ship was all alone on its whole wide, poisonous surface. He almost felt like blasting off right now, but he had a duty. None of his thoughts showed on his face, they never did unless he wanted them to. His voice was even as he turned to the other two and asked, "Has anyone an idea?"

Harrison shook his head.

Bennett said, "I've already activated a couple of diggers. They're on the way to the mine shaft now. They will be able to widen the tunnel enough to allow the grabs to get to the aliens. There aren't any lifts to worry about—the main shaft is in the form of a descending spiral with branching tunnels leading off it at different levels. It's very confusing—"

He stopped talking to snap down a few switches on his panel. On a screen before him a monster of flashing and rotating blades mounted on caterpillar treads nosed over into a small hole in the ground. Soil flew skyward. When it had sunk from sight the hole was much bigger. Other machines hurried in and came out filled with loose earth, then went back for more. Two grabs stood aloofly by, waiting for them to finish.

Bennett went on, a little apologetically, "This isn't such a hot idea, it may take too much time. Unless, of course, we can get them trapped in a dead end, and I don't think they'll let us do that. But I can't think of any other way of doing the job. How about you?"

Spence shook his head, then asked, "How many entrances are there?" He wanted the overall picture before he started making suggestions. Time was too short.

"Just the one," Bennett answered, and waited.

There was probably a very simple answer to this problem, Spence thought, but the terrible urgency of finding that answer so clouded his brain that he couldn't think at all. Performance data of the armaments carried by the ship, together with all the odd items of the Crawler physiology that they'd been able to pick up, tumbled through his mind like a pack of spilled cards, but nothing would make sense. Nothing fitted. And always there was the clock ticking—like a mouse scratching and nibbling away at their dwindling store of time.

He put his finger and thumb to the bridge of his nose and shut his eyes tightly. Steady now, he thought intensely, this is getting you nowhere. Take it easy. *Think*.

Question. How to catch five aliens hiding underground. Answer. Send robots to dig them out. That was logical, and the servomech officer had done the right thing. But any of the robots capable of taking the aliens were too big to traverse the tunnels. If, however, the tunnels were widened, and if the aliens stayed put until the grabs arrived, and if they were unarmed or incapable of damaging the grabs sent after them, then that solution might work out. Spence shook his head impatiently. There were too many "ifs".

Harrison had been figuring out something on his scratch-pad. He straightened up, looked at Bennett, then bent over his calculations again and began to check them carefully.

Finally he said, "This isn't going to work. The farther down we dig the slower we'll go. The way I figure it we won't even be able to reach the level the aliens are occupying before it's too late." He jerked his head upwards slightly. The movement took in their great flagship hovering impatiently out in space as well as the chronometer on the wall. There was something about the way he said the words, Spence thought. As if he'd been thinking about an entirely different matter.

Spence wondered if the other was getting an idea, and kept silent. Dragging it out of him half-formed wouldn't do any good, he'd spit it out himself if it amounted to anything. Meanwhile, how to get at five aliens two hundred-odd feet underground in a tunnel four feet wide?

All over the ship automatic machinery made small furtive, clicking noises, but the clock above his head sounded the loudest.

Harrison broke the silence. Strain made his first few words an almost unintelligible croak.

"We're going about this the wrong way. Robots are no good for this job. We—We—" He hesitated, then blurted, "We'll have to go after them ourselves."

Nobody said anything for a moment. Spence's mind raced ahead. It might work at that. It just might.

The tunnels were wide enough. They had suits, guns, means of detecting their prey, and this way they might even have enough time. But the crew, or any part of it, wasn't supposed to leave the ship during operations, especially if the ship was a Scavenger Fleet cruiser.

The crew on these boats was small, specialized, and interdependent to a high degree. They carried a thousand-odd cubic yards of near-human machinery which was designed to cope with anything that could conceivably turn up in the way of emergencies, so that the crew need never leave the ship at all.

But this particular situation was without precedent, Spence thought angrily, he'd just have to break the rules. He had a brilliant record up to now. He hoped desperately that nothing would go wrong.

But it was the job that mattered, not the individuals taking part in it. The problem now, he thought, was which member or members of the crew was the most dispensable.

Bennett spoke up, low-voiced and unhurried. He mentioned just how irregular was Harrison's suggestion, but seconded it. He also pointed out that when the robots could not be made to function efficiently, the job of servomech officer automatically became superfluous, or words to that effect. He ended by confessing to a yen to stretch his legs outside the ship.

Bennett's volunteering for the job beat Harrison's by

split seconds. The gunnery officer also gave reasons, good ones—the same ones in fact.

Spence sighed. He'd expected this. He said quietly, "We all volunteer, naturally, but someone will have to stay in the ship. Now," he argued, "two people will stand a better chance out there than one, but we've got to increase that chance as much as possible. The way I see it, Mr. Harrison and myself will attend to the Crawlers, while you, Mr. Bennett, will support us whenever possible with your servos. That way we will all be gainfully employed."

The captain wanted to go, too.

But Bennett had an objection. Supposing something should happen to the captain when he was outside. If he was killed, or injured maybe, what about the ship? The servomech officer couldn't handle it, that he was sure of. The cargo was far too valuable to risk leaving it stranded on the planet in the face of what was coming, or to lose in space because of an untrained pilot. The captain shouldn't go out.

He was right, of course. On a job like this the cargo came first, always. But Spence was annoyed. He showed it by being very sarcastic at first, but the mood left him quickly. This was no time to lose his temper.

"All right, heroes," he said, "get going. You'll need suits. The light-weight type will do here—the pressure is nearly Earth-normal. I'll give you the details while you're climbing in. Hurry it up."

The suits arrived. With rapid, practiced movements Bennett and Harrison dropped onto their backs, wriggled their legs into the lower half, then flipped over and began pushing in their arms. It looked like the donning of long flannel underwear, the hard way. Then came the fish bowls. In eighty seconds they were dressed. Pretty good going. Spence kept talking all the time.

"The air contains about thirty per cent oxygen. It isn't poisonous, exactly, but you'd strangle or burst your hearts through coughing if you had to breathe it for more than a few seconds, it irritates the breathing passages so much. Gravity is point six five Gee, so be careful—" He broke off and said sharply to Harrison, "Check that seam at your shoulder. Is it tight? Slap some cement on it and make sure. No, give it to me. I'll do it. Get the walkie-talkie strapped on."

Dressed, the two men began stretching and bending vigorously, testing for leaks. The captain continued.

"For weapons, better take gas guns and pistols firing nonexplosive bullets. Use the pistols only as a last resort. The reports will probably bring down the tunnel roof, and we've got to avoid damaging the things if possible. Concentrate on gassing them, we know enough about their body chemistry now to do that. There are a couple of gases in stock that will knock them out like a light. But if something should come up and you *have* to shoot, aim for the center of the twin flaps of muscle which cover their retractable eyes. These are at the top of their heads, which are very heavily boned, almost armor-plated, so don't miss them, the brain is located just behind the flaps. If you should come at them from the side, shoot at their hearts. They have two, located just above the second pair of gripping limbs and the fifth pair of walking limbs respectively. To do a good job you'll have to get both." He paused for breath as the weapons arrived via robot from the armory, then he went on.

"These three spots are their only vital ones. They are nearly all muscle, and you can make them look like sieves without slowing them down very much. Gas is best, anyway.

"Now git, and keep your suit radios on all the time. I'll be listening and I want to know everything as it happens."

Harrison and Bennett ducked out of the control room and made their way through massed piles of machinery to the tiny personnel lock in the great ship's outer skin. Two knights in shining plastic armor, thought Spence bitterly. He wondered if he would ever see them again. It was times like this that made him have doubts about the Force, and the Force's purpose, and whether it was all worth it.

The commissioning plaque on the wall said that it was. The clock beside it said it was twenty-five minutes before blast-off time, which was more important at the moment.

The captain took the servomech officer's seat. One of the plates showed a tiny picture of the two men sprinting for the mine opening. The sound of their breaths, amplified, came through the speaker. They paused on the brim for a moment without speaking, then dropped from sight.

Suddenly the commander's voice burst in on the silence. He sounded harassed, strained.

"Hello Fifty-Three. What progress?"

The captain jerked nervously. Then began to give his chief an account of the present state of affairs on the planet. The commander interrupted only once to ask incredulously, *"The men are off the ship?"* Then he let him finish.

Spence waited for the other's reaction. He supposed judgment would be deferred until the successful completion of the operation. But if it wasn't successful—He mustn't even think of that.

"You have exceeded your authority, captain. You had no business risking the ship like this, especially with fifty Crawlers aboard," began the commander harshly.

But before he could get warmed up Spence interrupted him with a level-voiced, "My orders were not to leave a live Crawler on the planet."

"I know that, captain. But let's not be greedy." Craig's tone was quiet, almost conversational, but Spence wasn't fooled a bit. The commander was about ready to blow up as he continued, "I've been looking at your record. It's a very good one. Somehow you've always managed to bring home the bacon, if you'll excuse the expression. This time it's different. Don't get overzealous, captain, that's bad. I am leaving shortly. You have another nineteen minutes. This had better work out, captain. Off."

Spence sat up at the mention of the time left to him. The rest of it he could worry about later, if there was a later. Nineteen minutes! What was the matter with Bennett and Harrison, struck dumb or something? Had the aliens sprung a trap, maybe? He was about to call them when Harrison's voice issued angrily from the speaker.

"Stay farther behind, Bennett. You're stabbing me with your suit antenna."

Subdued bumping and scraping noises came from the speaker, and an answering grunt. Very much relieved, Spence joined in with a faintly sarcastic reproof.

"Bennett. Please refrain from stabbing the gunnery officer. And isn't it about time you told me what was going on down there?"

"Nothing much, sir," Bennett's voice was uneven and a trifle breathless. He was wriggling at top speed along a tunnel and trying to talk at the same time. "We are well past the point in the tunnel at which the digger was stopped. It was a tight squeeze at first, but the tunnel is beginning to widen out a lot. We are about thirty feet above the alien positions. The detector shows four, close-grouped points of mind radiation about one hundred feet to our right and a single point almost directly below us. I expect it's a guard, but I'm nearly certain it isn't aware of us. The tunnel is widening out a lot now, we can stand up. We're going as fast as we can. Harrison is getting ready to knock over the Crawler."

Bennett stopped to get his breath back. Then he went on quickly, "I'll have to shut up in a minute. We're closing in on him fast, and I don't know if these things can hear or not. But seeing as the tunnel is wide enough for robots down here, wouldn't it be a good idea to start the digger again? With all of the tunnel as wide as this we could get some of the bigger 'mechs down here and speed things up a bit. Do you know how to control the digger?"

A little sarcastically, Spence said yes, he'd been able to pick up a few little things in his twelve years in the Force. He'd manage to do that all right. He pressed the necessary number of buttons and asked was there anything else.

Bennett didn't speak for several minutes. The scuffling noises from the speaker seemed to increase in volume. Then he said, with exaggerated lightness, "Yes, when the tunnel is wide enough you could send down a barrow for this alien. He looks untidy lying here."

Spence was in no mood for levity. "Right. So you got one. Was there any trouble?"

"No, but the vibration from the digger is shaking down

a lot of dust. The other Crawlers must know we're here by now. They'll be waiting for us."

"Can't be helped, I'm afraid, but it will be over any time now. The digger is almost through," said the captain. He was about to ask how they were standing conditions down there generally when Harrison's voice cut in. It sounded, thought Spence, decidedly uneasy.

"This looks bad, sir. I'm looking down the tunnel which the alien was guarding. It is perfectly straight, fairly roomy, and it widens to form a sort of room at the other end. The room is artificially lit and there are aliens in it. I can only see two, but the detector says they are all there. They are working at some kind of machine. I don't like the look of it," he ended and waited for the captain to speak.

Machines, thought Spence, it did look bad. He asked, "Can you tell if the thing is completed or still a-building, or guess at what it's for?"

"No, they're crowding round it. I can't even tell what it looks like. Only parts of it show."

A small pickup drifted into the tunnel beside Harrison and stared glassily over his shoulder. Back in the control room Spence saw the Crawler machine, too. It seemed to be a lot of queerly twisted plates built on four wheels. Baffled, he shook his head. He was beginning to wonder if it wouldn't be better to just pull out and forget the last handful of aliens when Bennett's voice came again.

"The digger's through. I turned it into a side passage and shut it off. And I hear the barrow coming for the stiff. You'd better send a few more down, we might need them in a hurry. Time is getting short, so we're just going to walk down this passage abreast until their room is in range of our gas guns. There's nothing else to do. Judging by the intensity of the lighting they use we might be able to get close enough without them seeing us. I hope so, anyway. Here we go."

The voice stopped. Over the speaker came the measured tread of two pairs of feet, slightly out of step.

Twelve minutes to go, thought Spence. The barrow carrying the Crawler guard rolled out of the mine opening and headed for the ship. He sent two others down to replace it. After that he never took his eyes off the scene being relayed from the tunnel. But there wasn't much to see, just two shadowy figures outlined by the light at the other end. The image wavered a little as the pickup moved to keep pace behind them.

Despite the intensity of his concentration, the screen couldn't fully occupy his mind. Not enough was happening on it. He kept thinking back. Back an hour, back two days, back a week. But, Spence realized with a start, a week ago he hadn't even heard of this planet. Nobody but a few obscure astronomers had even an inkling of its existence. Then everybody knew. In the same way as some quiet, unassuming neighborhood is brought suddenly into the limelight by a couple of juicy ax murders.

Five days ago the alarm had been given. Every unit of the Force in this sector had lifted itself from its base and made the twist into subspace. When it returned to the normal continuum it was eighty million miles from the Crawler planet and it was part of a fleet of two thousand.

It had been smooth. Not a single hitch anywhere, Spence knew. First had come the heavies. Twelve hundred fat silver cigars, each half a mile long, had hit the planet in a wave and washed around it twice. The first time they passed, not a single thing moved in the great Crawler cities. The second time took longer—but when they swept by, the cities were empty. Then, their holds crammed with the dominant life of the planet, they had disappeared en masse into subspace.

Then had come the clean-up squad, the Scavenger Fleet. The ships landed in cities which had been cleared of alien life by the heavies. When they took off again the cities blew themselves to pieces in their wake. It was a bit wasteful, Spence thought, using bombs on empty cities, but they had to keep the Crawler survivors from returning to shelter in them. There wouldn't be time to search them twice, because a common enemy would be along very shortly which would lap up Crawlers and humans alike with the finest impartiality.

With the cities out of the way, the Scavenger ships had scattered to route out the stragglers. It wasn't a very difficult job, but they had to hurry it a lot. There was no trouble in finding them. Any Crawler whose mind was working, even if he was asleep, registered on the detectors carried by the ships. Whether they cowered singly in caves or stood defensively at bay a hundred strong in some fortified position, it was just the same. A ship would flash over. Its projector would flicker invisibly down, then it would land and load the aliens aboard. Dead easy, thought Spence. Nothing to it. Routine.

Up to now, that is, the captain thought bitterly.

He was dragged out of his deepening mood of self-pity by the sight of Bennett and Harrison throwing themselves flat on the ground. Simultaneously the pickup showed the Crawlers moving their machine into the tunnel mouth. Muffled *plops* came from the speaker. The range was still too great, but the men were using their gas guns. A dirty brown fog grew in the tunnel as the gas combined with the alien atmosphere, blurring the view, but not before Spence saw that the enigmatic machine had started working.

Strangely enough, nothing much seemed to be happening. The machine was being pushed slowly down the passage towards the crouching men, with the aliens sheltering behind it as it crept long. The gas still obscured everything.

Suddenly Harrison's voice crashed out from the wall speaker as he shouted, "It's a fan. We're sunk. They're blowing our gas back at us."

"Stop shouting, Mr. Harrison," Spence said sharply, "I can hear you." The suit mikes were capable of picking up the lowest whisper. When Harrison had raised his voice it had been like sounding the heart of a volcano with a stethoscope. So now the aliens had a fan. That meant his men were powerless to use gas, and using anything else would be too risky, now that they knew of the shaky construction of the tunnel roof.

He'd had about enough of this, Spence decided, it was time to get out.

"Pull out, you two. Back to the ship."

"Captain, I've got an idea." It was Bennett's voice.

Low, unhurried, completely sure of himself he went on, "We can still pull it off. If we wait until they're real close and aim for the rotors, we could disable the fans and—"

"No shooting," the captain interrupted harshly, "You'd bring the roof down. And that's an order—"

A loud, vicious, *crack* came from the speaker. The sound was unmistakable. Spence gripped the edge of the panel before him and paled as he saw a few tiny rocks drop from the tunnel roof beside the two men. In a voice that shook with fury he exploded, "Mr. Harrison, I told you not to use your gun down there. If you've—"

"It wasn't us," Bennett cut in. "One of the Crawlers has a sort of gun. It's sniping at us. And the fan is speeding up, there's a small gale blowing in here now. I think they mean to rush us."

Bennett's tone wasn't quite so unruffled now. Talking rapidly, Harrison took up the troubled tale.

"The way I see it they mean to kill us and get out before the roof comes down completely from the gunfire. It's their mine so I suppose they know better than we do what the tunnel will stand. They're going to risk the shooting and—Down!"

There was another sharp report and simultaneously the screen blanked out. A direct hit on the camera pickup, thought Spence wildly, what a time to go blind. But that wasn't all. There was a close-spaced series of dull crashes from the speaker and the horrible gasping, choking sound of somebody strangling.

"Bennett. Bennett." Harrison was shouting again. A continuous, racking cough, unbearably amplified, drowned out his words.

Spence was reaching hurriedly to turn down the volume when the noise shut off and the gunnery officer's voice returned, low and urgent.

"Bennett's helmet cracked—a rock, I think. I've shut off his transmitter and slapped cement on the break. He's partly buried in the fall. I'm trying to get him free now, but the Crawlers are coming up fast." Harrison stopped as another explosion shook the tunnel. "Will you send a barrow here so's I can load him aboard. His suit is switched to pure oxygen now, but he looks bad. He's coughing a lot. And can I use my pistol? That Crawler is getting ready to pick me off."

"I can't see down there now. Do what you think is best. You're on your own." Spence answered.

He was beginning to kick himself for sending the men down there in the first place. It looked as if he was going to lose both of them. He thought briefly of cutting his losses and ordering Harrison back immediately, but he knew it would be no use. Harrison was the altruistic type. Besides, he wasn't so sure he could bring himself to abandon Bennett like that anyway. Maybe he was going soft, too.

Two more reports boomed from the speaker in rapid succession, Harrison's voice came again.

"That Crawler's finished. So is the fan, he fell into it when I shot him. It's ... it's made an awful mess. I'm gassing the others now. There wasn't much of a fall this time, though our guns make a bigger racket than theirs." He paused, his breath coming loud over the speaker. Then he said, "I can hear the barrow coming for Bennett. Send the other one in here while I get him onto this one. Maybe we can get a few Crawlers out after all."

The captain began talking rapidly. He told the gunnery officer not to be a dope. He used even stronger language. Harrison was to forget about the Crawlers. When the barrow arrived he was to pile in with Bennett and come up at once and not be a complete fool. Spence was beginning to repeat himself when a low, ominous rumble sounded, and the floor beneath him quivered slightly. Only then did he realize that Harrison had his transmitter turned off, and possibly his receiver, too.

"I'll break every bone in his body for this," Spence fumed helplessly. "What a stupid trick to pull. What if he had been calling the other names, it was for his own good." Spence was very worried about Harrison. He was new, he might do something very foolish, his voice had sounded funny just then, come to think of it.

When Harrison switched on his set and spoke, the captain knew that he hadn't been worrying for nothing.

"Bennett is on the way up. I want to stay here for a bit.

There's been another fall, a bad one. The Crawlers are all mashed up. It would take a bucket to load them onto anything, they're all over the place." For a moment Harrison sounded as if he was going to be sick. Then he recovered and went on, "But the detector shows one of them to be still alive, and I'm going to get it if I have to drag it out myself. You see, these last few days have gotten me down, captain. I'm sick of this job. I keep remembering things. All those cities we bombed, and that time the Crawlers came out of that cave and tried to contact us by drawing math symbols on the ground, and the way we gassed them without even acknowledging their signals."

"But we hadn't time," Spence argued. "You know that. And the only telepaths good enough to mesh with them were halfway across the galaxy, and couldn't have reached here in time to do any good. We had to make it a surprise attack or nothing."

"I know, I know. But we didn't even—" Harrison couldn't put it into words. He knew he was right, but the captain was right, too. He changed the subject. "How are we for time, sir?"

"Six and a half minutes," replied Spence, and thought incredulously, *six and a half minutes!*

Just then Bennett came into the control room, still wheezing and smothering an occasional cough. He wasn't much the worse for his near strangulation. Spence nodded at him without turning, and thought angrily that this was mutiny. All he said was, "Harrison. Bennett's here. Come back at once."

Harrison apparently didn't hear him. He said, "That's good." Whether he meant the time or Bennett was an open question. Then he went on in a low, conversational tone, "More stuff is coming down, mostly in the side tunnels which aren't very strongly built. I'm standing beside the alien which the detector says is alive. Funny thing. I tried to drag it out just now and it came to pieces in my hands. I don't get it. The detector says it is alive, but which piece of it is alive? I'm going to have a closer look—"

Harrison was beginning to talk to himself, thought Spence. That was bad. Next thing he'd begin to scream or laugh, and then he'd want to take off his helmet for a smoke. Quietly, coaxingly, the captain began repeating over and over the command to return to the ship, trying desperately to get hypnotic control over the mind that was so far gone that an appeal to reason was useless.

Suddenly Harrison said in a pleased voice, "Well, what d'you know," and burst out laughing.

The captain's eyes looked bleak. He signaled for Bennett to warm up the drive elements. He would try just once more.

But he didn't get the chance. The fleet commander's harsh voice burst in on them, wavering and fading in the way peculiar to a signal that is being transmitted from a ship in subspace.

"Flagship to Scavenger Five-Three. Report please—" The voice broke off as the commander gasped in unbelief, then he shouted urgently, "You're still on the planet, captain. Get off! Get off at once!"

The captain jumped to obey, but his hand froze on the firing key as Harrison's voice came again. It said simply, "I'm coming now, sir."

For seconds that seemed like an eternity the captain fought to reach a decision. Voices were shouting in his head about Service discipline, common sense, safety. Urging him to take off. Other voices were telling him to be a human being for once, instead of a soulless machine. He looked appealingly at Bennett, but the servomech officer wouldn't meet his eyes.

Bennett pointed suddenly at one of the screens. It showed the tiny figure of Harrison emerging from the mine shaft and sprinting for the ship. On one arm, from wrist to elbow, Harrison wore a beautiful, iridescent fur muff.

When Harrison burst into the control room the great ship was already climbing. He had time to get to his couch and settle his burden gently on his stomach before the acceleration started building up, then he couldn't move.

"Seventy-five seconds," Spence whispered, "Oh, come on, *Come on.*" It sounded almost like a prayer.

Slowly the air around the ship thinned. The huge, pock-marked sun, its corona clearly visible, glared in at them through the starboard screen. The sky was black. They were in space, the warp drive could take over.

Twelve seconds after they had twisted themselves into the safety of subspace, the furiously expanding sphere of annihilation brought about by the detonation of the system's sun vaporized the Crawler planet.

Harrison lifted the furry bundle and shook it in the air. "I found it underneath one of the dead Crawlers. It's a youngster. Cute, isn't he?"

"Cute, he says," said Bennett in disgusted tones. He choked, and a fit of coughing took him.

Spence said, "Better put it in suspended animation with the others. This air of ours is bad for it."

He was pleased with Harrison. The gunnery officer was going to turn out all right. Unavoidably, they'd had to kill a few aliens, but Harrison had been able, personally, to rescue one of their young, so that more than made up for it. He had no intention of resigning now, Spence knew; he probably felt quite a knight in shining armor.

The captain had felt that way when he was a new boy, he remembered. Somehow, the feeling never quite wore off. It came of belonging to an organization dedicated to the job of protecting, assisting, and keeping the noses clean generally of every race in the galaxy that walked, wriggled, or flew and had intelligence. We're just a flock of space-going guardian angels, he thought a little cynically, all we need are halos.

He came down out of the clouds with a start to hear Bennett saying, "You know, I'd hate to have the job of explaining all this to the Crawlers when they wake up on their new planet. I wouldn't be a telepath for anything, too dangerous, for one thing—"

If a planet of the pre-nova stage sun is found to contain intelligent life, the Force will assemble an adequate number of transport units to evacuate the planet in question, having first informed the natives of their danger through operatives of the Department of E-T Communications.

Should no ETCOM telepaths be available at the time, the natives must be evacuated forcefully and taken to the planet assigned them by the Department of Colonization, where the situation will be explained to them when they are revived.

From the "Force Handbook," section on Special Duties.

Occupation: Warrior
❖❖❖❖❖❖❖❖❖❖❖❖❖❖❖❖❖❖

Chapter I

FROM HIS position six paces front and centre of the men who were drawn up in open column of threes behind him, Dermod watched the slow approach of the closed ground-car out of the corner of his eye. Driven by a bored looking Earth-human in Guard green it contained two large, cater-pillar-like life-forms—the warm-blooded, oxygen-breathing, multi-pedal and furred beings who inhabited the planet Kelgia. Because they required no other body covering their insignias of rank took the form of dyed patches of colour on their sleek, silver-grey pelts.

So this, thought Dermod, *is the enemy!*

Slowly, inexorably, the vehicle bore down on him. Dermod's mouth felt suddenly dry. It was nearly time for him to act, and he was hoping desperately that his act would be convincing.

In the rigid lines of men behind him tension was mount-ing also. At any moment now there would be a supposed-ly spontaneous and uncontrolled demonstration of hatred against the crawler officers in the groundcar. There always was such a demonstration, Dermod thought with a gri-mace of distaste; it was designed to impress the enemy with the fine, fighting ardour of men who were in reality nothing but a bunch of cowards, weaklings and big-mouthed braggarts. But if these men could convince the crawler officers of their bravery then they would not be picked to fight in the coming war, because given the chance an enemy picks the weakest opponents to fight against and not the strongest.

The groundcar was so close now that Dermod could see dust streaks on the bubble canopy. Now was the time, he thought, and started his lips to quivering and allowed a rapidly increasing tremor to shake his arms and shoulders. In the old days he had been one of the leaders in his Drama Group. His face would be pale now, he knew, and well beaded with sweat. Dermod reached the climax just as the car drew level with him and he slumped bonelessly to the ground.

His action surprised the men behind him as much as the enemy officers because the demonstration got off to a late and very ragged start. But the first few isolated shouts built up quickly into general uproar, then Dermod's world—viewed through slitted eyes at groundlevel—became a maelstrom of dust, stamping feet and sheer organic noise.

Dermod allowed the shouting, fist-waving men to surge around and over him for a few seconds, then he fought his way upright and joined them in hurling abuse at the enemy. The effect he wanted to produce was of an officer who could faint at the mere sight of the enemy even before hostilities began, but he did not want to overplay the role ...

Half an hour later Dermod was summoned to the camp administration building and shown into an office which contained a green-uniformed officer seated behind a large, cluttered desk. The Guardsman indicated a chair.

"Major Dermod," he said briskly, "you have been chosen to fight in the coming war. What is more, your display of funk out there so impressed the Kelgian inspection team that they took you without even consulting your dossier. However, it is my duty at the moment to instruct you regarding the rules of conduct for the coming war.

"As the subject will be of necessity a somewhat blood-thirsty one," he added, smiling sardonically, "please try not to embarrass me by fainting again . . ."

As the meaning of the other's words sank in Dermod had to fight to keep the flood of relief and sheer jubilation he felt from showing in his face. *He was in!* Instead he tried to look shocked and apprehensive, the way an ordinary Earth soldier would look after being given such news.

The site of operations, the Guardsman explained, would be the usual one and the number of combatants had been fixed. No reinforcements would be allowed to make up losses in Humans or Kelgians, and in the unlikely event of an extended war only food supplies and replacements for war material already in use would be allowed. There would be no medical facilities except those furnished on request by the Guard.

The weapons allowed the Human side were chemically-powered rifles and pistols firing solid projectiles, and grenades. The Kelgian equipment would be basically similar but of a more advanced type firing explosive bullets . . .

Dermod half-rose out of his chair at that point, mouth open to protest. The thought of what an explosive bullet could do to a man gave him a suddenly unpleasant feeling in the pit of his stomach. He stammered, "But . . . but . . ."

"We consider," the officer continued firmly, "that the physiological disadvantages of the Kelgian life-form makes an advantage in fire-power only fair. You were about to say?"

"Only that you might have given them something more—well—humane."

"That is a word which does not apply in these circumstances," said the other coldly. "If acting humanely was your primary concern, the whole miserable bunch of you should have decided to stay at home. Now, do you have any other questions?"

Dermod had, but it would have been a dead give-away if the cowardly, frightened personality he was trying to portray had asked them. But he might be able to ask a few.

"The planet we'll be using has several large islands," Dermod said timidly, "I was wondering—"

"If you'd be allowed to play around with boats," the Guardsman broke in. "Well the answer is no. This will be strictly a land war."

"How about air support?"

The Guard officer shook his head again. "No fighter or bomber aircraft. A few light reconnaissance machines perhaps, if you can find anyone fool enough to fly them. Also, there will be no artillery, bombardment rockets or any other type of long-range weapon. You've started a big war this time and we mean to see that it is made as bloody and unpleasant as possible for each and every one of you.

"Any other questions? No? Then goodbye."

Inwardly seething, Dermod left the building where every look directed at his uniform was one of contempt, or scorn, or sardonic amusement. He was heartily sick of turning the other cheek to these sarcastic and sour-faced tyrants in Guard green; it was humiliating, infuriating and intensely frustrating, and this last session had been the worst yet. The only thing which stopped Dermod from taking a swing at one of those hateful faces—a very unwise thing to do in any case—was the thought that his days of submission to them would soon be over.

The first step in a bold and far-reaching plan had been successfully taken this afternoon when the man who called himself Major Jonathan Dermod had been picked for combat. The next step would be harder, because that same Major Dermod would somehow have to win a war. But the third and final stage would be the simplest of all, Dermod thought; nobody has to *help* an avalanche downhill ...

All around him the mighty Guard helicopters were dropping like great angry insects onto the landing areas. Others already down were disgorging long flat cases of rifles, and stores personnel busied themselves checking and carrying under the watchful eyes of tight-lipped Guardsmen with lading bills in their hands. Dermod swore under his breath in sheer helplessness as he watched. The men doing the fetching and carrying were those who had *not* been picked for combat, and these non-combatants would have all the hard work of getting the Seventeenth Earth Expeditionary Force ready for departure three weeks hence while the Combat men would be on leave until embarkation time. All of which was a nice illustration of how the outwardly benevolent Guard did its dirty work.

By rights the Combat men should have been kept hard at it, instead of being free to worry for three solid weeks about what was going to happen to them in the coming war.

It had not been like this in the old days, Dermod knew, and the choking ache of yearning caught once more at his chest and throat. In his mind the roar of the freight helicopters became the thunder of a thousand heavy bombers darkening a sky white-splattered with flak, or the Jovian rumblings of a massed artillery barrage. His association channels widened suddenly, his mind slid back to that distant, half-legendary past when life was bright and full and exciting.

The slipstream howled through the rents blown in his cockpit canopy by the enemy tail gunner, and a smear of oil on his goggles made it hard to see the instrument panel of the little fighter plane. But the big red button atop the control column was under his thumb and the only thing that mattered was the expanding image of the bomber centring his gunsight, seemingly pinned there by his eight white lines of tracer. His cannon fire bit, gouged and bludgeoned its way through the enemy's fuselage. Control surfaces tore free, shredded away, and a sudden glare of orange fire marked the end as fuel and bomb load let go together. The tiny plane rocked and shuddered as it ran into the expanding sphere of the explosion, then Dermod found himself being jolted about on the bucket seat in an even more cramped interior while he shouted instructions to his crew through the din and dust and hot oil smell of a tank engagement. Earth and stones fountained skywards around his ponderous mount, flying rock and shrapnel whanged off its armoured flanks and the cannon-shells of a ground-strafing aircraft tore up a furrow scant yards away from its churning metal treads. His machine-gunner was hammering away at the aircraft now, and all of Creation seemed to be made up of peal after peal of thunder and clouds of sharp-smelling blue smoke. And Dermod was striding the bridge of his heavy battleship while broadside after broadside crashed out and all around him was spread the most beautiful and inspiring sight of all, the tremendous, irresistible might of a naval task force deploying to meet the enemy ...

War, thought Dermod sadly as his mind returned reluctantly to the here and now, *had been fun in those days.*

When he returned to his quarters Dermod tried to make himself rest for a few hours, but it was no use. He felt an urgent need to talk over plans with the General again, especially *the* plan. But most of all he thought that he wanted a friendly hand on his shoulder and a confident voice to reassure him that what he planned to do would ultimately end in the greatest good for the largest number of intelligent beings. The General, unfortunately, who was a very reassuring person indeed, was on Kelgia at the moment picking the worst caterpillars he could find to fight against, and he would not be back on Earth for at least a week.

Abruptly coming to a decision, Dermod changed his uniform for civilian-style lounging overalls; he would submerge his doubts and uncertainties in work. For he knew that among the poor, confused but tradition-loving minority which comprised the lowest social strata in present-day Earth culture he was unique, possessing as he did knowledge of military tactics and strategy normally restricted to student Galactics. Further, he knew that the manner in which the coming war was fought depended on the morale of his men and, the Guard being what it was, Dermod knew that he personally would have to do his utmost to see that that morale remained reasonably intact until embarkation time. After that ... well, he had a few ideas which he was keeping to himself.

Dermod left the camp area and drove to the town which lay a few miles away. It was dusk and the streets were crowded with civilians, sensation-hunting Galactics and a liberal sprinkling of soldiers whose broad white belts proclaimed the fact that they had been picked for combat. At least one admiring female was attached to every uniform in sight so temporarily there was no morale problem there, Dermod thought. He parked and made for the nearest bar.

There were several combatants in the place, he saw as he took a table and worked the menu console briefly for a drink, most of them at the centre of noisy, excited groups. But at the table next to him sat a lieutenant with a preoccupied expression listening with great care to the words of an overweight and over-loud civilian who was buying him drinks. Dermod couldn't help eavesdropping.

". . . It was when we were fighting the Brelthi a few years back," the fat man was reminiscing loudly. "A small affair compared to this, you understand, but hot while it lasted. Those Brelthi octopoids are so big and awkward, you see, that the Guard allowed them anti-gravity belts— only one per being, of course, and the amount of lift pre-set—to give them more mobility. Well, what do you think the so-and-sos did? They started pooling belts—some of them doing without while others, wearing three or four of the things, took off and tried to pot at us from a couple of hundred feet up in the air. . . ! But we'd have won even then if the lousy Guardsmen hadn't . . ."

Looking at this veteran of the Brelthi-Earth incident Dermod decided that he was one of those worthless types who always manage to live through a war without actually fighting in it. Either that or he was a very low and dirty form of life indeed, because the point of his narrative had begun to shift subtly, and in a direction which Dermod did not like.

". . . But if you want my advice, friend, you grab yourself a nice safe job at Headquarters—you can usually find a spot in Catering if you're smart—and sit tight in it. The General Staff are just as anxious about their hides as anyone, and you can be sure that they'll run the war from a safe place." He paused and hunched himself closer, then dropped his voice meaningly. "I shouldn't be saying this, you know, but if you can't wangle anything like I mentioned and the going gets really sticky, well, I heard that if you contact the Guard and . . ."

"May I buy you a drink, Soldier?" Dermod cut in

quickly at that point, indicating the Lieutenant's two-thirds empty glass and dialling for two of the same. To the fat man he said harshly, "I heard what you've been saying to the Lieutenant here, and I'm ashamed of you! He's going to *fight* this war, aren't you, soldier, and if the rest of the Earth force looks as tough and competent as he does it won't be a long one!" Furiously, he added, "What are you anyway, an undercover Guardsman? You certainly talk like one!"

The fat man protested indignantly at this insinuation until the Lieutenant, still looking rather startled at the idea of anyone thinking him tough and competent, told him to go away. When his drink popped into sight before him he smiled faintly at Dermod and said "Thank you."

Chapter II

The Lieutenant was an imposing sight, Dermod thought; his tall, rather spare figure was well-suited to the maroon and grey uniform that had been designed for the Earth Expeditionary Force, and with the glittering, thigh-length boots and broad white belt—a hand-down from the traditional webbing worn with oldtime battledress—he made a splendid picture. Only the face surmounting that trim uniform was not soldierly and that bore, to express it in the kindest terms possible, a look of extreme anxiety. Again Dermod cursed the fat man under his breath, then in an effort to undo some of the damage the other's big mouth had wrought he said aloud, "Forget what that yellow slob's been telling you. You're going to fight, soldier, and what is more, you're going to win—this time things will be different.

"I'd like to talk to you for a bit," Dermod went on in tones of one who is asking a great honour. "Not for long, though, as I expect there's a girl or two waiting for a good-looking fellow like you and I wouldn't want—"

"No girls," the Lieutenant interrupted. "You see I'm married . . . just recently . . . and I, she . . ." He choked off into silence, his features working with emotion. For an awful moment Dermod thought he was going to burst into tears.

Dermod could see the whole pitiful picture. Young man picked for Combat, scared; young wife scared, forbids him to go. Dilemma. He quarrels, leaves to find courage in euphoriacs. *No guts, no backbone, no nothing,* Dermod thought disgustedly. And he was expected to fight a war with material like this!

Oh, *damn* the Guardsmen . . . !

For the Guard was motivated, they claimed, by a great and noble ideal; the granting of the maximum amount of freedom to every individual entity of every Galactic race. A being was free to engage in any activity whatsoever providing such activities did not infringe on the freedom of other beings. And if two groups of entities felt so strongly that their differences could be settled only by war, why then, the Guard arranged a war for them!

But life, the Guard proclaimed piously, was precious, and if it was to be lost at all then it must be lives of the least worth. With special teams from both sides picking out the worst soldiers in their opponent's forces—the Guardsmen obligingly put complete psychological dossiers at the disposal of these teams, in the interests, they stated, of fairness—this desire was achieved. Stated simply it meant that the best soldiers never got a chance to fight, that training such soldiers was therefore a waste of time, and that the individuals who did become soldiers and who were later picked to fight were the dregs of the dregs.

The reasons for a man joining the army these days, Dermod thought bitterly, ran the gamut from hysterical or weak-minded patriotism to the simple desire for a uniform with which to increase the chance of success in amatory adventures. If a soldier wasn't a moral louse then he was a psychological wreck.

But the Lieutenant could not help being what he was, and he was, after all, one of the officers on whom Dermod would have to depend in the weeks to come. A little psychological first-aid was indicated here, and quickly. Dermod ignored the imminent water-works and began to speak quietly, confidently and apparently casually about the coming hostilities. And gradually the other began to look less sorry for himself; he began putting in comments of his own and to show more and more interest. Too much interest, perhaps, because he grew suddenly suspicious.

Interrupting Dermod with a jerky wave of his hand, he said, "You keep saying that this war will be different, that the whole campaign won't just fall apart, as it usually does, into an unresolved and inglorious mess—a piece of farcical entertainment for the amusement of the Guardsmen! You keep telling me this over and over. How do you *know*? Who are you anyway ... ?" The Lieutenant stopped short at that point, his eyes lost their alcoholic dullness and became bright and penetrating. He said, "I've seen you somewhere, and recently. Yes! You . . . you're the Major who passed out when the crawler officers came by . . . !"

Dermod felt himself tightening up. This was bad, very, very bad. The Lieutenant might lack many qualities but his intelligence and powers of observation were certainly not at fault. And his voice had been growing steadily louder, and this—the story of the Major-Who-Fainted coming dressed as a civilian to give pep-talks to Combat men—was the sort of gossip which would spread around . . .

No smallest inkling of The Plan must become apparent until the war had actually begun. Everything depended on that. Somehow the Lieutenant had to be shut up.

". . . You," the other was continuing derisively, "are a fine one to talk about—"

"Silence!"

Dermod spoke quietly, but the rasp of authority was suddenly in his voice. "Listen to me, and when you answer keep your voice down!"

It was a desperate risk he was taking, but there was nothing else he could do. He would have to tell a little—just enough to insure the other's silence—in order to keep the Lieutenant from blabbing a lot of apparently senseless information which could, if it reached the ears of the wrong people, be pieced together to reveal The Plan in its entirety. He said curtly, "I fainted—rather, I *appeared*, to faint—deliberately. Consider, please, the implication behind that statement—if you're not too drunk, that is. When you have you will realise why this conversation must be kept secret, because you'll know that if the Guard even suspected what I have done ..."

Deliberately he left the sentence unfinished.

But the Lieutenant wasn't too drunk. Surprise and anger at Dermod's suddenly abrupt manner gave place to dawning comprehension. "You must have pulled a faint because you *wanted* to be picked to fight!" he said excitedly, and straight-away began jumping to wrong conclusions to follow his single right one. "And from what you've been saying, the way you seem so confident about everything, there must be others who have done the same thing ... !"

"You've got it," Dermod said quickly. "Now keep it to yourself. Another drink, soldier?"

The Lieutenant stood up, very straight, very proud, very serious. He said, "I don't think I will. It might make me talk too much tonight and give me a fuzzy head in the morning. From tomorrow on ..." His eyes shone and he seemed to be listening to the distant sound of bugles. ".... I want to be in top condition. I think I'll go home. Goodnight, sir."

His hand jerked spasmodically at his side in the beginnings of a salute before he remembered that Dermod was supposed to be a civilian, then he wheeled and marched out.

Dermod had a pleasant feeling of accomplishment as he rose and followed the Lieutenant out. He had allowed the man to think that there were others on the Earth side like Dermod, but that was the sort of misunderstanding which could help morale so he had let it pass. Mostly, however, he had succeeded in making one frightened man in uniform into a determined and enthusiastic soldier.

As Dermod left the bar, however, the reaction set in. Maybe it was the sight of a Guardsman stalking like a dark green spectre through the noisy, excited crowd, or perhaps it was seeing so many Galactics in the streets. The Earth-human Galactics—their proper designation was Galactic Citizens—regularly visited the settlements where their poor relations gathered because they thought the inhabitants romantic, swashbuckling figures who lived dangerous and colourful lives. The thought that an over-whelming majority of Earth's population was made up of these spineless and degenerate intellectuals filled Dermod with shame and disgust, the more so because he had once counted himself to be one of them. But mainly Dermod felt low because of a growing conviction that he was a single and very puny force trying to move the classic immovable object.

He had to remind himself repeatedly that the object *wasn't* immovable, only very, very big. And that it was so delicately balanced that a very small force indeed, if properly applied, would send it toppling.

Not only on Earth but on practically every other world in the Galactic Union the set-up was essentially the same. At the bottom of the social scale were the malcontents, who were generally neither too ethical nor well-educated, and grouped into settlements which varied in size from a large town to tracts of territory which took up a respect-able slice of a continent. And they were intensely, almost fanatically, proud of their glorious past. Because they believed that only among themselves was to be found the drive, idealism and sheer ruggedness of character that had typified the race in the past, they thought of themselves alone as being truly representative of their respective spe-cies.

However, in the case of Earth, which was a fairly average one, over ninety-five percent of the population consisted of Galactic Citizens. Apart from a small propor-tion of scientists and medical men, who admittedly did useful work, they were nothing but a great mass of ineffectual, pleasure-loving aesthetes who did not feel strongly about anything, least of all who ran things in the Galaxy. The Galactics, therefore, together with their hu-man and non-human equivalents on the other planets of the Union could be discounted as an effective force, which left only the Guard to be dealt with.

Dermod smiled mirthlessly to himself. *Only the Guard...*!

The force whose word was law in the Galaxy was not

stupid. Where the Galactics were concerned their control was practically non-existent, there being little likelihood of revolt from that quarter. In the settlements, however, the undercover and uniformed Guardsmen swarmed like flies. All over the Galaxy the settlements were trouble spots, potential foci for revolt, and the Guard knew it and took what it thought were the necessary precautions. But this time, Dermod was sure, the trouble piling up was more than even they could handle.

Straightening his shoulders Dermod threw off the last vestiges of his fit of depression; he had work to do. Turning into another bar he surveyed the place quickly. Two Combat NCOs were at a table discussing something in worried undertones. Dermod went across to them and sat down. He said, "May I buy you a drink, fellows . . . ?"

It was in this and many other ways that Dermod got to know a sizeable number of his men during the succeeding three weeks. He was not impressed. But he believed himself a good enough psychologist to think that his talks with them had done some good—his subject at the Galactics university, before the accident which had allowed him to make a clean break with his former life, had been History and Psychology. It was as if the restless young man of those days had possessed a precognitive faculty, because he could not have chosen a better combination of subjects to prepare him for the task which lay ahead.

Then all at once, with the embarkation of the Earth Expeditionary Force, the task was no longer of the future but of the immediate and urgent present.

Wafted upwards on the ghostly blue pillars of their pressor beams the twenty-seven Guard transports carrying the combatants and their equipment left Earth. Ten short days later—during which Dermod bullied, exhorted and shamelessly tricked the officers under him into accepting his new and alarming ideas on waging war—they were dropping onto War Planet Three, the world which had been set apart as being most suitable for use in wars between the warm-blooded oxygen-breathers of the Galaxy. But it was another two days before the emptied transports took off and the last of the Guard propagandists, who had insisted on travelling with the Earth force, left for their own base some five hundred miles away. Only then did Dermod breathe easy and, with the knowledge that no part of The Plan had been discovered by the Guardsmen, begin the opening moves of stage two.

He had at least four weeks in which to do pretty much as he pleased—that was the time normally taken for the officers and men to settle in, get used to their weapons and generally coax themselves into something approaching a fighting mood. Or conversely, that unfortunately large number of men who had taken seriously the demoralising stories of the propagandists planned ways of deserting. At the end of this period another Guard psychologist would come around with more unsettling talk, Dermod knew, and then the war would finally get under way.

That was the *usual* way the thing was done ...

Chapter III

On the first day free of Guard interference Dermod carried out a general inspection of the men. It was a deadly serious occasion, but as he slowly paced along the rigid lines of men he could not help feeling amused at the perplexity and sheer astonishment in the eyes which met his own. They all knew him, of course, to be the Major who had fainted at Enemy's Inspection—why now was he strutting around with a Colonel's insignia on his collar? And why was this recipient of such amazingly rapid promotion carrying out the inspection with only two NCOs attending him instead of a tail of junior officers? Why, for that matter, was there not a single commissioned officer to be seen on the whole parade ground ... ?

When Dermod had the men stood easy and mounted the small podium to address them it would have been the understatement of all time to say that he had their undivided attention. He stood silent for a few minutes, looking at them and hefting the microphone he carried from hand to hand, then he spoke:

"You men are curious about me," he began quietly,

"and with reason. Well, I'm not going to satisfy it. That job I'll leave to your officers for later this evening. Let it suffice to say that there have been certain things going on which had to be kept from the Guardsmen for a while, but now the need for secrecy where you men are concerned is gone. What I am now going to talk about is your enemy, his physical make-up, weapons and the most efficient methods of killing him. I will also touch on the tactics and strategic principles which will insure our winning this war."

Quite a few mouths dropped open at this cool assumption that they could accomplish something which had not been done for centuries. Dermod ignored them and continued:

"In a straight fight between a crawler and one of us there simply would be no contest," he said. "The Kelgians are nothing but great shapeless sacks of tegument and fur suffused with blood and other fluid matter, with no skeletal structure to speak of. A deep wound anywhere on their bodies if not treated quickly by special medical equipment causes them to bleed to death fairly quickly. We on the other hand are tough, which is why the Guard in an effort to even things up have given them explosive and us solid projectile ammunition. Even with this advantage in fire-power, however, I am still convinced that there will be no contest . . ."

They were not liking this part of it, not one little bit. He was forcing them to think in terms of a possible gory end for themselves. Hastily Dermod moved onto a slightly less morbid point, thinking bitterly as he spoke of the other Commanders throughout history who had harangued their men before battle: Henry at Agincourt, Montgomery at El Alamein, Claudius before the climactic battle which was to give him all of Britain. Those men had inspired such love, loyalty or idealistic fervour that their followers would willingly have given their lives for their superiors.

But these days it was not ideals a Commander stressed, nor did he exhort his men to Death or Glory. He promised instead to take good care of them; he guaranteed not Glory, but Safety.

". . . Make no mistake about it, men," Dermod went on, "the strategy I have in mind is going to cost lives, enemy lives. Where the safety of you men and myself is concerned—I intend to fight this war in front with you and not from the base here—there is a saying I have which covers the situation: We can't live forever, but we'll have a damned good try!

"Oh yes, you will be safe, men," he continued in a grim tone. "But safety does not lie in avoiding decisive contact with the enemy, in running away or in deserting. It lies in being able to kill your enemy before he can kill you; efficiently, quickly and with the minimum of fuss. You must fall on him while he's least expecting it—at feeding time, while he's asleep, and especially when he's thoroughly convinced that you're nowhere within a hundred miles of him. You must rise out of the very ground he's walking on and slay him before he even knows that he is being threatened. Look there!"

At a signal from Dermod the missing officers began moving onto the parade ground in a straggling single file, and immediately a howl of laughter went up from the men. But their usually resplendent and immaculately tailored officers continued to slouch past, out of step, crouching slightly and with heads moving restlessly from side to side. They were a ludicrous sight with their blackened faces, their shapeless, drab yet oddly familiar uniforms whose outlines were made vague by haphazard blotches of brown and green and dull yellow paint, not to mention the grimy netting draped from their helmets and the odd scraps of vegetation sticking to it. The only thing clean and shining were the rifles they carried.

Watching, Dermod gave himself a small pat on the back. His address to the men, up to now anyway, had not been the wheedling, cajolling and over-flattering kind that they had been expecting. Instead it had been so short and to the point that it had left most of them feeling stunned. But now was the psychological moment for a little comedy relief, the time to relax the tensions which had been built up and at the same time to teach a very important lesson . . .

The ragged file of officers spread out into line abreast and walked a few yards into the scrub which bordered the parade ground, then quietly, incredibly, they disappeared. The laughter died as if it had been switched off.

"I've very little more to say to you," Dermod resumed conversationally. "Not next month or next week, but to-morrow, you will begin learning how to become invisible— how to kill and how to be safe from the enemy. You will take those pretty uniforms you're wearing and rip off all the fancy work, and chop off those elegant boots below the calf—and if any of you spit and polish experts try to keep a shine on what's left I'll personally skin him alive. Then you'll daub paint and sew rags and hang greenery on yourselves until I won't know whether any one of you is a tree or just a bump in the ground of this God-forsaken planet. In short you'll learn the art of camouflage. And when the Guard psychologist comes round a month from now with his lying, unsettling talk, you will be well on the way towards winning the war.

"Because the enemy will not expect us to act so quickly, you see. They will still be busy just working up courage for a fight. So you will have the advantages of surprise, of tactics and fighting methods that are a complete departure from recent tradition as well as the purely physical ad-vantage—"

Someone started to cheer then and it was taken up. Dermod broke off, surprise and a mixture of other emo-tions silencing him momentarily. His every word had been calculated, a psychological push-button, but he had not expected such a strong response so quickly. He felt pleased yet at the same time contemptuous of these men who could be swayed so easily, and he was angry with himself for no good reason at all. Suddenly he bellowed, "Silence!"

When they had quietened down he went on, "As I was about to say, this purely physical advantage is of least importance. You are no longer human against caterpillar— you must sink all your softer emotions and instincts for the duration and become cold, merciless and efficient killers. From this day on you transcend the purely physical in that your job is a training and a philosophy and a way of life. You are such that no other race in the entire Galaxy will stand before you, for your occupation is . . . Warrior.

"And the cheering," he added, "will keep until you've won the war. Dismiss!

But they cheered their fool heads off anyway.

General Prentiss was waiting for him when he returned to the Operations Room. The General had done nothing since leaving Earth beyond conferring on Dermod the brevet rank of Colonel as had been previously arranged so that he would be the ranking officer on active service. Though possessed of a keen brain he neither was nor looked the part of a soldier, having risen to his position through politics. But it was Prentiss, when he had first met Dermod and realised the potentialities of the other's unique talents, who had put to him the first rough outlines of what was later to become The Plan.

Returning Dermod's salute casually, the General said, "I was listening to you, Colonel, and you have them practically eating out of your hand." He smiled slyly. "Now what?"

Dermod felt a brief resurgence of the awkwardness he sometimes felt before this small, podgy man with the restless eyes who was the political and military leader of all the non-Galactics population of Earth. He would have been happier if Earth's leader had been made of sterner stuff, but supposed that the Guardsmen took good care to see that the strong-minded individuals did not rise to positions of power. But he wished the General would be less ingratiating towards his subordinates, and not smile so much, and generally act more like a General . . .

Hastily pushing such thoughts out of his mind as being unjust and unworthy, Dermod replied, "Next we will have a Signal Victory. Nothing big, you understand—it may be only a clash between patrols—but it must be decisive enough to convince the men that they are unbeatable. If they firmly believe that, then they *are* unbeatable. What I had in mind was something like this . . ."

"Sounds all right," said the General when Dermod had finished. He got to his feet, smiled his sly smile again and left. Dermod, who had been about to suggest that the General go over some of the longer-term plans with him, shook his head irritably, then went over and locked the door. He settled down for a long, uninterrupted think.

War Planet Three—nobody thought enough of it to give it a proper name, though it had several improper ones— was one of several uninhabited worlds set aside by the Guard for the business of conflict on the purely physical level. The others had environments suited to chlorine-breathing life-form, or underwater species, or even forms of life which lived by the direct conversion of solar-energy. But Three was suitable, just barely, for warm-blooded oxygen-breathers so it was here that the Guard had dumped the Earth-humans and Kelgians to fight their war.

The planet had nothing at all to recommend it beyond its atmosphere. The single vast, diamond-shaped continent which lay along its equator was nothing but a monotonous expanse of near-desert broken by low, barren mountains and criss-crossed by ravines and gullies and dried-up river-beds. The few islands which made up the rest of the planet's land mass were simply smaller editions of the one and only continent. Yet vegetation grew with surprising profusion on this bleak terrain—thick, coarse-leafed plants that carpeted the surface with brown and dull green and sickly yellow. But the plant-life was unable to support any animal species above a couple of inches in size, nor was it profuse enough to keep down the dust.

This, then, was the battleground.

A little over two hundred miles eastwards lay the Kelgian base, and approximately five hundred miles due North was the small establishment maintained by the Guard. All of the area in between was simply a vague blur to Dermod at the moment, a very hazy battleground indeed. Until he could draw accurate maps and obtain detailed photographs of the intervening territory there was very little he could do.

Having decided that no planning was possible until such details were available, Dermod decided to call it a day.

Chapter IV

Next morning the campaign got under way. Formed up in four battalions of roughly two thousand men each, with Bandsmen and their reproducers positioned at intervals along the lines, the Earth Expeditionary Force marched smartly out of the Base. The four columns gradually drew apart as they headed for their separate areas of operation until they were hidden by the dust of the supply trucks tailing them. Dermod stopped watching them at that point and returned for consultations with his Air Arm.

This consisted of Lieutenants Dowling, Clifton and Briggs together with about thirty maintenance men. The latter were included in the two thousand or so supply, transport and clerical personnel which Dermod had decided would be absolutely hopeless as fighting men—they were the cowardly cowards as opposed to the potentially brave cowards who had just left, though even they would be given the same training when their duties allowed it. The three Lieutenants, on the other hand, were special, hand-picked cowards.

All three possessed the type of personality which functioned best when alone, all at one time or another had owned helicopters and so were not afraid of height, and all were individuals who developed enthusiasm quickly and were easily led. Lieutenant Clifton, the man Dermod had encountered in the bar on the night after he was picked for combat, was particularly impressionable and he had been made the leader.

"Sit down, gentlemen," Dermod said when they had filed in. "I don't want to hang around here any longer than necessary so we'll keep this brief.

"While we were landing in the transports," he began briskly, "I had you men at the viewports photographing the terrain, and although some of the results were good they only give a rough idea of the surface of the continent we are at present occupying. Now I require the *fine* details—every mountain, pass, hole in the ground, or bush.

This data is of vital importance if I am to formulate tactics that will ensure the irreducible minimum of casualties on our side. I suggest also that you do your mapping in the early morning or late afternoon, when longer shadows will give a truer idea of surface contours." He paused then, and made his tone at once serious and faintly apologetic as he went on. "You men have a lonely, hard, at the same time boring job, but you are three of the most important people in the whole force. On your work depends our whole future strategy.

"Your first assignment is to map the territory between here and the enemy base but without—I repeat, *without*—going near that base. We do not want them to suspect that we've already commenced operations against them.

"That is all," Dermod ended, smiling, "except that I want Lieutenant Clifton to fly me out to the heads of the four columns. The rest of you tag along and practise your formation flying for the general edification of your ground-bound brothers. Thank you, gentlemen. Dismiss."

Dermod flew out to the four battalions, now spread over thirty miles of territory, and said a few words of encouragement to the officers in charge. The visits were not strictly necessary but Dermod had promised that he would fight with and lead his men, and he did not want to give a bad impression by staying at the base. While Clifton and himself were thus engaged the other two aircraft performed clumsy aerobatics at an extremely safe height. The hypno-tapes which the flyers had taken gave complete knowledge of how to operate their machines—but knowledge was not skill, that only came with practise. At the conclusion of his visits Dermod signalled the planes to form a V-formation and they headed in the direction of the enemy base.

An arrowhead of jets screaming and thundering towards the enemy lines would have been much more stimulating to the eyes of the men below, Dermod thought sadly, but even in these three small aircraft there was powerful symbolism.

From two thousand feet Dermod thought that his command did not look like anything much. Each column had been allocated three half-treads—for scouting ahead and on each flank—and twelve balloon-tyred trucks for supply duties. The scouts were in their proper positions even though there was no chance of the crawlers attacking so soon, but Dermod had wanted his officers to learn good habits early. The number of supply vehicles had been nicely calculated to allow proper service without giving surplus space for the lazy types to hitch rides; he wanted everybody to be as hard and fit as possible.

And the battalions themselves were no longer orderly columns of marching men, they had become like chopped-up worms with little eddies and patches of men either pacing or motionless behind them. Training had begun and the combatants were already learning how to shoot, how to throw rocks—they were still too butterfingered to be allowed to practise with real grenades—and how to attain the invisibility of the perfect chameleon. Dermod had had the idea of sending each company forward in turn with instructions to ambush their marching comrades, and this seemed to be working out very well indeed: it taught the marchers to be observant and the ambushers to be quick in concealing themselves, because they had to run fast to get ahead of the column and in the heat of the afternoon they did not feel like running too far.

Dermod watched until the units of his command shrank and disappeared over the horizon behind him, then he turned his attention forward.

Immediately on his return to base Dermod called up the General, because during the flight a disquieting thought had occurred to him. He said, "Sir, we were allowed three aircraft for our use. What did the crawlers get extra?"

"How should *I* know," said the General, and laughed. "Possibly anti-aircraft guns. Are you worried?"

"No, sir," said Dermod shortly, and rang off.

He was angered at the other's light-hearted dismissal of the matter. Couldn't the General see that if it *was* A-A guns, those same guns could also be used as ground artillery? But it would hardly be anti-aircraft weapons,

Dermod told himself; that would be too straightforward a solution for the Guard. For the Guardsmen were fair, fiendishly fair, and Dermod was now sure that if they had not told the Earth side what they were giving the Kelgians to balance the three aircraft, then neither had they told the enemy that the Earth forces possessed those aircraft. Dermod resolved to keep his possession of the planes a secret for as long as was possible.

But as he retired that night he could not help wondering what surprise the crawlers would spring on them. It quite ruined his sleep.

Two days later Lieutenant Clifton returned from a flight fairly stuttering with excitement. When Dermod had him calmed down he reported that he had observed an enemy column leaving the Kelgian base. Their direction of movement was not towards the Earth forces, but inclined southwards by an angle of about forty degrees. He had not been near enough to get an accurate idea of their numbers or composition but . . .

Dermod cut him short at that point, making no attempt to hide the anger he felt: "You were ordered not to go near that base!"

Pride and the confident expectation of a pat on the back changed to growing dismay as Clifton said hurriedly, "It was a navigational error, sir. But I stayed west of them all the time, in the sun. And the updraught from a mountain let me stay there with my engine shut off so they didn't even hear me. I could have glided there all day—"

"How close exactly were you?"

"Six, maybe seven, miles."

At a distance of six miles and his machine hovering silently in the glare of the sun, Dermod thought that it was next to impossible that Clifton had been spotted. As he thought of the Lieutenant simultaneously holding his plane in that updraught, keeping it between the sun and his objective and somehow managing to keep that objective under observation through his glasses, Dermod found his anger evaporating. Clifton had displayed considerable cleverness and initiative. But at the moment he looked as one momentarily expecting the wrath of God to descend on him. Dermod smiled suddenly and said, "Relax, Clifton. You did the wrong thing but used your head to turn it to our advantage. I like that. Do you think you can do it again?"

Clifton nodded eagerly. "It's very mountainous and there are always up-currents just before sunset."

"Good. Then you will keep that enemy column under observation at that time every day, and report their movements to me wherever I am. But," Dermod concluded with great emphasis, "if there's the slightest risk of your being seen, pull out at once. Understood? Very good, Clifton, dismiss."

When the Lieutenant had gone Dermod settled back to think. So the crawlers had sent out a column, the numbers and composition of which was still unknown. Dermod could, however, make a good guess at the type of beings making it up, as well as the reasons for their commander sending them out so soon. If Dermod had been the usual type of Earth officer he would have been doing something similar at the moment.

In every army these days there was a proportion who, besides being just no good themselves, exerted a very bad influence on the others—the bad apples in a barrel of already over-ripe fruit. While the training and general morale-boosting of the others went on in and around the base, these individuals were usually sent out on some mission of small importance—such as scavenging for material abandoned in previous wars—to get them out of the way. Usually they hid out or deserted and their commanders considered them small loss. But Dermod had done the reverse to this, keeping his bad apples at base and his best men in the field from the start where, if things worked out as he hoped, his best would soon make contact with the worst of the enemy . . .

After a second report from Clifton next day, Dermod angled his first and second battalions southward to head them off—though as yet his men knew nothing of the enemy force. Training continued steadily and without pause. On the third day out from the base it began to lose the aspect of being a new, exciting game to the men as muscles and joints protested against such highly unusual exercise. From the fourth to the sixth day the effects of their training were beginning to show in their quicker responses to orders, their great physical stamina and their increased self-confidence, but they were becoming so stiff and weary that they were about ready to mutiny.

But Dermod kept hounding them. When a party from the third battalion found, while scavenging, a crate of peculiar, alien-shaped brackets he decided that whatever they had been used for once they would make perfect entrenching tools now, so to the training syllabus was added instruction on how to dig a foxhole actually while under fire from an enemy—by pushing a mound of earth up in front and using this rough cover to dig in deeper. The men did not object too much to the exertion or dirtiness of the process, but the soil in the area was crawling with insect life which seemed to be all teeth.

The personnel in the scout cars were definitely the most comfortable men in the whole army, until one of them found a wrecked and half-buried oil tanker from some previous conflict. Dermod salvaged enough scrap metal from it to armour the cabs of his scout cars against everything but a hand-grenade lobbed in at close range. But the driving cabs became unbearably hot at midday and just bearably so for the rest of the time between dawn and sunset, so the result was that the drivers felt ten times safer, performed their jobs much more efficiently because of this and grew as murderously angry as everyone else.

By the ninth day they were all so tired, sore and irate that they were ready to fight with each other. But on that day Dermod had lined up for them a small force of the enemy . . .

Chapter V

On the face of it the whole plan looked so easy—Clifton insisted that it possessed Classic Simplicity—that Dermod felt a little ashamed of it. He had had the crawler column under such close observation for the past six days that he could almost tell the direction and distance they would travel to within a couple of miles and a few degrees of arc. As well as knowing the enemy's mind he also knew every hill, gully and potentially useful patch of vegetation in the area where he had decided the first clash would take place. So the trap he set—using the men of the second battalion and positioning them in the underbrush along both slopes of a valley which the enemy column was almost certain to use—was fool-proof, and as well as possessing the element of surprise his men outnumbered the crawlers by about six to one!

But to make absolutely certain, to be *sure* the enemy used this valley and not the slightly more difficult pass to the south or the dried-up riverbed to the northeast, the trap had to be baited.

Dermod gave a lot of thought to the type of person who would best fill the role of cheese in the mouse-trap. Everything hinged on this first blow at the enemy being successful. Finally he decided that the only person whose abilities and understanding of the situation he could be absolutely sure of was himself.

So that was why, on the ninth day after leaving Base and two hours before noon, Dermod and the Sergeant driver of the scout-car which was concealed some distance behind them lay motionless in the undergrowth watching the approach of the crawler column. The Sergeant, a man called Davis, kept up a continual and luridly derogatory criticism in whispers: the Kelgians were like unprintable snails, they made his skin crawl the way they humped themselves along, and how such slow-moving, awkward and generally loathsome creatures had the nerve to think they could fight Humans was beyond the Sergeant.

Dermod let him continue unchecked, knowing that Davis was merely trying to reassure himself by negating the importance of the enemy, until the crawlers were within two hundred yards of them. At that distance the enemy column, which had resembled nothing so much as a sluggish river of mercury rolling towards him, was beginning to show as separate, silver-furred entities; and the low, eerie humming which, to a form of life which undulated on its stomach was probably the equivalent of a rousing quick march, was plain enough to make his scalp prickle.

Dermod said, "Quiet, Davis. Back to the car!"

With Dermod in the observer's seat Davis sent the scout-car charging out of its concealment and into full view of the enemy. He halted it momentarily as if taken by surprise, then turned and made off in the direction of the valley where Dermod had set his trap. Looking through the rear observation slit a few seconds later, Dermod confidently expected to see the crawlers in hot pursuit of what they must think was a lone enemy scout-car taken by surprise. But instead it was the crawlers who were surprised apparently, and frightened. Instead of giving chase the sudden appearance of the car had thrown them into confusion—they were milling about in disorder and some of them had even begun to move back . . . !

Dermod swore. "Outside, quick!" he ordered. "Lie down and pretend to tinker with the engine, pretend we're in trouble. No, better still," he amended hastily as Davis was dropping to the ground beside him, "spill some oil on the bushes there and set fire to it . . ."

A few seconds later Dermod could not see the Kelgians for yellow, greasy smoke—Davis certainly had not spared the oil! But the crawlers had at last caught onto the idea that the Earth scout-car was in trouble. Bullets began whining at them through the smoke to explode somewhere far ahead. Then two hit the side of the armoured cab above them, loosening one of the sections of plating.

"Inside!" Dermod shouted. But the Sergeant had anticipated him and if Dermod had been a split-second slower Davis would have been away without him.

The explosive bullets were bursting all around them now, pelting the sides of the car with an erratic hail of flying earth, rock-fragments and shrapnel. But the direct hits were the worst—the noise of exploding projectiles expending their force against the metal of the cab jarred his brain like a physical blow. He was tossed about in his seat like a rag doll by the jolting of the car, the cab interior was stifling hot and the place reeked of fuel from a sprung oil line somewhere.

In an odd, objective corner of his mind he wondered how he could have been such a fool to think this sort of thing pleasantly exciting, while at the same time he used his foot to kick Davis's off the accelerator so that they would not outpace the enemy. The Sergeant's instructions had been to keep just beyond grenade range and to handle his vehicle in a manner which would suggest to the enemy that he was alone and panic-stricken. Because he really was panic-stricken by this time Davis tended to ignore the first half of his instructions while unconsciously obeying the second half to the letter. So this vicious game of footsie continued until the slopes of the valley where Dermod's men were posted went jerking past the observation slits, and still the scout-car fled.

All of the enemy column had to be inside the valley before the trap was sprung; Dermod had stressed that part repeatedly. Now he wished that he had not been so definite in the matter.

For the constant stream of explosive bullets was picking and tearing at the armour plating surrounding the cab, and the damage being done to unarmoured sections of the vehicle could only be imagined. The smell of fuel was so strong now that it hung like a choking, stinking fog. Then suddenly there was a sharp *clang*. Something metallic screeched across the back of his bucket seat, a violent tug at his shoulder-padding slewed him round and simultaneously something else tore a line of fire across his cheek. Bright, glaring sunlight flooded into the driving cab where sunlight had no right to be, and the fact of the gaping hole which had just been blown in the protective plating had barely registered in Dermod's noise-numbed brain when a sickening vibration shook the vehicle. With a scream of stripped gears it ground to a halt.

Davis, his mouth wide open and face contorted was clawing at the door handle. Dermod shouted at him to stay inside, but couldn't even hear his own voice above the noise, and grabbed his arm just as he succeeded in getting it open. An explosive bullet caught the Sergeant full in the face, his whole head burst into bloody jam and he fell back inside. Dermod let go his arm hastily ana slammed the door shut again.

But the cab's interior was getting hotter and hotter despite the air blowing through the great tear in the plating. Dermod's feet were burning, the floor was beginning to glow red and fire shone through the sprung seams. He would have to get out of here, and risk the crawler bullets—the alternative was to be burned alive. He yanked frantically at the door handle. For a heart-stopping second it stuck, then Dermod tumbled out and wriggled and rolled frenziedly away from the scoutcar. He was only a matter of yards away from it when the fuel tanks caught and it went up with a roar.

As he rolled away from the blistering heat a new sound battered at his senses, the thunder of nearly two thousand rifles crashing out as one. He lay still then while the Human rifle fire gradually slackened off and the peculiar mewing, bubbling noises which came from no human throat had also died away. Then slowly he rolled onto his back and sat up.

Singly and in tumbled heaps the crawler column lay like so many bulging, shapeless sacks that leaked bright pink—crawler blood was an improbably pastel shade compared with Human—and excited groups of his men surrounded them. He would have to order the crawler dead buried, Dermod thought tiredly, and their transport camouflaged for future use by himself. Most important those deadly, explosive-projectile rifles would have to be cached away safely, and men trained to use them. No smallest trace of what had happened here must be left for possible discovery by the Guard. And he would have to say a few congratulatory words to his men.

All at once Dermod felt an intense aversion towards doing any of those things. He wanted only to get away from this place, and the memory of Davis's head. He wanted to go back to Base and surround himself with books and maps and the theoretical problems of war, because the practical side of it had turned out so much less pleasant than he had expected. But he had his duty to perform, he told himself as he climbed slowly to his feet and walked away from the burning scout-car, he had a war to win.

The victorious Second marched back to base and were joined there within a few days by the others. Training continued with undiminished intensity in the vicinity of the base, the only difference being that the men wore their spare full dress uniforms of maroon and grey instead of the new combat garb—the Guard psychologist was expected daily and Dermod did not want him to notice anything too unusual. For the Guardsmen had sharp eyes and there were enough inconsistencies for him to spot even as things were.

And the Guard psychologist did spot something wrong, something terribly, inexplicably wrong from his point of view. He came bursting into the Operations Room, then occupied by the General, a Lieut-Colonel (Supply) called Simons and Dermod, and he was in a towering rage.

Apparently he had just finished addressing the men, having given them the usual guff about his organisation being both benevolent and at the same time champions of the ideal of maximum freedom for the individual, and that while the Guard would naturally allow them to make war if they wanted to, it felt grave concern over the fact that so many promising young men were intent on getting themselves killed. He had dwelt at length and in gory detail, as only Guard psychologists knew how, on the manner of death which could overtake them if they persisted in their folly. He had appealed to them to take instead the intelligent, more civilised course and continue to live instead of dying horribly in screaming agony . . .

Normally a quarter of those present could be expected to desert after an address like that, the Guardsman knew, and the rest would be so demoralised that the war would simply peter out in a matter of weeks. But this time he wasn't getting through to them at all. And when he had tried to tackle some of them individually they either laughed at him or walked away!

Dermod cursed under his breath when he heard that part of it. He had told the men over and over how to behave when the Guard psychologist was talking to them. But the men of the Second had been blooded in battle—

they strutted about the base like conquering heroes—and the men of the other battalions were begging Dermod to lead them to similar or even greater glories. There was scarcely a man in the whole base who looked or acted like the coward which he in fact was.

But they could have tried harder, Dermod thought angrily as he listened to the Guardsman's tirade.

". . . Just what is happening here, anyway?" the psychologist was shouting. "Those men have become *fanatics!* That's the only word to describe them. I don't like that, it's not our policy to allow—"

"You were late in visiting us," the General interrupted slyly, "so I presume you spoke to the crawlers first. How many of them did you get to desert?"

"None of *our* men will desert," Lieut-Colonel Simons put in boastfully, "so that means we'll start the war with a numerical advantage. We'll eat them up!"

Simons was in charge of catering and supplies—being a senior officer possessed of several well-developed neuroses, which included panic reaction to sudden noise, the inability to sleep outdoors and the impossibility of sleeping at all without a light in his bedroom, that was the only duty he was capable of handling—and had never been off the base. But he, too, had been caught up in the martial fervour currently suffusing the place. Dermod swore again. Both Simons and the General had been told that they must eat humble pie with the Guardsman—also grovel, lick his boots and scurry at his beck and call—so that he would take himself off as soon as possible and let them get on with the war in peace. Instead of that they were actually *baiting* the psychologist!

And by their stupid, unthinking boastfulness they were jeopardising the whole Plan . . .

Dermod mumbled something hastily to the General, excused himself and left the room. In the outer offices were Clifton and two NCOs. He told them exactly what he wanted done, then waited the ten minutes necessary for their astonishment to abate sufficiently so that they could do it. There might be no need for the precautions he was taking, but from the way the meeting next door was being mishandled ... He shook his head and angrily re-entered.

". . . Somebody or something has infected these men with delusions of heroism," the Guardsman was saying in tones equally mixed with anger and contempt. "Well, we'll see how that delusion stands up when the Kelgians start blowing chunks out of their bodies with explosive bullets and—"

"They'll stand, don't worry!" Simons broke in again, so carried away with excitement that his voice had gone falsetto. "We licked them once and we'll—"

"*Simons!*" Dermod barked suddenly, unable to contain himself any longer. "Shut you're blasted trap!"

The Guardsman looked startled, then suddenly thoughtful. Finally he stood up and said quietly, "The whole situation here is wrong. From a slip just made by the Lieut-Colonel I've learned that you have fought an engagement with the Kelgians which even their commander does not know about! Yet I am convinced that it occurred from the high morale of the men here. Also, I do not know of any army where a Major can tell a Lieut-Colonel to shut up. So until these points are cleared up I am calling this war off. The necessary transports will be sent for just as soon as my copter takes me back to Guard Base—"

The General and Simons both started to protest, their faces pale with the realisation of where their over-confidence and loose talk had landed them. Dermod took a grim delight in watching them stew in their own juice. It was General Prentiss who became coherent first:

"But you can't do that! The rules say that if you don't dissuade a certain proportion of us from fighting then the war can go on without interference from the Guard until one or both forces decide to—"

"What I see here," the Guardsman cut in, "smacks of a well-planned and extensive conspiracy, so the rules can go hang. We made 'em so we can break 'em. Good-day, gentlemen."

Dermod had unobtrusively placed his elbow on the outer office buzzer when he saw how events were shaping. Now he got up quickly and held open the door for the Guardsman. He smiled when the psychologist stopped dead in the doorway, then turned and said stiffly, "Very dramatic. What does it mean?"

Closing the door again on the six men wearing combat garb, purposeful looks and rifles carried at the port who formed a threatening semi-circle outside it, Dermod said awkwardly, "I've never done this before, so don't know the formula. You're under arrest. Now I think I'm required to disarm you."

The Guardsman actually smiled. Indicating the caduceus on his collar, he said, "The Med and Psych branch don't carry arms, except as protection against non-intelligent carnivorous life-forms." He gave a meaningful look that took in the base and everyone in it and added sardonically, "My mistake."

The General and Simons were looking utterly stunned by Dermod's action. He left them that way and trailed by the guard detail, conducted the psychologist out of the building. As they were crossing the parade ground the Guardsman's copter—useless so far as Dermod was concerned because he had no hypno-tapes on how to handle it—was being wheeled out of sight, and Clifton's aircraft took off . . .

Next day the Earth Expeditionary Force was on the move again.

Chapter VI

Dermod had addressed them very briefly while they had been drawn up in marching order just before leaving. He had said that the Second Battalion had covered itself with glory already, but only because they had been the ones nearest to that crawler column—it could have been any one of the four. They all had been given equal training and now everyone would get a chance to use it on the enemy. He wasn't going to exhort them to fight, or coax or flatter them into it, or even use full-blown phrases about their duty to their planet and that he expected every man to do that duty. As men of Earth, some of the few left who were still conscious of their world's glorious, pre-Space Age traditions, he did not expect them to fight. As beings who in the past had been the greatest race of warriors ever known, he knew they would.

He had added that the heroic Sergeant Davis had been the only casualty so far, and that if they all remembered everything they had been taught and kept cool when situations arose which seemed to be dangerous for them, then it was quite conceivable that Davis would be the only casualty. That was the way he and, he was sure, everybody else wanted it. Dermod had ended sternly with the warning that if any stupid over-excitable idiot did something silly and got himself shot then he would personally strangle him with his own two hands.

They had marched out then, cheering, and Dermod had taken off with Lieutenant Briggs to check on the disposition of scout cars and flanking parties. Clifton had not returned, of course, and as the shadows of Dermod's plane flickered back and forth across the columns of marching men two thousand feet below he wondered if he would ever see the Lieutenant again. He was depending on Clifton for a really vital mission, and if the flyer was dead, if his mangled or charred body was even now lying amid the wreckage of his machine somewhere en route to the Guard base, Dermod did not know what he was going to do. When Briggs set him down beside his scout-car nobody had any idea just how unsure of himself their commander was feeling.

Dermod pulled himself into the unprotected back of the scout-car and banged on the cab plating for the driver to start. The car moved off with a lurch which sent Dermod flopping into the vacant seat beside the Guardsman. He had decided to take the psychologist along rather than risk holding him prisoner at the base where some of the impressionable types might have been talked into letting him go. At the moment the Guardsman was watching everything with an intense, almost clinical curiosity. His eyes had an absent look, as if in his mind he was already working on a paper about all this for one of his professional journals.

Suddenly the psychologist spoke:

"How did you do it, Major—I mean Colonel?" he said sardonically. "I've heard some of your men talking about you, and you're nothing less than a legendary figure. And I'm interested in this great battle you won . . ."

"It wasn't a great battle," Dermod said irritably. He was feeling strangely dissatisfied with himself and anxious about Clifton, not to mention the fact that he was worried sick about the effects of recent events on The Plan. And the General was acting like a frightened old woman and not backing him up at all—Dermod's arrest of the Guardsman, the only move he could have made in the circumstances, had scared the General nearly to death. But as Dermod continued he had his feelings enough under control to keep his voice pitched too low for the driver to overhear him. He said, "We outnumbered them nearly six to one and we took them by surprise. It was a victory, but not a battle."

"Call it what you like," said the Guardsman, "my chief concern is the casualty list. There were two hundred and fifty-three beings in that column you ambushed—I found that out at the Kelgian base—and that life-form is easily damaged as you know. What percentage was killed, and where are the prisoners?"

"There were no prisoners."

"You . . . you killed them all?"

Dermod nodded.

For the rest of the day the Guardsman did not speak. His face was pale and he did not look at all well, and he sat as far away from Dermod as he possibly could.

The Guardsman remained untalkative for the four days which followed, during which Briggs and Dowling kept the crawler base under aerial surveillance. They reported that the enemy was scattered in groups of five hundred or so in the hills which surrounded their base, apparently engaged in general training manoeuvres. Except for the evening of the second day when they had set fire to a sizeable area of vegetation—very likely through carelessness with their explosive bullets—there was nothing unusual in the reports.

It had been on that same evening that Dermod had

decided it was no longer necessary to hide his possession of aircraft from the enemy, because Dowling had returned from his flight with two bullet holes in his wing-tip. Dowling, pasty-faced with fear, had told Dermod on landing that if those bullets had connected with the structural member instead of going through the fabric without exploding they might have wrecked the plane and he would have been killed. His colleague Briggs was present at the time and agreed with him. Both informed Dermod that they would not fly again.

It had taken three hours and all of Dermod's powers of persuasion to make them change their minds, and when they did it was only on condition that they did their observing well beyond the range of crawler fire. Reports on bulk movements of the enemy continued to be accurate but in the finer details—specifically data on what it was the crawlers had been given to balance his three aircraft— Dermod knew nothing. If only he had Clifton ...

All his plans and operations so carefully being worked out in advance were like structures raised on sand if Clifton had been unsuccessful. Yet he had to keep on, knowing all the time that at any moment a Guard warfleet could come screaming down to wreck everything.

And gradually he was coming to hate the General for a weak-willed, frightened old woman: Prentiss was continually ordering him to send the Guard prisoner back to the Earth base, obviously to arrange some sort of deal with him. He was beginning to hate himself also for his part in this great and noble crusade to release the Galaxy from the tyranny of the Guard, because he more than suspected that the bulk of the population were just too apathetic to care one way or the other. But most of all he hated what he was doing to his men.

Dermod was in the state of mind where he did not know whether he wanted a soft shoulder or a whipping boy when on the fifth day the Guardsman decided to re-open conversation—almost at the point where he had previously left off.

He said quietly, "You must understand, Colonel, that we Guardsmen get around a lot. In our perhaps peculiar view nearly all forms of intelligent life are of equal worth, so that the death of so many Kelgians affects me as strongly—or to be completely honest, very nearly as strongly—as the slaughter of an equal number of Earth-humans. Why was it necessary to kill them all, do you contemplate doing the same thing again, and how do you manage to sleep nights?"

"Taking your questions in reverse order," said Dermod heavily, "First, none of your business. Second: I plan to attack the enemy again, and often. Finally, it was not necessary to kill all of them, but the safest course was to do so. Furthermore, I could not have stopped—"

"I know, I know," the Guardsman interrupted. "I've heard all about Davis and yourself and the exploit in the scout-car. But could you not have given orders to take prisoners instead of simply butchering two hundred and fifty—"

"I could not!" Dermod cut in angrily. "Put yourself in my position for a moment. If I had ordered that the column be ambushed but not all of its members killed— that only the crawlers who resisted strongly were to be killed and the others who appeared to be demoralised or frightened were to be taken prisoner—and remember that you forbid us the use of Translators, or even radio for communications between ourselves—I would have been introducing a multiplicity of objectives into the operation, which invariably causes confusion. Some of the crawlers being taken prisoner would have misunderstood what we were trying to do and panicked, or even tried to rally, and a large number of humans would have been killed or injured.

"I can't allow that to happen to my men," Dermod ended grimly, "because if they sustained casualties in anything but very small numbers they would take to their heels. The only way to make soldiers of them was to train them to fight with safety. That means few or no prisoners I'm afraid."

"You certainly have your problems," the Guardsman said in tones oozing with mock sympathy. He was silent for several minutes while the car bounced and lurched across a dried-up river bed and ploughed through the scrub on the other side. Then he asked suddenly, "Do you realise what you're doing?"

Dermod sighed. He said tiredly, "Yes. I am taking men who are lacking in all the finer qualities—courage, self-discipline, unselfishness, a code of ethics—and encouraging them to get used to and like the killing. And as you know yourself it is the cowards, weaklings and bullies who, once they have been shown how, make the most vicious and sadistic killers. That was demonstrated at the ambush . . ."

"You must feel real proud of yourself," said the Guardsman drily, "to have accomplished so much."

Dermod regarded him levelly for several seconds, then said, "What do you think?"

The Guardsman looked thoughtful. "A couple of minutes ago I would have said yes, you do, to that. Now I'm not sure what I think . . ." He trailed off into silence and remained that way for the rest of the afternoon.

Chapter VII

Two days later Dermod's army was traversing the rising ground below the foothills of the ring of mountains which surrounded the crawler base, and his plan was to contact—and eliminate a sizable portion of—the enemy on the day following. He was forced to direct operations from the ground now, the terrain being impossible for landing aircraft. Dowling and Briggs had to drop their reports to him on the way to the spot a few miles back which they used as a landing ground. For reasons of fuel economy Dermod no longer allowed them to return to the Earth base after each flight, so that the only contact he had with the General was through the supply trucks, which meant a two-day delay in each direction. Not that that mattered, because Prentiss was still jittering about his temerity in arresting one of the all-powerful Guardsmen, and his messages were no help to Dermod at all.

There was still no news of Clifton.

It was while they were moving off after the midday meal that Dermod said, "If you would tell me what it was you gave the crawlers to balance out against our three aircraft, I could alter my strategy accordingly and perhaps save a number of lives."

"Human or Kelgian?" asked the Guardsman derisively.

"Human, of course."

The other shook his head. He indicated the marching men, the music, everything, with a wave of his hand. Each Bandsman's equipment had been programmed for the same piece—not the rousing, cheerful and light-hearted marches of their training period but a slower theme which used a nice blend of muffled drums and distant bugles, what Dermod called eve of battle music. The men were drab, black-faced apparitions hung with grenades and rifles—some of them the awkward-looking type which had been captured at the ambush, with the curled stock designed for crawler appendages—and their every movement told of complete self-confidence and even eagerness to do battle. "Look at them," the Guardsman said, "every one a hero! Or maybe hysteric is a more accurate description—a weak-willed individual temporarily overwhelmed by his own delusions. A few nice, gory casualties might shock them back to reality. That is why I won't tell what the little surprise is the Kelgians have waiting for you, or even how close you were once to discovering what it was yourself. What I am hoping is that when the heroism of the hysteric meets the courage of the cornered rat plus the X-factor I've been speaking about, this war will end shortly afterwards."

"You hope for a lot," said Dermod angrily.

"I'm hoping," the Guardsman corrected him gravely, "for a miracle."

"Listen," said Dermod, suddenly impatient, "and I'll tell you exactly what I have planned for tomorrow. Just so that your disappointment won't be too great when the miracle doesn't come off . . ." He went on quickly to say that there was a long, steep-sided valley about fifteen miles ahead and running almost due north and south. His air observations had shown that there were three training groups of crawlers, two small and one fairly large and totalling about nine hundred beings, occupying it at the present moment. The mountainous country would allow him to bring his forces quite close to the valley without being seen, but to be doubly certain of retaining the element of surprise he was going to rest the men from mid-afternoon to dusk, then have them take up their positions during the night.

The men of the First and Third battalions would take up positions at the north end of the valley and, soon after dawn, would begin to advance along it. The first group of crawlers they would meet would number only a couple of hundred, and if they did not wipe these out completely the survivors would fall back on the second group which was also a small one. The remnants of these two groups, by this time fleeing in panic, would run into the third and final bunch and infect them. The result should be a general stampede towards the south end of the valley where, among the rocks and criss-crossing ravines at a point where the valley widened out, the Second battalion would be waiting for them.

And just to help things along, detachments of the Fourth would be stationed at intervals along the high ground on each side of the valley to snipe at the fleeing crawlers and to drop grenades on any who tried to climb out of the valley at the very few points where this was possible. The Fourth battalion would also deal with any look-outs which the enemy might have posted above the valley, though Dermod thought that they would have little to do in this respect as the crawlers would not be expecting contact with the enemy for weeks to come.

"... The only point where we might meet resistance is with the third and largest group of the enemy," Dermod concluded. "But I don't expect it—especially not since Dowling identifies them as the bunch which set fire to their range at weapon practice! We shouldn't have much trouble taking a group as stupid and careless as that."

"I suppose not," said the Guardsman.

Dermod looked at the psychologist sharply. The other's tone had been completely flat and emotionless, his face totally devoid of expression as he had said the words. Had Dermod said something of importance, and was the Guardsman trying to hide the fact? Or was he merely staging abnormal reactions to make Dermod feel unsure of himself and so undermine his self-confidence? The last was more likely the correct assumption, he thought.

"They won't all be killed of course," Dermod said, deliberately getting in a thrust at what he had learned was one of the Guardsman's sensitive spots. "I'm hoping a few will escape to spread alarm and despondency among the rest of the crawler forces, and so make our succeeding battles that much easier."

The Guardsman was silent for a long time, then he said seriously, "Kelgia is a highly civilised, cultured and scientifically advanced world, ninety-seven percent of whose population are galactic citizens. Your enemy are only the Kelgian equivalents of yourselves, of course, but they have feelings and emotions which can be understood and shared by you. Their system of marriage and familial relationships are exactly the same, for instance, which when you consider it deeply enough shows how near us they are. Does the thought of taking the lives of so many of these intelligent beings not affect you?"

Dermod said shortly, "War's a dirty business."

"Oh, so you admit that now, do you?" said the Guardsman sarcastically, then suddenly he shot out, "But did you always think that? Or did you think that war was something thrilling, exciting, romantic?"

Dermod did not reply.

"You are a highly unusual and talented man, Colonel Dermod," the psychologist went on in more thoughtful tones. "In fact I would say that you aren't what you pretend to be at all, that somehow you managed to switch identities with the real Dermod . . ."

All at once Dermod's mind was rushing back to that section of space and time where a jetliner, its aerodynamic stability destroyed by an explosion in one of the power plants, was tumbling seawards. There had been a slight, rather timid individual called Jonathon Dermod in the seat next to him who had talked interestingly and excitedly about joining an officer's training school. The young man had been killed when the ship hit the sea and for some reason—perhaps it was with the idea of contacting his next of kin—he had taken the other's identification plaque. But when he discovered that there was no next of kin and that none of the other survivors had known him previously, he had taken Dermod's identity along with the plaque. Now he felt himself tensing at the thought that this Guardsman was so near to guessing his secret.

But then, he reminded himself sharply, what difference could that make now. He was in too deep.

"... I see I am correct," the Guardsman, who had been watching him closely, said. "From what I have seen of your abilities I would say that you were once a bright but lazy young man studying for his Galactic Citizenship who became bored with such dry and difficult subjects as extra-terrestrial history, sociology and ethics—as well as the subjects which must be mastered if a Citizen is to meet with and understand the alien and at times visually horrifying entities making up our civilisation—and turned to the history of Earth for escapist reading. You had access to books and records ordinarily denied to all but students as being unsane, but instead of evaluating them properly you began to actually live in them, have day-dreams about them, and so on.

"This sort of mildly insane behaviour would not have mattered in an ordinary man," the psychologist went on. "But you were a potential Citizen possessing very danger-ous knowledge and the ability, gained from your psycholo-gy and sociology classes, to guide and influence large masses of people. In the end I would say that the inhabi-tants of the settlements appealed to your romantic ideas in the same way as had the fact and fictional records of the past, and joining their army was the final act of stupidity.

"But now that you've discovered killing civilised beings is neither thrilling nor romantic why not demonstrate your sanity—your *humanity*, I should say—and call the whole thing off?"

For a moment Dermod felt his purpose begin to waver. Why, he asked himself, should he subject himself to physi-cal danger and increasing mental discomfort in his desper-ate attempts to salvage The Plan? Especially when the General had taken cold feet and sounded as if he was ready to scrap it himself. The way the Guardsman told it, calling the whole thing off seemed the sane and logical thing to do. But then, he reminded himself abruptly, this was a Guardsman talking, and Guardsmen could talk anybody into anything given enough time.

"You're wasting your breath," said Dermod. He leaned out of the car and bellowed the order to halt. As it passed back along the line the Bandsmen's reproducers fell silent one by one and the quiet became filled with the sounds of scuffling feet and low-voiced conversation as the men began clustering around the supply trucks. In the near-silence the Guardsman's voice sounded unnaturally loud.

"But *why* . . . ?"

"Because," said Dermod quietly, "I consider everything you say worthless. You're a hypocrite, the whole Guard is nothing but a pack of hypocritical, supercilious tyrants who—"

"Tyrants!" the Guardsman burst out. "But you're *free*, man! Freer than at any other time in all of history. You do exactly as you please. You can ride to Hell on horseback if you want to—we'll even supply the horses—so long as you don't insist on taking others with you who do not really want to go. That is something we don't tolerate—"

"What happens when we want to fight a war?" said Dermod sourly. "The Enemy's Inspection insures that only those of least ability fight, Guard psychologists ruin the morale of these and the whole thing becomes a farce in which we're made to look ridiculous. Do you call that freedom?"

"We are scrupulously fair about it," the Guardsman insisted quickly. "You have to admit that. Besides, our chief purpose in these wars—if we can't avert them altogether—is a twofold one; to see that as few people as possible are killed and to argue or scare some sense into the combatants. There is nothing like the threat of death to shock minds into sanity and give them a truer sense of value, especially the weak-willed, over-impressionable type who have got caught up by somebody else's sense of injustice or wounded pride so that they think they want to fight a war over it. And we usually find that the man whose pride has suffered is someone who will be nowhere near the front when the fighting starts . . ."

Dermod waved his hand irritably for silence. He said, "We, and our opposite numbers on other planets and of other species, are a persecuted minority which you are obviously bent on wiping out because we are proud, stubborn, independent and a source of annoyance to you because of these qualities—"

"You're all wet!" the Guardsman broke in vehemently. "Any one of you can become a Galactic Citizen provided he studies and shows himself capable of mixing, without friction, with extra-terrestrials."

"Very few of us consider the effort worth the goal," Dermod said drily. He had the other rattled now, which fact pleased him very much. He terminated the discussion by climbing out of the car and walking rapidly back towards the main body of his column.

But he had not ended it. The Guardsman was at his heels, fighting to draw enough breath both to keep up with his pace and talk at the same time, and he kept plugging away. Dermod had to admit that if nothing else he was a tryer.

A large proportion of the Galactics on Earth did tend towards degeneracy, the Guardsman admitted freely, but that was because the cream of Earth's galactic citizens left the planet while still young and generations of inbreeding had further lowered the quality of the stay-at-home. But at least they did not have to be continually watched in case they caused trouble, and among them were some of the Galaxy's great creative thinkers. The majority of Citizens, however—not only on Earth but all over the Galaxy —were averse to performing the necessarily unpleasant jobs connected with law enforcement, he explained; they were so sensitive, intelligent and pacifically inclined that to all but a few of them the very thought of taking action, even police action, was abhorrent. But entities did occasionally go off the beam, both singly and in large groups, and corrective action had to be taken to preserve the peace. That was why the Guard . . .

At that point Dermod halted for a few words with his

Lieutenant of Bandsmen regarding the music to be played during tomorrow's fighting. The Lieutenant, a thin-faced, intense and very earnest young man, was in favour of the Mars movement from Holst's Planet Suite. Dermod said no, he wanted something noisier, less subtle and with plenty of percussion. The Chief Bandsman suggested Tchiakovsky's 1812. Dermod said that that was better, but that the cathedral bells would sound a bit out of place. What had they by Wagner in stock . . . ?

The Guardsman kept breaking in every chance he got, and when Dermod moved along to say a few words of encouragement or crack a joke with groups of men who were now lying about wherever they could find shade, he continued talking. And he sounded so logical, so persuasive, so damnably *right!*

The present war had been caused by a so-called trading mission composed of non-Citizens from Earth. By rights, the Guardsman affirmed, no-one who was not a Galactic Citizen should be allowed to mix with other cultures, but forbidding interstellar travel to non-Citizens who could afford it would have been violating the Guard's prime tenet of maximum freedom for the individual. So the trade mission was allowed to go to Kelgia. The Kelgian Galactics would have nothing to do with them, naturally—they considered, and rightly, that non-Citizens tended towards avariciousness and were lacking in business ethics—and the humans were forced to trade with Kelgian non-Citizens like themselves. Misunderstandings through sheer ignorance, harsh words and a certain amount of double-dealing on both sides had resulted in a disturbance in which two humans and at least the same number of Kelgians had died, plus a fair number of injured on both sides. Feeling had run so high after that that both sides demanded a war as the only course that would satisfy them. Reluctantly the Guard had granted their wish, the psychologist said seriously, because it valued life so highly.

According to him the Guard was a body of dedicated men without whom the present galactic civilisation would fall apart. It was composed of humans because only in that species was to be found the mental toughness which could force a man to do unpleasant, even wrong, things for the greater good. Some of the things they had to do seemed harsh to those who did not understand, but ...

Suddenly Dermod could not take any more of it.

"Sergeant!" he called abruptly, and waited while the nearby NCO jumped to his feet and came forward. "Put a guard on this man," he went on, indicating the psychologist, "and under no circumstances allow him to talk. If he insists on talking, kill him."

As the Guardsman was led away Dermod realised with amazement that he had meant every word of what he had just said, and that he was literally shaking with anger. He turned to find a shady spot where he, too, could rest until sundown, but he found it impossible to sleep. Every time he emptied his mind of the myriad details connected with the campaign and closed his eyes he saw the tumbled, flaccid bodies of two hundred and fifty-three Kelgians, and wondering how it would have felt if they had been human dead. And he saw the beautiful, simple thing that was The Plan. Supposing he was successful and won this war, the General would then take over again. What sort of a mess would that shallow, weak-willed old woman make of things then ... ?

And all the time the voice of that accursed Guardsman kept gibbering silently in his brain. On and on and on, coaxing, arguing, demanding. And this time Dermod could do nothing to shut it up.

Chapter VIII

By dawn next morning Dermod and his Second Battalion were strung out across the mouth of the valley, and presumably his other units were in position also by this time. Slightly forward of the main line and concealed behind the safest cover there was available were four small special duty parties. These were composed of men who had shown most aptitude in handling the captured enemy weapons, and Dermod was hoping that these men

with their explosive projectile rifles would be the answer
to whatever surprise weapon it was that the Kelgians
possessed. Behind Dermod the valley widened out into a
saucer-shaped basin with steep, unclimable sides, then
narrowed sharply into another valley which was little
more than a ravine on the other side.

Dermod had the Guardsman with him again, but the
psychologist's whole bearing now was one of utter
hopelessness. And he had not said a word for the past
three hours. It was simply as a means of passing time, and
to keep from thinking too much, that Dermod spoke:

"Another thing I don't like about you people," he said,
"is your manner. And to be the ruling clique of the Galaxy
you're a singularly sour-faced, sarcastic and angry-eyed
bunch. Don't you ever laugh?"

For a moment he thought the other would make an
angry retort, but then his shoulders slumped dejectedly.
Dully, he said, "You must realise that we're very frustrated
men. There are some people and things which we would
dearly love to spank, and we're not allowed to. Also there
are some of us who feel guilty over past sins."

"I can imagine," said Dermod.

"You can't," said the Guardsman, and the conversation
stopped right there.

As it grew lighter Dermod looked more and more frequently at his watch, his ears alert to catch the first sound
that would tell him that the First and Third had started
their attack from the other end of the valley. But the first
sound he heard was of aircraft engines!

Cursing, Dermod looked wildly around. He had given
strict orders to Briggs and Dowling to stay away from this
area today, to divert interest from this valley by concentrating their attention on a crawler group fifty miles
away. And now one of the stupid fools had turned up at
the worst possible moment. Suddenly the aircraft's motor
cut out and Dermod saw it come gliding in over the rocky
edge of the basin. The fool was trying to *land* . . . !

Then abruptly Dermod was up and running. He had
seen the plane's registration number. Clifton's.

There was only one flat stretch in the basin and it was

strewn with large and small rocks, and how Clifton avoided them as he touched down and rolled forward was a miracle. Flaps full down, rocking madly and with the brakes already beginning to check its speed, Clifton's aircraft travelled nearly fifty yards before disaster struck. A projecting rock tore away the port landing wheel, it slewed around and went into a cartwheel which ripped off both wings and ground the tail section into ruin. The fuselage and engine, upside down now and moving backwards, kept on skidding and bouncing until friction with the ground dragged it to a halt.

Dermod was still ten yards from the wreck when Clifton came out to meet him on his hands and knees.

"You lucky so-and-so! What *happened* man? Did you get to the Guard base? Are you hurt ... ?" Dermod babbled, pulling the Lieutenant to his feet and shaking him in sheer excitement. "Tell me quick!"

Slurring his words slightly because he was still a bit dazed, Clifton made his report. By stripping down his machine and carrying all the reserve fuel containers he could cram into the passenger's cockpit he had reached the five-hundred miles distant Guard base as ordered. There he had acted and talked exactly as Dermod had told him, and the Guardsmen had fallen for it hook, line and sinker. They had even given him some of their gadgetry to take back with him—a radio and a Translator for the Guardsman who was still supposed to be at the Earth base—and told him what a smart fellow he was for seeing things their way. Headwinds and engine trouble on the way back forced him to land two days march from the Earth base, and then he had to take a truck back to his grounded plane with fuel and spares, hence the delay.

But on his way here he had stopped over at the base for some food, and purely by accident discovered that the General was no longer there! The other officers knew about it and had continued to send Dermod orders left behind by General Prentiss for that purpose, and had succeeded in concealing his absence from the men. The General had left a week ago—just the day after Dermod had left, in fact. That was why Clifton had risked both his own neck and Dermod's plans for surprising the crawlers by his crash landing. What were they going to do?

"*How* did he leave?" asked Dermod sharply.

"In a one-man, unarmed scoutship supplied by us," put in the Guardsman, who had just come up. "We secretly gave the commanders of each of the belligerents such a vessel, just in case things got too unpleasant or boring for them and they wanted to go home. This is normal procedure, the desertion of the supreme commander has a bad effect on the morale of the combatants, which in turn shortens the war ..."

"We'll win the war, with or without the General," Dermod cut in, speaking quickly to Clifton. "But at the moment I haven't time to thank you properly for what you've done—there will be a battle here any minute. Find some good cover right away and stay in it." To the Guardsman he said viciously, "You think of everything, don't you?"

Whatever the other said in reply was drowned by the crash of rifle fire which came rolling thunderously down the valley. Dermod sprinted back to his position, the Guardsman pounding close behind. The attack had begun.

Magnified and distorted as they were by the steep walls of the valley, Dermod could still pick out and analyse the separate sounds of individual weapons: the short, sharp *crack* of Earth rifles, the slower boom of grenades and the flat, double-report of crawler guns—one made by the weapon and the other by its bullet exploding on the target. After the first few minutes the volume of firing diminished considerably, which was what he had expected. What Dermod did not expect, however, was for the Guardsman to choose this time to renew his arguments

"... The General's taken cold feet at you arresting me," he was shouting. "He's got out from under it all, and I'll bet you anything you like that he's blamed everything on you! Now's your chance to call the whole thing off. We both know that you can beat the Kelgians, why kill thousands of them just to prove it?" When Dermod seemed not to be taking any notice of him, the psychologist's voice thickened with sheer, impotent fury. "You blood-thirsty maniac, you ... you butcher, *why* ... ?"

"I am not bent solely on massacring Kelgians," said Dermod coldly. "In fact I hope a lot of them escape to tell what will happen here, so that when I use the Translator sent you via Clifton by your colleagues to call on their high command to surrender unconditionally, they will be too terror-stricken to do otherwise but agree. And my winning this war is but a step—a very necessary one, I admit—in a much greater plan ..."

Two thin, wispy stems of smoke rose from somewhere further up the valley and burst into gaudy bloom; signal rockets, one orange and one blue. Orange following blue signified that the enemy was attacking from an unexpected quarter, and blue after orange that the Earth forces was outnumbered. Both rockets going up together was a meaningless signal. Dermod, who knew the exact placing and numbers of all the Kelgian forces, decided that one of his men must have let them off out of sheer excitement. But he couldn't help worrying a little even so ...

"... My winning this war," Dermod continued a trifle absently, "would have been enough. Nobody has ever accomplished that much for hundreds of years, and the fact that humans had won over extra-terrestrials in a Guard-controlled war would make the Guard's position untenable—beings all over the Galaxy would be convinced that the Guardsmen, who were also human, had assisted the Earth forces. The result would be a wave of anger and rebellion which would end the tyranny of the Guard for good.

"Or can you see a flaw in that plan?"

It was obvious from the Guardsman's face that he could not. "Our one weak spot," he said, then appealingly, "but we had to be strictly fair—we were outnumbered so greatly. And to maintain that reputation we had to lean over backwards, behave more harshly than was strictly necessary sometimes, towards members of our own species ..."

The firing was definitely closer now, and far up the valley Dermod thought he could make out traces of smoke. He said, "When I was forced to arrest you to keep you from stopping the war I thought the whole plan might fizzle out. But Lieutenant Clifton made it to your base with the story that you were negotiating with both sides for a cease fire—a rather ticklish job which might be ruined if anyone other than yourself butted in on it. They swallowed that and sent him back with their blessing, believing that he was one of the smarter types who had decided to aid you by carrying your hands-off message.

"Now when we march the disarmed Kelgian forces back to our base, their belief that you helped us win will be made a certainty by seeing you riding alongside me in the command car. Naturally you will not be allowed access to a Translator to explain, and by the time the people at your base find out what has been going on they will not be believed."

Dermod looked from the utterly defeated and impotent Guardsman to the tiny, undulating shapes of the distant and soon to be defeated enemy which were beginning to emerge from the haze of smoke. This was his hour of glory, the successful end of perhaps the greatest crusade in history was only minutes away. But he felt only anger, impatience, dissatisfaction and gnawing self-doubt. He wished fervently that he could get the whole thing over with and go home. Or did he wish that, for if the campaign was finished he would have nothing to fill his mind and keep him from thinking too deeply on the consequences of what he had done . . . ?

Chapter IX

Signal rockets climbed skywards and burst, soiling the pure blue with daubs of orange, green and yellow smoke. There were seven of them, their pattern and sequence completely meaningless, and these were followed in erratic succession by five more. Dragging his field glasses out of their case Dermod wondered fulminatingly if his men guarding the valley slopes had decided to have a fireworks display . . . !

Or, he thought with sudden foreboding, were those nonsense signals indicative of panic?

But his glasses showed only a steady stream of crawlers rounding the distant bend in the valley, and behind them a thickening haze of smoke. Dermod could hear Bandsmen through the shooting and knew that his First and Third had advanced along the valley as planned, having stampeded the two smaller enemy groups into the large one, which was now in full retreat also. There was nothing visible to cause alarm ...

Suddenly he caught his breath. From somewhere amid the heaving mass of crawlers a spear of flame shot upwards to wash against the valley rim momentarily and then spill backwards down the slope. Where it had passed it left furiously burning vegetation and clouds of oily smoke.

Flame-throwers!

In the instant he identified the crawler surprise weapon Dermod was up and running towards his special duty men, though every instinct in him screamed for him to go the other way. To his three groups equipped with crawler rifles he could only tell the truth, ignore the strained attitudes and suddenly pale faces and give what advice and encouragement he could. The enemy had flame-throwers, he told them; a short range weapon much less terrible than it looked. But explosive bullets outranged this weapon so that his special duty men must concentrate all their fire on entities using flame-throwers—they would know them by the tanks strapped to their backs—and leave all others to the Earth-type rifles of their comrades. When Dermod returned to his position the crawler bullets were already banging off the ground around him. He shouted, "Hold your fire men, wait until they're closer ... !" Then viciously aside to the Guardsman, "You gave them flame-throwers, and you call *me* inhuman ... !"

Dermod wasn't listening to the Guardsman's reply, he was more horribly, abysmally afraid than he had believed it possible for a human being to be. And underlying that was another fear, the gnawing, corroding, soul-destroying fear that what he was doing was *wrong*, criminally, insanely wrong. If only there was some way of pulling out so that he would have time to think it all out again. But the sides of the basin were too steep to climb easily and the only other escape route was the ravine which was too narrow to let his men get away quickly—either way he would lose all but a fraction of them, because once the Crawlers saw the Earth forces in retreat they would rally and take the offensive. Dermod swore silently, reminding himself that it was *his* force that had the enemy on the run at the moment, that *he* possessed the initiative . . . ?

". . . And we are not, therefore, inhumane," the Guardsman was protesting when Dermod heard him again. "Those things are tricky to work, and you had observer planes. We expected that the Kelgians would be afraid to use them in case they blew up and that you, once you got to know about them, would refuse to face them. Not even a hero likes to face a flame-thrower. But things went wrong; your observer spotted a flame-thrower being used and reported it as an accidental setting fire to a rifle range, and the Kelgians—either through fear of them or because they knew they were being observed—stopped using them.

"Now, however, they are desperate."

Dermod shook his head violently, as if by sheer physical movement he could shake some order into his mind. The enemy was now within rifle range, but obscured by the smoke which blew down the valley from their rear. Dermod licked his lips. They were rushing headlong into his ambush, the forces he had so carefully set in motion were now out of control, and that was wrong. He had not thought enough about the pain and fear and killing, or about the long-term consequences, or about anything at all except his stupid, juvenile urge to play soldier. He needed time, and time had run out. But he must do something, he must at least *try* . . .

The first sound he made was an unintelligible croak scarcely heard above the firing. Dermod swallowed and tried again; "Men, listen to me! Hold your fi—"

The long crash of the first volley drowned him out. Tensed up to fever pitch and with their ears ringing with the sound of gunfire from up the valley they had misheard and misunderstood his order. The Bandsmen joined in then with "Ride of the Valkyries" at maximum volume and the riflemen settled down to rapid fire-at-will. Dermod had chosen it finally for three reasons; it was a stirring piece, the gunfire would not sound quite so frightening to his men if they mistook some of it for over-enthusiastic percussion and the cries of the wounded—a very demoralising sound, he had read—would be blotted out.

He was very much afraid that there would be a lot of wounded this time.

The rifle fire of the Second was taking terrible toll—the narrow floor of the valley seemed to be carpeted with enemy casualties—but still they came on, pushing around and over the bodies on the ground until they, too, became similar obstructions to those who came behind. Despite the withering fire of his men and the fantastic pile-up of bodies at the mouth of the valley they kept on coming, fleeing in blind panic from the advancing First and Third. The men of the Second who were strung out across the valley mouth could not kill them fast enough.

Beside him the Guardsman was being sick.

Dermod shook his shoulder savagely. "We've got to stop this!" he yelled through the din. "Help me, there's a Translator in Clifton's plane . . ."

At that moment Dermod's eyes spotted a crawler squirming its way across the bodies of its comrades, its progress hampered by the heavy tank strapped to its back and the long-nozzled pipe clasped in its forward eating appendages. Fire vomited suddenly from the nozzle and a patch of vegetation close to the special duty group near Dermod burst into flames. The volume of firing diminished abruptly, it being no longer possible to clearly see the targets. Dermod shouted for the special duty men to stay in their positions, but his vocal chords were no match for Wagner and they probably would not have obeyed him anyway.

He saw them rise and run back towards the main force, saw another gout of liquid hell engulf two of them and watched in sick horror as one of them, a living torch, tottered a few steps before crashing to the burning ground. He, unfortunately, had been unable to make himself heard above Wagner.

Driven from the rear the crawlers poured through the screen of smoke and rolled over the middle of the Second's line, then streamed on towards the ravine at the other side of the basin. Dermod could do nothing to stop them. He didn't *want* to stop them now, because apart from everything else his control of his men was practically non-existent and they were rapidly becoming a disorganised rabble on the verge of panic themselves.

"The wreck, quickly!" Dermod shouted, dragging at the Guardsman. "Help me with the Translator . . . !" He didn't try to read the expression on the other's face, he was too busy searching through the smoke for the spot where Clifton's plane had come down. Suddenly he saw it.

By this time the crawler vanguard were actually at the mouth of the ravine. The flame-thrower expert who had been the cause of their break-through was still in their midst when a lucky shot from one of the surviving special duty men connected with its storage tank. The tank went up with a roar and flung liquid fire over a radius of fifty yards, igniting the tanks of two other flame-thrower operators and incinerating crawlers and humans alike in one vast lake of fire.

At the middle of which was Clifton's plane.

The mouth of the ravine was now a raging, impassable inferno. But the crawlers kept on coming, milling about in indecision before their hoped-for way of escape, then divided and sought to climb the rim of the basin. But crawler physiology was not suited to rock climbing so they turned inwards again. The basin was rapidly filling with crawlers.

Then the exultant First and Third, in hot pursuit of the last of the crawlers, came charging in. They had had it easy up to now, no crawler having stopped its flight long enough to direct a flame-thrower back at them, although they had passed an unusual amount of burning ground. They soon found out what it was like, but like the crawlers preceding them they could not go back because of the press of their own men behind. The inside of the basin was fast becoming a bloody shambles, with crawlers retreating from what seemed like a locally developing attack by humans only to run into another group of humans who fled thinking they were attacking. Blistering heat and oily black and yellow smoke filled the basin. Dermod could see men crouching and firing in all directions; they coughed and choked, their eyes streamed so that they could hardly see and they fired at every shadow which moved in the poisonous fog rolling around them. Maybe half the time they guessed right and shot at a crawler instead of one of their own. And weaker now that so many Bandsmen had perished beside them in the ravine, but still blaring out above the din of battle, *Die Valkyrie* went on and on ...

Somehow he had to get a nucleus of organisation around him before everybody killed everybody else off, he told himself feverishly. The Translator had been destroyed in the ravine fire, but if he could make his own men obey him that would be something, at least. If only he could stop that ghastly music!

There must be only one reproducer left in operation now, Dermod judged from the way the echoes bounced back and forth from the slopes, and it was somewhere close by. With the Guardsman he began to search desperately, coughing and choking, stumbling into patches of burning vegetation and crawling on, beating at his smouldering clothes as he went. Bullets cut the air around him and tore and gouged at the ground. When he came to the crouched, quivering figures wearing a Bandsman's pack he wanted to cry with sheer relief.

Viciously he yanked out the music tape and switched it to Public Address. "Men, this is Colonel Dermod ..." he croaked, and the ghastly, distorted voice roared out over the basin. But that was as far as he got, because a stray Earth bullet smashed into the reproducer mechanism.

"You're change of heart comes a little late," the Guardsman yelled. His left arm hung limp in a uniform sleeve which was just a bloody rag and his face was chalky with horror, shock and pain. Dermod could not meet his eyes. "I hope you're satisfied."

Dermod bowed his head.

"Even though you now realise your error," the Guardsman continued wildly, "the damage is done. Humans are tougher than Kelgians, so they will come out on top even from this shambles here—and the Kelgians will surrender. Your war is won, the influence of the Guard will shortly be gone and we can look forward to galactic civilisation falling apart into a mass of single, mutually antagonistic worlds. You've done it, God help you. And us."

From his depth of guilt and self-loathing some odd portion of Dermod's mind noted the fact that the Guardsman was not talking so loud, yet he was making himself heard without difficulty. That was curious, Dermod thought, and looked up.

Gradually the firing had slackened all over the basin, and a few minutes after he realised that fact it stopped altogether—even the crawlers had stopped shooting. Through the clearing smoke Dermod could see humans and Kelgians in isolated groups still clutching their weapons, tense, strained and every one of them looking up.

And vast, dark shadows were sliding in over the rim of the basin, despite the fact of the sun being still high in the sky. Dermod looked up to a sky darkened by the monster shapes of descending Guard transports and felt so profoundly thankful that he could not say a word, and he only half heard the Guardsman babbling excitedly about General Prentiss having taken fright and blabbing to Guard Headquarters on Earth and then immediately sending ships to cope with the situation . . .

" . . . And I suppose you're wondering what will happen to you," the Guardsman ended, "when I tell them all about your conspiracy?"

Dermod shook his head dully. "I hope they shoot me," he said. He meant it, too; the way he felt about himself at the moment that would have been a reward rather than a punishment.

"You won't get off as easy as that," the psychologist said, and there was a trace of something that was almost compassion tinging the sternness of his tone. "I know exactly what will happen to you. The Guard does not destroy when it can salvage . . ."

A close-spaced series of loud plops sounded from all

around them and the ground was suddenly covered with wide damp patches which steamed faintly. The Guardsman looked up, then said appreciatively, "Gas-bombs, good! They're putting everybody to sleep rather than risk further casualties ... But I was engaged in telling your fortune, Colonel," he continued. "The first job will be to clear up the dangerous situation you have created here and, though there is enough high-powered help in the fleet upstairs, you will probably be allowed to help in that. But even when that is settled, you—and that fellow Clifton, and a few others among your men who feel bad over the things they have done—will decide that you have not yet made amends. You will spend the rest of your lives trying to make sure that a similar situation does not arise again. Your former friends will hate you for this and the Galactics, while properly appreciative of the job you are doing, will feel uncomfortable near you.

"You will be frustrated by the apathy of some beings," the Guardsman went on, his words somewhat slurred now because the anaesthetic gas was beginning to take effect, "angered and impatient at the thoughtless cruelty and stupidity of others, and you will never completely get over your own feeling of guilt from your past sins. Altogether you will be a pretty sour-faced, sarcastic and unpleasant fellow ..."

Dermod was never sure later whether it was the psychologist or himself who went to sleep first. He only remembered feeling briefly and tiredly startled at the last words he heard before his mind dived into unconsciousness.

"... But then, people expect that of a Guardsman ..."

ROBERT A. HEINLEIN

The greatest science-fiction storyteller of all time!

Available at your bookstore or use this coupon.

____BETWEEN PLANETS	27796	$1.75
____CITIZEN OF THE GALAXY	28911	$1.95
____FARMER IN THE SKY	27596	$1.75
____HAVE SPACESUIT—WILL TRAVEL	26071	$1.75
____RED PLANET	26069	$1.75
____ROCKET SHIP GALILEO	26068	$1.75
____THE ROLLING STONES	27581	$1.75
____SPACE CADET	26072	$1.75
____THE STAR BEAST	27580	$1.75
____STARMAN JONES	27595	$1.75
____TIME FOR THE STARS	29389	$1.95
____TUNNEL IN THE SKY	28195	$1.75

BB BALLANTINE MAIL SALES
Dept. AL, 201 E. 50th St., New York, N.Y. 10022

Please send me the BALLANTINE or DEL REY BOOKS I have checked above. I am enclosing $. . . . . (add 50¢ per copy to cover postage and handling). Send check or money order — no cash or C.O.D.'s please. Prices and numbers are subject to change without notice.

Name_____

Address_____

City_____State_____Zip Code_____

08   Allow at least 4 weeks for delivery.   AL-4